# The Gay Mardi Gras Murders

## A Mia Ferrari Mystery

### SYLVIA MASSARA

## License Notes

This novel is entirely a work of fiction. The names, characters, and incidents portrayed in it are the work of the author's imagination. Any resemblance to actual persons, living or dead, events, or localities is entirely coincidental.

Published by Tudor Enterprises
Australia
(61) 419 492 623

Revised edition 2016
First published by
Tudor Enterprises in 2013

ISBN-13: 978-0-9808350-9-0

Copyright © 2011, 2016 Sylvia Massara

Sylvia Massara asserts the moral right to
be identified as the author of this work

# Dedication

*To my darling cat, Mitzy:*

*I lost you just after I finished writing this
novel and, therefore, I want to dedicate this to you.
Thank you for the last 20 years. You were the
best and most constant companion I ever had.
I love you forever and you will always live in my heart.*

# Author's Note

The character of Amanda Wilson in this book is the invention of my dear friend and author colleague—Carol E. Wyer.

Carol is the author of the quirky and humorous fiction novels featuring Amanda Wilson: "Mini-skirts and Laughter Lines" and "Surfing in Stilettos". She now has a vast array of titles to her name. For more information on Carol and her novels, please visit www.carolewyer.co.uk

We go through life making friends, and in this case it's wonderful that Carol's fictional character, Amanda Wilson, and mine, Mia Ferrari, are the best of friends. This gives yet another dimension to cyber-friendships.

# Titles by Sylvia Massara

Romantic comedy:

*Like Casablanca*
*The Other Boyfriend*

General fiction:

*The Soul Bearers*

Mia Ferrari mystery series:

*Playing With The Bad Boys*
*The Gay Mardi Gras Murders*
*The South Pacific Murders*

Sci-fi romance:

*The Stranger*

For more information on Massara's novels, both in eBook
& paperback editions, plus participating retailers;
or for latest novels or to contact the author, please visit:

**www.sylviamassara.com**

# CHAPTER 1

Starting a new year always brings a sense of renewal and hope; and for me, this was the case in more ways than one.

While on my duty manager's shift for a New Year's Eve function at Rourke International Hotel Sydney, I watched some three hundred revellers waiting to greet in 2013. I stood for a moment to take in the festive atmosphere around me while I counted both the losses and blessings that had been my lot during the past twelve months.

I had finalised the divorce proceedings of my eighteen-year marriage to Nathan, my cheating ex. This meant that while I lost thousands of dollars on legal fees plus my lovely home, which I had had to sell because I couldn't afford to keep up with the mortgage repayments, I was at the same time grateful I had liberated myself from something that had been holding me back for years. As a result, I found a new sense of being and independence; and I went on to rent a lovely Art Deco apartment near work. This meant I could kiss Sydney traffic goodbye and simply walk to the hotel. The highlight of the year, however, had been the purchase of *Mia*, as I call my red Ferrari Spider 360. *Mia* means "my or mine" in the Italian language of my ancestors—and *la mia machina* means "my car". So *Mia* was not only "mine", but she also shared her name with my own: Mia Ferrari. I thought this rather serendipitous when I made the decision to buy her.

The past year had not only touched me personally, but also professionally. I had helped a woman who hadn't been able to help herself and who plunged to her death from the tenth floor of our hotel atrium, landing on top of the baby grand in the cocktail bar. Linda Liu had not lived to welcome in the New Year, but I hoped she was now resting in peace after I had finally managed to solve her case despite the trouble I had caused for my archenemy, Detective Sergeant Phil Smythe of the Kings Cross Police Department.

A smile touched my lips at the thought of how I outwitted Smythe at every step of the way. Of course, I had received a huge amount of help from the hotel's security manager, and my best friend, Guy Dobbs; and my pseudo-son, Chris Rourke—son of David Rourke, owner and CEO of Rourke International Hotels.

An image of David flashed into my mind. He had also lost in the last year—his marriage to the "ice queen", Elena, had broken down completely. This brought a promise of renewal for the love David and I had shared briefly, so long ago in Venice, before Nathan had come into my life.

I came back to the present when I noticed the music in the ballroom had stopped playing and the countdown to the New Year began. ".... nine... eight... seven... six..." The crowd yelled at the top of their voices. Tears rose to my eyes; I had no one to hug and kiss. I was an outsider, looking through a window into a world that was not a part of me.

"... two... one... Happy New Year!" There were echoing shouts all around the ballroom before the orchestra started to play again and the crowd broke into "Auld Lang Syne".

I stood ramrod straight and looked very official in my black pantsuit that was my uniform. My arms hung down in front of me, wrists crossed over, with one hand holding a walkie-talkie in manner of the secret service. Then I jumped as a pair of arms engulfed me in a bear hug, and a kiss was planted on my cheek. "Happy New Year, Ferrari!" A deep American voice shouted close to my ear.

I pulled away to look at the black face of my dear friend and work colleague—framed by frizzy grey hair, with large brown eyes and white teeth, he was smiling at me. "Dobbs!" I exclaimed with sudden joy and hugged and kissed him in return. "Happy New Year to you, too, my man. I didn't know you were on duty tonight, you sneaky thing." I arched an eyebrow at him and added with mock severity, "What's Eileen got to say about this?"

Dobbs smiled and pulled at my sleeve. "Let's get out of here," he yelled above the noisy crowd. "We can't talk like this." He started to make his way toward the ballroom doors, jostling past groups of merrymakers, and I followed close behind.

Once outside we took the lift down to the hotel lobby and

slipped into a corner of the café, which was now closed even though they still served us coffee from the cocktail lounge nearby. Compared to the function in the ballroom the rest of the hotel was dead quiet. Most guests were either at the function or safe asleep in their beds.

"So what gives, Dobbs?" I threw him an accusatory look. "You should've told me you were on duty so we could've had dinner together before the party in the ballroom got going."

Dobbs waved a hand in order to pacify me. "Hold it right there, Ferrari. How can a guy get a word in edgewise with you flapping your gums non-stop?" The look of thunder on my face made him clear his throat. "At least, let me explain," he added in a conciliatory tone.

I leaned forward and rested my chin on one hand while I pinned him from across the small marble-topped coffee table with icy blue eyes. "I pulled a double shift today because most of the duty managers asked for time off to be with their families, and as I'm the only one without family I was nice enough to offer to work all day plus this evening. So don't play games, Dobbs, or else I'll start treating you like I do that prick, Smythe!" I felt my temper rise at the thought of the man.

"Whoa!" Dobbs placated me with a charming smile. "I didn't mean it that way, Ferrari. Girl, you do beat all, don't you? Just listen for a moment," he insisted.

I expelled a sigh to calm myself and sat back in my chair to wait for his explanation while at the same time I acknowledged I was being unfair to him. It wasn't his fault that he was happily married, and a recent grandfather; while I was divorced, soon going on forty-nine years of age, and I had no living family. Dobbs was my family now. He was the closest thing I had to a father seeing as mine had been his best friend when they were on the force years ago.

I missed my dad so much it hurt, and this was one reason why I hated the holidays. I had no one with whom I could share the special moments, at least no blood relatives to speak of. I lived all alone in Australia, having lost both parents years ago and being an only child. I did have some cousins in Italy, but we didn't really keep in touch except for the odd email.

"I only came on duty about an hour ago," Dobbs explained; and once again I came back to the present.

"Why did you?" I was curious now, my sulking mood forgotten. "We have security covered with Robert and Nat."

Dobbs looked a little shy all of a sudden. "Well, I couldn't leave my girl alone now, could I?"

I felt the pinprick of tears at the back of my eyes and gulped down some coffee in order to regain my composure. "Oh," I managed to say.

Dobbs gave me a knowing smile. He had obviously known how I was going to be feeling tonight of all nights—New Year's, and no one to kiss. At least, Christmas had been different. I'd spent it with Dobbs and his family. His daughter, Maggie, was over for a visit from Hawaii with her husband and six-month-old baby Rose. We had a grand time as we were regaled with great stories from the time Dobbs had been a homicide detective with the Honolulu Police Department.

I was touched that Dobbs had thought of me tonight and I reached out and placed my hand on his. "Thank you, Dobsy," I said with my pet name for him. "I don't know what I'd do without you." I wasn't sure if he blushed under his dark skin, but I was fairly positive he did.

"That's okay, Mia. You know you're a part of our family."

"Yes," I replied. "Yes, I am, and I appreciate it. But I suppose Eileen isn't going to be too happy with me." I didn't think Dobbs's wife would have liked him away from home on New Year's Eve on my account, but Dobbs dispersed my doubts when he let out one of his deep belly laughs. "What?" I asked, watching his strong but stocky frame shake with mirth.

"Eileen was happy to see me go, girl," he explained. "She wanted Maggie all to herself after Ted volunteered to bathe baby Rose and put her to bed."

I thought of Maggie's husband and his devotion to his new daughter. The man was a lump of sugar and he would do anything for Maggie and baby Rose. "I presume Ted's catching up with his movies while his father-in-law is at work?" I smirked.

Dobbs nodded and we laughed heartily. Ted was a martial arts freak and loved to watch Bruce Lee and Steven Segal movies. Seeing as no one else liked them, he took every opportunity to catch up with his viewing whenever the family was otherwise engaged.

"I'm just going to call the boys and make sure all is well in the ballroom," Dobbs announced, rising from the table. "What about another round of coffees?"

"Sure," I nodded. "Go and make your call while I order."

When Dobbs returned we sat down to cappuccinos and Danish pastries. "I'm starved," I declared.

"And I shouldn't even touch these," he replied, casting a longing look at the pastries. "Eileen forbade me from having any sweets since I put back on the weight I lost when I went to visit baby Rose in Hawaii last year."

"Never mind, Dobbs." I smiled conspiratorially. "I won't tell her if you don't. Besides, it's now a new year and you deserve to spoil yourself a little." Dobbs needed no further encouragement and attacked the pastries with gusto. "So tell me," I said as I watched him take a bite from an apple Danish, "how's Smythe these days? I haven't seen him since the Linda Liu case."

"Good thing, too," Dobbs replied in between bites. "He's not too happy."

His comment instantly aroused my curiosity and I was really glad Dobbs still attended the poker nights with Smythe and some of the boys from the force. I hated it that he was still friendly with Smythe, seeing as Smythe treated us like civilians; plus the fact that Dobbs played poker with scum like him used to really get my goat. Nowadays, however, I had learned to tolerate contact with the enemy, especially since the boys talked about cases when they got together, and often Dobbs came back with useful bits of information. The poker nights had paid off while I'd been working the Linda Liu case and they could prove useful in future.

"So why isn't he happy?" I asked, secretly relishing the thought that not everything was going well with Smythe.

"He's been assigned a partner," Dobbs informed me.

I shrugged my shoulders. "What's the big deal about that?"

Dobbs finished his pastry and picked up a plum puff. "He's always worked alone in the past."

I smiled gleefully. "Well, you can tell *Dirty Harry* that his lone wolf days are over and he has to become a team player." Then I added with hope written all over my face, "I don't suppose you're really going to make my night and tell me the new partner is a woman."

Dobbs shook his head and sighed. "Ferrari, how many times do I have to tell you to let go of this animosity you have for Smythe? The guy's a decent sort, you know. He cut you a lot of slack in the Linda

Liu case, if you care to remember. I mean, he could've thrown you in jail for interfering with the investigation!"

I laughed. "You can't be serious. Without me he wouldn't have had an investigation!" I stated fiercely. "Besides, you very well know he was the reason I didn't get into the police force all those years ago."

Dobbs rolled his eyes. "How could I forget when you keep bringing it up time and again?"

"I will never forgive him!" I frowned in anger. "No matter what he does for me in future, I can never forget what he did back then. He can even pave the streets with gold in my honour, but I still won't forgive the bastard! And to top it all off, he reminds me of my ex; so every time I see him I want to blow his head off."

"You Italians and your thoughts of revenge," Dobbs chastised me. "You're so angry all the time."

I didn't take any notice of what he said. I just hated Smythe, and that was that. "So, do tell. Is the new partner a woman?" I persisted.

Dobbs sighed again. "Unfortunately for you, no. It's some young guy."

I felt disappointed. Smythe hated women in the police force. He had made this much clear years ago when he was responsible for the rejection of my application on the technicality of height restrictions. At the time, the restrictions had just been removed; but despite this, Smythe had found a way to block me from joining the force and I had never forgiven him since.

"Well, whatever," I dismissed the whole Smythe thing, but not before I savoured the fact that he would be pissed off at having to babysit some young gun.

Dobbs finished eating his pastry and glanced at his watch. "It's past one," he announced, "and I've had it. I'm going home. Do you mind?"

"Why should I mind? I'm happy you came to be with me in the first place." We stood and walked toward the lifts, and I gave him a big hug and kissed his cheek. "Thank you for coming toning; you know it means a lot to me."

He hugged me back. "You mind you get some rest, okay?"

I nodded with a cheeky grin. "Yes, father Dobbs."

He gave me one last look and, when he seemed satisfied that I didn't look too tired, he winked and walked off in the direction of the stairs, which led down to the back-of-house area. I punched the button for the lift and decided that after a quick check on the ballroom I was going home to bed. The night manager had been in charge since eleven, and now that the function was beginning to wind down I felt confident he could handle any eventualities that may arise.

The lift doors slid open and my heart skipped a beat when David Rourke, CEO of Rourke International, and my ex-lover, stepped out. "Mia!" He greeted me with a smile that stirred my heart. "Happy New Year." He then reached out and hugged me to him, planting a chaste kiss on my lips.

"Happy New Year, David," I managed to sound casual. "I thought you'd left for Hawaii to check out the new site for Rourke's."

"I was going to fly out this morning, but I didn't fancy spending New Year's on a plane," he replied. "So I rescheduled for tomorrow, or today, I should say," he corrected, glancing at his watch.

I wondered whether he had spent the New Year with anyone special, but it was not my place to ask. After the split with his wife, I'd thought we might pick up from where we left off all those years ago, but neither he nor I had been ready for this. On top of which, he was still my boss and this would further complicate matters. His son, Chris, however, thought differently and confessed to me that I should have been his mother and that David should have married me. I didn't want to speculate on this further, not with David standing in front of me, so I banished the thought from my mind.

"Where's Chris?" I asked with a feeling of motherly concern. I considered Chris a friend, even a son, and as our hotel was located in the red light district of Sydney, which was also a huge tourist area, I always worried when he was out late.

"He's asleep," David answered. "We had New Year's dinner with his grandmother and then came back after watching the fireworks at midnight."

I was surprised David still socialised with Elena's mother, but it wasn't the old lady's fault that her daughter had decided to abandon her own son and fly off to Switzerland to start a new life. Elena had never been close to her son; hence Chris's attachment to me.

"Good thing he didn't go carousing with his friends," I remarked. "You know how crazy the streets get on New Year's Eve."

David nodded and regarded me with attractive green eyes. "There is one thing I wanted to talk to you about before I fly off. Do you have a moment?"

With those eyes and that smile of his, I had a lifetime; but I wasn't going to admit to this. "Sure," I replied. "How about a New Year's 'non-alcoholic' drink?" I suggested, knowing none of us drank alcohol while on duty.

We made our way to the cocktail lounge and ordered a couple of Pellegrino waters. "Chris decided to move in with me now that Elena's gone," David commented.

I supposed this made sense seeing as Chris had been living on campus at his university while his mother lived in the hotel's penthouse with David. Chris never got along with Elena and therefore chose to live on his own. He only came home during holidays, when he also worked on a casual basis for the hotel. Now, with Elena gone, it made sense that he and his dad should share the huge penthouse.

"I know what you're going to ask me," I pre-empted before David had a chance to speak. "And the answer is, yes. I'll keep an eye on him while you're in Hawaii."

"You're an angel, thank you." He smiled and my stomach fluttered with butterflies.

"How long will you be away?" I stuck to business so I could shift my focus from what was going on inside my body.

"A couple of weeks at most," he replied. "I'm checking out two sites; one in Maui and the other on the big island. I'm not yet sure which one will be better for the project."

No one in the group knew about David's expansion plans for the hotel chain, except his son and me. It felt good that he had taken me into his confidence. "Well, I hope all goes well for you; and don't worry about Chris. I'll make sure he behaves."

David regarded me with a doubtful look that sent me on the defensive automatically. "What's that for?" I sounded suspicious, but his gaze, I realised, held warmth in it.

"Ferrari," he stated in the style of Dobbs, "and who's going to make sure *you* behave?" There was a gleam of amusement in his eyes.

"I take exception to that," I complained, knowing all the while he had been teasing.

He patted my arm. "Well, don't. After all, trouble seems to

follow wherever you go. I only hope," he added, "that this time you'll stay away from dead bodies."

Little did we know at the time how prophetic his words would turn out to be.

# CHAPTER 2

After an uneventful ten days, David returned from Hawaii with good news on his part while I had no *dead bodies* to report, much to his relief. He had identified a suitable site for the building of a Rourke International hotel-resort in Waikoloa, on the big island. As a result, he had to leave almost immediately again and I didn't see much of him during the next few weeks as he flew back and forth between Sydney and Hawaii to deal with the purchase of the site and hold negotiations with architects and builders. During this time, I continued keeping an eye on his son and we became closer than ever. So much so, that we pretty much settled into a mother-son relationship before too long.

"You know, Mia, you don't have to come here and cook dinner for me," Chris protested one evening while I prepared homemade gnocchi with Napolitana sauce.

I handed him a couple of plates and some cutlery. "Just set the table," I said. "You must realise you can't have junk food all the time, Chris, or your father will kill me when he comes back from one of his trips to find a big, fat blimp sitting in his son's place." I grinned and Chris laughed. We both knew that with his tall athletic physique and the amount of sports he played, this was an impossibility.

"I don't eat junk food all the time, you know," Chris nevertheless argued. "The hotel kitchen sends me lots of healthy meals."

"Good thing that I talked to them," I retorted, "otherwise, you'd be ordering burgers and fries every night."

Chris sighed and knew he couldn't win the argument. "Fair enough." He shrugged and set the table while I put on the final touches to our meal before joining him to eat. I didn't always dine with him, but whenever I worked a day shift, I made time for dinner when his father was away so I could keep him company.

Chris had many friends and was often out. Despite this, we caught up at least twice a week, and I ensured he ate well. During these times, he peppered me with questions about "my next case" and I constantly had to remind him that I wasn't an investigator but a hotel duty manager. This didn't seem to matter to the nineteen-year-old. He loved to hear what went on in the hotel and how Dobbs and I dealt with it.

I perceived Chris idolised us as a result of his own involvement in the Linda Liu case, where he assisted greatly by hacking into certain computers to obtain information we needed; and because Dobbs and I treated him like a member of the team. So after the case was solved, he began to pester me about the next case. Just because he studied IT at university, and was very talented with computers, it didn't make him the FBI; but he seemed to think so.

"What's happening these days," he asked when we started to eat. "Any news I should be aware of?"

"You're joking, right? If you think I'm going to involve you again in any kind of investigation that comes my way you've got rocks in your head. For God's sake, I almost got us both arrested last time!" I admonished him.

He didn't seem fazed by this and as he attacked his gnocchi he remarked, "You know you need me, Ferrari. You're not computer savvy when it comes to gathering information."

I set down my fork and glared at him. "Hacking is illegal; you know that. And while it comes in handy, you could get yourself arrested. You were lucky last time Dobbs spoke on your behalf, and that's why Smythe chose to let you off the hook."

"Okay, okay," Chris tried to pacify me when he realised I wasn't going to go along with him. "But you must admit, having someone on the inside can really help."

I sighed, picked up my glass of Coke and took a long swig to give myself time to calm down. Much as I loved Chris and his assistance with computers, I wasn't about to make a habit of exposing him to danger. It was bad enough that I had allowed him to work the Linda Liu case because I kept hitting dead ends and his information had helped to clarify a number of issues.

"Someone on the inside?" I questioned, and firmly set down my glass on the table. It was imperative he understood we were not playing cops and robbers, at least not where he was concerned.

"Chris, there is no *inside*," I stated. "We are not detectives, and even if I decide to look into something I'm not about to involve you in it again. Not only would I be endangering you, but you'd be committing a crime; and both Smythe and your father would have my hide if they ever found out!"

A smile played on his lips. "That's what it is, isn't it?" he exclaimed with alacrity. "You don't care about exposing me to danger, Ferrari. You're just afraid Smythe and Dad will find out."

"That's enough!" I chided him rather abruptly. "I refuse to discuss this any further, so eat your dinner before it gets cold."

He looked crestfallen at my outburst, but I couldn't help it. He had come close to the truth in that I was afraid of being found out by Smythe and David if I used his skills, but he was wrong about my not caring by exposing him to danger. I loved him as my own son and I would kill myself before I jeopardised his safety. I was a grown woman who knew the ways of the world and the crazy people in it, and if something happened to me, so be it; but I wasn't about to endanger a young man who was trusting, loving and full of life, and who idolised me enough to get himself involved in something that could harm him.

"Why don't we change the subject?" I suggested gently, aware that my temper always got the better of me.

"You're right," he agreed. "Sorry; I didn't mean to be so pushy. I just want to help where I can."

My heart softened toward him and I wanted to hug him. I was so proud of him and how he had turned out. He was a young man who knew where he was going, and he had his head firmly planted on his shoulders. Not like his flighty mother, who had spent most of Chris's childhood away from him.

"You must be excited about this new hotel venture in Hawaii," I remarked to change the subject. "Your dad's been so busy with it; and I'm sure he's going to be very successful with the expansion plan."

Chris nodded. "Dad always wanted to expand into the US market. After all, he was born there and still has family scattered all around."

I forked a gnocchi and popped it in my mouth, trying not to look too concerned as I asked, "Do you think he might base himself over there one day?"

"I don't know," Chris answered. "He's lived in Australia a long time now and it's pretty much his home. Besides, my whole life is here; so even if he decides to go back, I intend to stay in Sydney."

I looked down at my plate and suddenly lost my appetite. The thought of David going away was unthinkable, and yet I had nothing with him. Our love affair consisted of that one very special night in Venice almost twenty years ago.

"What's the matter?" Chris's voice broke into my thoughts.

I pasted a smile on my face and regarded him. "Nothing." I pushed away the plate from me. "I'm full, that's all."

"And I'm finished," he stated, patting his tummy. "But I still have room for dessert."

I stood up, happy to have something to do and blow away the cobwebs from the past. "I was prepared for this eventuality and that's why I managed to swipe a slice of tiramisu from the kitchen, just for you."

Chris was up and clearing the table before I asked him to do it and I made coffee. We sat down on the leather lounge near an expansive window that looked out toward the city skyline and while I drank my coffee, Chris demolished his dessert.

"Hey, how's the Ferrari going?" he asked, setting down his empty plate on the coffee table and wiping his mouth with a napkin.

"Fantastic," I replied, a tone of excitement in my voice. I loved driving my car. "In fact, I'll get a chance to show it off soon."

"Oh. To whom?"

"To a good friend of mine who's coming out from the UK for a visit. She's never been to Sydney, so I'll be playing tour guide with the car. She's coming over in time for the gay mardi gras."

Chris looked interested. "Is she gay or something?"

I laughed. "No, no. Amanda's married and has one grown son, probably around your age or a little older. Anyway, she just needs a break."

"A break from what?" Chris queried.

"A break from her husband," I informed him, my tone sounding somewhat bitter as I suddenly thought of my scumbag ex.

Chris obviously picked up on my change of mood and didn't pursue the subject of husbands. "When's she arriving?"

"Second week in February."

"Is she a cool chick like you?" He smirked.

I laughed, feeling my mood lift. "Yes, I guess she is. I've known her now for almost twenty years. I met her in France, when I was travelling through Europe," I informed him, "and we hit it off straight away. So we kept in touch since. Amanda's going to love Sydney, and she'll absolutely adore the mardi gras."

"Why's that?"

"She has a real lively mother that's best friends with a gay couple who do fashion design in Cyprus. The mother lives in the UK but often goes off to Cyprus to be with her 'adopted' boys," I explained. "Anyway, Amanda intends to photograph the parade on mardi gras night and send off the pics to her mum and the boys. They'll get a real kick out of the outrageous costumes and the parade floats."

"Excellent," Chris remarked. "I look forward to meeting this Amanda. If she's as cool as you say, I'm going to be hanging out with two cool chicks instead of one."

I laughed. "Well, don't get any ideas that somehow you're going to fit into the car with us. You already know it only seats two."

"Yes, but while you're working I could always take Amanda sightseeing in the car, if you lend it to me." He threw me a sheepish look.

"Nice try; and no can do, Chris Rourke!" I rebuked him gently. "Mia is mine and unless I'm dead or unconscious, no one else drives her."

Chris lifted his hands up to his chest, palms outward. "Okay, I get the message."

"Besides," I added, "I think Amanda will want to hang out in the hotel sometimes when I'm on shift."

"Why's that?"

"We have the female impersonator show coming up for the mardi gras festival. They'll be performing from late Feb right through to the end of mardi gras."

"Oh my God!" Chris gave me a look of mock excitement. "Just think, queens in King's Cross. What a rarity."

I grinned. Being in the red light district, we had seen it all before. "Well, these queens are quite talented, and they've been touring overseas. The fact that they're putting on a show at Rourke's is going to give us a lot of publicity. The hotel's already full for the duration of the show I'll have you know."

"And the queens are staying with us, I suppose?"

"Of course," I replied. "I think we're in for an interesting time."

Chris gazed at me with certainty. "Of that I'm one hundred per cent sure, Mia Ferrari. All we need now is a grisly murder to really spice things up." His tone sparked off a premonition of impending doom that struck me in the stomach. "Are you okay?" he asked when he saw my paling face.

I took a few moments to compose myself before I replied. "Don't even say that in jest, Chris. You know the old adage 'be careful what you wish for'."

He smiled to put me at ease. "You know I'm only kidding."

I knew he was, but something dark seemed to hang in the air all of a sudden, and I had the feeling we were all going to be swept away on a rollercoaster ride that would end by crashing into the house of horrors.

# CHAPTER 3

Dobbs arranged for extra security through an external contracting company in readiness for the upcoming female impersonator show. "I've gone over budget," he complained to me one morning when we were both on shift, "but it's money well spent."

I agreed. "I think you did the right thing, Dobbs. Full house in the hotel, the show totally sold out, and we're in the middle of the red light district—I just hope we don't have any gatecrashers, like bikie gangs, wanting to lynch the drag queens."

Dobbs made a cross with his index fingers. "Pssst! Don't even say it, Ferrari," he warned with a shiver. "That's the last thing we need."

I grinned and replied with sarcasm, "Well, if something happens, we can always rest assured that we're under the protection of Smythe and his sidekick." I raised a querying brow. "By the way, what did you say his name was?"

"I didn't," he answered. "But if you must know, it's Sean Webb."

"You already met him?" I glowered at him all of a sudden.

Dobbs nodded with a grin. "Last Friday; at the boys' poker night."

I pulled him by the sleeve of his jacket and made him follow me from the reception area, where we had been standing, to a quieter corner of the lobby. "You didn't tell me this." I pinned him with an accusatory look.

He pulled his sleeve free of my hold and smirked. "You don't need to know everything that goes on, you know."

"Smartarse!" I did an about face and walked off, leaving him standing alone. Dobbs followed me, however, and tried to catch up as I headed for the back-of-house area and toward the staff restaurant.

"Hey, wait a minute!" he called out, slightly out of breath.

I stopped and waited for him. "You're rather unfit," I remarked, still feeling miffed.

"Be quiet, Ferrari!" he berated me.

I gave him a wicked smile. "You know I'm only pulling your leg, Dobbs; but you deserve it for keeping secrets, in any case. I just thought we'd agreed to share our information."

We made our way into the restaurant and ordered coffee and croissants for morning break. "I was going to tell you, but I've been so busy with arranging the security for this drag queen business that it slipped my mind," Dobbs said by way of apology when we sat down with our food.

"Okay." I accepted his explanation. "But there's nothing stopping you now from telling me all about it." I wasn't exactly upset with him; though I wanted him to think so. Ever since we had been working together, around five years now, we'd always shared information.

"Sean," Dobbs commented, "is a youngish cop, late twenties or early thirties, a bit gung-ho for my taste, athletic-looking—in fact, when I think about it, you'd like him because he's a bit of an asshole."

I laughed at his pronounced American accent when he tried to make a point about something. "Really, Dobbs, you should know better. I don't go for 'bad boys' anymore. My last ex was enough to cure me from arseholes, trust me."

"Well, this is all I can tell you about Sean Webb. I only met him briefly at poker night. He had to leave early because he was on shift with Smythe."

This time, I laughed louder. "I bet Smythe really loved that. Having to babysit a rookie, and on poker night to boot. Serves the bastard right!"

Dobbs sighed, probably about to tell me off regarding my feelings of animosity toward Smythe. Instead, he changed the subject altogether. "Chris told me about your friend, Amanda."

"Yes." I grinned. "I think he's trying to get you to coax me into lending him the Ferrari so he can take Mandy sightseeing while I'm on shift." I took a bite of my croissant before I went on. "He'll do anything to drive that car."

Dobbs gave one of his deep belly laughs. "That's young Chris for you. I guess now that the boss flies off to Hawaii so much, he wants to have a bit more fun."

My eyes clouded at the mention of David.

"What is it?" Dobbs asked.

I shook my head in a helpless gesture. "I don't know, I guess it's the change in general. Things are always changing and we can't stop it." Dobbs didn't know about my love affair with David; this was the only secret I had ever kept from him. "Do you think you'll go to Hawaii once the hotel's built? You'd be closer to your daughter and baby Rose," I said to dispel my thoughts of David.

"Maggie lives in Honolulu, so what am I going to do on the big island?"

"You could always fly back on your days off," I suggested but hoped he didn't take it into his head to leave. I hated the thought that I might lose two of my favourite men.

"No, I won't be going back. Eileen and I made a life for ourselves in Australia." His reply brought relief flooding through me. I wasn't going to lose my family after all. As for David, this remained to be seen. "Now, tell me more about the drag queens," Dobbs prompted.

I took a sip of my now cooling coffee and glanced briefly at my watch. "Time to get back to work," I informed him. "Not much to tell about the female impersonators," I added as we made our way out of the staff restaurant and headed down the corridor toward the lobby area. "All I know is that there are four of them plus their manager, and the show is called *The Tit Elating Follies*." I raised my eyebrows at the name while Dobbs simply grinned. "They're checking in on the same day Mandy arrives and unfortunately, I have to be on duty."

"I can watch the pager for you," Dobbs offered.

I gave him a grateful smile. "As tempting as that sounds, I still have to be here to greet them personally. They're on the VIP list. But once I get them settled, I could take you up on your offer so I can rush to the airport and pick up my friend."

We reached the lobby, which was rather quiet after the morning's checkouts. "Done deal," said Dobbs. "Well, I'm off to my operations meeting."

"Okay," I replied. "I'll probably catch you at lunch."

In the days that followed, we were so busy that I often worked double shifts to help out with the volume of work generated by the continuous full occupancy leading up to the gay mardi gras. Each day blended into the other and before I knew it the day arrived when the female impersonators were due to check in.

I greeted them at Reception and was surprised to see three young males, all of them slim and with an effeminate look about them. They were accompanied by a short and stocky middle-aged man, whom I assumed was the group's manager, and a breathtakingly beautiful young woman who looked around thirty. I had no idea who she was, but she was a real head-turner. She stood at approximately five feet ten with long auburn hair, large hazel eyes and supermodel looks. She was truly stunning, and I felt dwarfed when I stood close to her, being five feet nothing.

I introduced myself. "Welcome to Rourke International. I'm the senior duty manager, Mia Ferrari."

The woman extended a hand to shake mine and I couldn't help but notice the elegant, slim fingers with long pink fingernails. Her grip was firm as we shook hands. "My name's Ophelia," she said in a husky voice, "but on stage I'm known as Clee Torres."

My stunned expression must have caused amusement among the group because I saw the merriment in their eyes as they regarded me. "Don't take any notice of my darling Clee," the stocky, middle-aged man stated when he stepped forward and shook my hand. "I'm Jim Casey, the manager. Clee likes to shock people," he explained, and seeing the puzzled look on my face, he added, "Darling, Clee is the real McCoy." He eyed me knowingly.

Understanding dawned upon me. "Oh, you mean..."

"Yes," one of the young men jumped in and shook my hand. "Clee's got herself a real clit."

It took every effort for me to keep a straight face. "That's nice to know, and you are?"

"I'm Ayna Liscious," he said with a naughty smile.

I wasn't amused and could only pray the bikies didn't get to these primping young men that were dressed in skin-tight jeans revealing— unlike the gorgeous, young Clee—that they had not had "the snip" and, therefore, were not the real McCoy.

The other two impersonators introduced themselves by their

stage names of Felle Ashio and Zsa Zsa Lahore.

I took our guests through the express check-in service and allocated each of them a suite on the top floor near the penthouse. At the back of my mind, I made a note to warn Chris to stay away from the impersonators unless he wanted to be sexually molested. I wasn't sure that the young men were gay, as not all drag queens were this way inclined; however, I had a feeling that if Chris wasn't careful he'd soon find out.

Dobbs caught up with me when I returned from escorting our guests to their suites and took my pager from me. "Thanks, Dobbs. I only have half an hour to get to the airport and pick up Mandy. I'll settle her at my place and then come back to work."

"Why don't you take a few hours off?" he suggested, noticing the tired look on my face.

I acknowledged the double shifts I'd been working lately had taken their toll and was grateful for his offer. "Are you sure you can handle it? I don't want to leave you to deal with all this," I offered, but secretly hoped he wouldn't change his mind as I needed some relaxation time before this evening, when The Tit Elating Follies would be performing their first show.

"Off you go, girl." Dobbs made to push me out the door. "You look beat."

"Thanks. I owe you one." I smiled and took off.

Although Kings Cross wasn't that far from the airport, I put my foot down on the accelerator and prayed I didn't get picked up for speeding. I figured Mandy's plane would be touching down by now, but she still had to go through customs so this would give me enough time to get to the airport and park the car.

I made it to the arrivals lounge just in time to see her walking through the sliding doors. She caught sight of me and started to wave madly while trying to navigate her luggage trolley with one hand. "Mia, at long last!" she called out.

I reached her and gave her a big hug. Mandy was six inches taller than I, so she had to bend a little to return the greeting. "It's so good to see you!" I declared, happy to finally have my friend with me. "Did you have a good flight?"

"Yes," she answered. "I managed to get some sleep, which is always a good thing."

I stood back to take a good look at her. "Why, Mandy, you look great!"

She smiled bashfully, but I could see she seemed pleased by the compliment. She was wearing an elegant, off-white pantsuit with a red blouse that set off her blonde-streaked, shoulder-length hair and green eyes. Somehow, she looked different from the photos we had been exchanging online, and then it hit me. "Oh my God! You finally did it. You're wearing contacts!"

She grinned. "Yes, I managed to overcome my fear of lenses and decided it was time for a new look."

"I love the blonde streaks, too. My, my, you look like an Aussie chick already." I led the way out to the car and helped her steer the luggage trolley. "Hey, you brought so much luggage, I hope I can fit it into the car," I observed. The Ferrari had a decent sized boot for a sports car, but I wasn't sure if we would be able to fit in all of Mandy's things.

"If worse comes to worst I'll get a taxi to take me to your place," Mandy suggested.

As it turned out we managed to stuff the boot with her bags and before long, we were at my apartment, stretching out on the sofa with a glass of red wine. I felt tired, but I wanted to catch up with Mandy before I took a nap. I planned to take her to the female impersonator show this evening and wanted to look rested.

After about half an hour of girl talk, both Mandy and I started to nod off so I pulled out the sofa bed where she was to bunk during her stay and then went to my bedroom to take a nap. We planned to go to the hotel at around six and have dinner before the show, which was starting at eight.

I wore my usual black pantsuit uniform that evening as I was still on a double shift, but Mandy changed into a forest-green pantsuit with a cream blouse. I thought she looked quite elegant and sleek for a chick of fifty-one years as I introduced her to Dobbs and Chris, who had both turned up to meet us in the lobby when we arrived.

Mandy knew all about them through our frequent correspondence and she was particularly interested in Chris since I had described him as a young version of David. She wasn't disappointed, either. When the boys left us to our dinner she remarked, "He's gorgeous with that dark, wavy hair and green eyes, Mia. Of course, I never got to meet his father; but you had enough photos of him when I first met you."

"Just a warning before I forget," I told her. "Dobbs doesn't know about David and me. Only Chris knows because David told him some time ago, and now he sees me as a kind of pseudo-mother."

"Your secret is safe with me, you know that," she reassured me. "And how lovely that you have a son of sorts."

I smiled, thinking Chris could very well have been my real son had I married his father instead of that idiot, Nathan. "Chris once told me his father should have married me; it was very touching," I confided.

"What kind of mother would you have made, I wonder?" Mandy regarded me with merriment in her eyes. She knew all about the computer hacking in which Chris had been engaged during the Linda Liu case.

"Never mind," I replied. "Eat your dinner or we'll miss the beginning of the show."

Promptly at eight, I found a table for us to sit and enjoy the show, but I warned Mandy that if my pager went off I would have to leave her to it. She was fine with this as long as she had some wine to drink. I grinned, knowing her love of wine, and ordered her a bottle of a fine South Australian Shiraz from our functions supervisor who happened to come over to ask me a question. For me, I asked for a bottle of Pellegrino. Mark, the functions supervisor, smiled at us and left to get our order. Mandy and I sat back and waited.

"I'm so looking forward to seeing this show," she whispered as the lights went down and a spotlight hit the makeshift stage, which had been erected for the sole purpose of the show. There were around three hundred guests sitting at tables set for two and four people respectively; and the ballroom was filled to capacity.

The first person to appear on stage was the stunning Clee Torres impersonating Cher right down to the pouty lips, long black hair and superfluous make-up. She wore an outrageous see-through, black mesh bodysuit with the smallest pieces of satin covering her crotch and nipples; and with a thin strap at the back that acted as a kind of G-string. Her feet were encased in high-heeled leather boots that came up to the knee and on her upper body, she wore a leather jacket. On her head, she had on a soldier's cap that was covered in glittering stones of all colours, encircled with a black stone-covered band that held a single stone in place just above the visor. This was a sparkling pink stone the size of a large strawberry.

Mandy leaned forward to get a better look as Clee strode around the stage lip-syncing the words to Cher's song *If I Could Turn Back Time* against a backdrop prop symbolising a navy ship, and re-enacting Cher's video of the song. "Oh my God," Mandy declared above the music, "is she/he for real? Where is his... uh... his you-know-what?"

"You mean her cock." I smirked. "She doesn't have one; she's the real McCoy," I informed her in a dry tone, thinking of Jim Casey's description of his star.

Mandy didn't bother to reply. Her full focus was on the bits of satin covering Clee's crotch and nipples.

When the song finished, Clee took a bow and the prop changed to one of a spiral staircase with satin curtains hanging on either side. Clee scurried off stage just as the other three queens appeared at the top of the stairs and commenced their descent, each wearing a crest of long white feathers attached to the back of their skimpy costumes and with a smaller crest worked into a diamante tiara on their elaborately-coiffed wigs. They were dripping in fake diamonds, mainly at their ears and wrists, and they wore string upon string of pearls that ran over their breasts and travelled over their flat stomachs, ending in the smallest triangle of pearl-studded satin that covered their crotches.

This time, the song was *I Will Survive* by Gloria Gaynor, and the queens paraded around the stage a-la-Ziegfeld Follies. Halfway through the song, Clee joined them on stage, this time dressed in a long-tailed tuxedo jacket, top hat and cane, and wearing nothing else except a satin bowtie and tiny bikini pants made of strings of pearls. Her breasts were bare and perfect. In her role, she symbolised a male figure; and she had pasted a small moustache on her upper lip, with her long hair hidden under the hat.

I raised my brows at the intense energy in the room. The audience seemed captivated by the sensual display on stage as the queens rubbed up against Clee's body, only to be pushed away by her as if rejected. Mandy's eyes were glued on Clee; so much so, that she hadn't touched a drop of wine. This was a first for her, I thought with amusement.

"You okay?" I asked in jest.

She turned to me with eyes the size of saucers and declared,

"Amazing breasts! I must ask her who her surgeon is." Then, we burst out laughing.

The show ended around ten and I had to help Mandy out of the ballroom as the wine she had consumed once the show finished hit her jetlagged body and brain. Dobbs was still hanging around the hotel and when he saw me struggle with her, he came over to give me a hand. Between us, we propelled Mandy toward the lifts.

"She's not always like this," I explained when I saw the query in his eyes, "in any case, she won't remember a thing. She needs to rest now."

"I'll say." Dobbs grinned. "Hey, some show, huh?" He raised his eyebrows when he said this.

I laughed. "Dobbs, don't tell me you were ogling Clee's breasts."

He threw me a look of indignation. "Ferrari," he barked, which made me laugh even more, "I don't go for gay men!"

I could barely speak for the laughter. "It's a *she*, Dobbs. I met her in person when she checked in, and her manager informed me she has a real 'clit'." I wrinkled my nose at the word, but I liked shocking Dobbs; and from the look on his face, I had been successful.

"C'mon, where's the friggin' lift?" he complained.

I smirked at his discomfort and looked away to give him a chance to recover his composure. Meanwhile, I happened to gaze in the direction of the ballroom and spotted the female impersonators coming out in their regular clothes and making their way over to the lounge bar. Jim Casey was with them and much to my surprise, so was Mark, the functions supervisor. He was hanging onto Clee's arm and whispering in her ear. I cocked an eyebrow in curiosity and followed the two with my eyes. Mark was gay; so what was he doing with a transsexual, unless he was bi-sexual himself? Or perhaps Clee was the bi-sexual one. I shook my head and dismissed the thought just as the lift arrived.

Mandy fell asleep fully clothed when I deposited her on the sofa bed at home, and I almost followed suit because I was so exhausted after the big day I'd had. Thankfully, I managed to slip into pyjamas before I fell asleep immediately my head touched the pillow.

Something seemed to be vibrating and ringing at the same time, and I made a mental note to punch out the neighbour above my unit because it was his habit to vacuum late at night. I turned in bed and placed the spare pillow over my head. The noise stopped for a few seconds and everything was blissfully quiet. Then, it started up again; the vibrating and ringing. I turned once more, this time opening one eye and peering at my electric bedside clock. It was 3.57am. The noise stopped again and I thought I must have been dreaming. I closed my eye, but before I could sink back into blissful slumber, the vibration and noise started up yet again. This time, both my eyes opened and I realised that vacuum cleaners didn't ring. The noise was coming from my mobile phone, which was resting on my night table.

I sat up, still half asleep, grabbed the phone before it stopped ringing and saw it was Dobbs on the caller ID. "What's wrong?" I asked with concern in my voice. My mind was still foggy with sleep, but I was alert enough to realise that unless something was horribly wrong, Dobbs would never ring me at this time.

"Finally!" he declared with relief. "I've been ringing you for half an hour or more."

"I was asleep," I retorted. "What the hell is it?"

"You'd better get your ass over here," he exclaimed. "Your lady friend, Clee, is in the bathtub—"

I didn't let him finish as anger swept over me. "Is this a joke? What do I care that she's in the fucking bathtub?"

"Oh, you'll care about this one, Ferrari," Dobbs replied tersely. "She's swimming in a pool of blood and with pieces of her floating around."

# CHAPTER 4

Although I lived within walking distance of the hotel, I jumped into my Ferrari and arrived at the scene within five minutes with a very sleepy Mandy in tow.

She had awakened during my conversation with Dobbs as a result of the noise I made while moving about my bedroom, opening and closing drawers, looking for something to wear. All my uniforms were with the hotel's dry cleaner so I threw on a T-shirt and an old pair of jeans.

A drowsy Mandy appeared in the doorway while I was dressing. "What's going on?" she asked, rubbing her eyes.

"I've been called in for an emergency," I replied, putting on my sneakers. "Go back to bed; it's still early."

"What kind of an emergency is it that warrants getting you out of bed at this hour?" She fixed me with a look of suspicion.

I sighed, knowing I was going to have to tell her the truth. Mandy knew me too well for me to gloss over the reason as to why I was rushing in to work in a pair of old jeans, and not a bit of make-up. "Clee's been murdered," I announced and saw the shock in her eyes mixed with a kind of excitement. I knew that expression only too well because this was how I looked when I sniffed a mystery to solve. "Oh no!" I stated firmly, shaking my head. "You're not coming with me."

Mandy made a beeline for the lounge room and called out over her shoulder, "You try and stop me, Ferrari!"

When we arrived at the hotel, Dobbs met us in the lobby. He was in full uniform and looking haggard. "This isn't a sightseeing tour, you know!" he exclaimed when he saw Mandy.

I shrugged. "Too bad, Dobbs. I couldn't stop her even if I tried.

What gives?"

We started to move across the floor toward the lifts and I noticed a few police officers posted at the hotel doors. Dobbs saw the question in my eyes. "They're making sure no one leaves the hotel until the forensics process the murder scene."

The lift arrived and we stepped in. As Dobbs punched the button for the tenth floor, Mandy remarked, "Of course, I am sorry someone was murdered; but I'm glad I'm here to experience this first hand."

I smirked at the look Dobbs threw her and knew I would have to keep her out of the way before he throttled her. "Is Chris in the penthouse?" I asked, ignoring Mandy's comment.

"I guess so," Dobbs replied, looking none too happy with Mandy.

"I'll get Mandy to stay with him while we go over the scene." I saw from the corner of my eye that Mandy was about to protest and I shook my head at her. Thankfully, she had the sense to remain silent.

When the doors slid open, I stepped out and almost collided with Smythe who was about to step into the lift. He paused and took a long look at me from his great height of six-two; then, he clapped eyes on Mandy. "I'm not even going to ask, Ferrari." His official police voice held a tinge of surliness to it. This was his usual way of telling me I was a pain in the behind.

"Good." I grinned and replied back in my own official duty manager's voice, which had a bit of a bitchy tone to it, at least where Smythe was concerned, "As the senior duty manager of the hotel, I was called in. You know very well that I have every right to be here." I made to walk past him, but he caught hold of my wrist and stopped me. I bristled. "What now?" My eyes threw daggers at him.

"The floorshow was over hours ago," he remarked sarcastically, "so what's with 'pixie' over here?" He pointed toward Mandy with his chin.

I pulled my wrist free of his grasp and noticed for the first time that Mandy had tied back her hair in a short ponytail, which made her look like a five-year-old. Not only this, but her eyes were bright as she gazed at Smythe, and she wore a silly smile on her face. For the first time since I'd known her, I wanted to slap her. Mandy was sweet on Smythe! It took all of my willpower not to whack her one and then grab Smythe's Glock and blow his head off for being a smartarse.

"Detective Sergeant Phil Smythe, this is Amanda Wilson; my good friend from the UK visiting Sydney for a few weeks." I made the introduction as if we were at a garden party instead of a murder scene.

To my great surprise and horror, Smythe extended a hand toward Mandy and she placed hers in his. "Welcome to Sydney, Amanda," he said smoothly, and I suddenly wanted to puke.

"Please, call me Mandy," she gushed, lowering her eyes and blushing.

I took a step between the two and broke their grip while they were shaking hands. "Can we get on with this?" I glared at them in annoyance.

Smythe cleared his throat and did not offer any comment, which was strange for him; and a feeling of rage rose up from my toes to my stomach. Dobbs must have sensed the pent up energy within me and took hold of Mandy's arm as he declared, "Mandy, this is official police business so I'm going to ask you to stay in the penthouse with Chris. He'll look after you while Mia and I finish up here."

Mandy looked disappointed, but she followed Dobbs when he started to move toward the penthouse, located at the other end of the corridor from Suite 1009, where Clee's body was supposedly in pieces and swimming in a bath of blood.

When they moved off, a young detective walked up to Smythe. "Phil, do you want me to go downstairs and wait for the coroner?" Even though he addressed Smythe, he glanced in my direction with a look of expectancy.

He looked to be in his late twenties or early thirties, about five feet ten with an athletic build, gorgeous almond-shaped eyes, spiky black hair and light chocolate-coloured skin. It occurred to me that this was Sean Webb, Smythe's new partner, but I had never imagined him to be Eurasian. Dobbs had never mentioned this even though he'd told me he was a "bad boy" type, just as I liked. He was right. Webb was very attractive in an exotic way, and I felt instantly drawn to him.

"I'm Detective Sean Webb," he introduced himself, shaking my hand.

His grip was cool and firm, his tone confident. A bad boy all right, my mind screamed out. "Mia Ferrari," I returned, "senior duty manager of the hotel."

Smythe watched our interchange as if he was in deep thought about something, and then he snapped out of it and punched the lift button. "You go, Sean. I'll take Ferr... I mean, Ms Ferrari to the scene."

The lift arrived and Sean stepped in, throwing a look of amusement at his partner. "Will do," he said as the lift doors slid shut.

"Arsehole," Smythe murmured under his breath, but I heard him loud and clear.

"What's the matter, Smythe, you miss your Dirty Harry days already?" I gave him a wicked smile.

"Shut up, Ferrari," he replied tersely. "We'll wait for Dobbs to get back so I can get this over and done with. I don't know why I have to show you what happened when Dobbs already documented the events on behalf of the hotel."

I couldn't help but smirk. He was really pissed off, and I loved it. "Dobbs might have documented everything, Smythe, but I have seniority here; and in the absence of the general manager and the CEO, I'm in charge. I need to see what happened for myself."

Smythe didn't deign me with a response as we made our way to Suite 1009. He obviously had other things on his mind because normally he would have come back with some snappy remark even though what I had just said was true. In the absence of the general manager and the CEO, the policy was that the senior duty manager should be in charge. Right now, Peter, our general manager, was away on annual leave and David Rourke was in Hawaii, so Smythe was stuck with me.

I struggled to keep up with his stride as we approached the murder scene and once there, he handed me a pair of booties and latex gloves. "Don't touch anything," Smythe warned as if I didn't know any better.

Dobbs reached us just as we were about to enter the room. "I'll wait for you out here. I've seen all I need to see."

I followed Smythe into the room and espied forensic technicians dusting for prints while others collected fibres, took photographs and looked for any other evidence they could get their hands on. Smythe moved through the large bedroom and approached the bathroom where other forensic people were working the scene.

I prepared myself for whatever was waiting in the bathtub. Despite this, what met my eyes turned my stomach and I was sure I was going to faint. I must've swayed because Smythe automatically reached out and grabbed hold of my arm to steady me. I stood up straight and mouthed a silent thank you to him.

Clee's face was as beautiful in death as it had been in life, but the rest of her was right out of a horror movie. Her head and torso floated in the tub with her perfect breasts peeking out through the bloody water. The killer had cut her body in half at the waist and her pelvis floated at a weird angle to the torso, revealing a pierced bellybutton with a small silver hoop and shaved, orange pubic hair at the groin, forming the figure of a heart. Her long legs were left untouched except for the feet, which now floated freely around the tub. I swayed again and the last thing I saw before I fell into Smythe's arms was the blood-spattered tiles around the bathroom walls and floor.

There were voices all around me, but my eyes remained shut. I was lying on something soft and someone was holding my hand.

"Should I call for the doctor?" Chris's voice asked from somewhere above my head.

"Yes," replied Mandy, and I felt her hand tighten on mine.

"She's only fainted, for God's sake." Smythe's unconcerned remark came from the vicinity of my feet.

"Call the doctor, Chris." This was from Dobbs, who must've been standing behind Mandy and looking over her shoulder at me.

I made a strong effort to open my eyes as the last thing I wanted was to give Smythe the satisfaction of seeing me at my weakest. It was bad enough that after this episode he would have ammunition to tease me and call me a fainting lily for the rest of my days.

Mandy's grip on my hand tightened even more. "Wait, wait!" she called out. "I see her eyelids moving. I think she's coming to."

"Pour her a whiskey, Chris," Dobbs commanded.

"I have to get back to the scene, Dobbs," Smythe said. "Let me know how she's doing, will you?"

I heard the door open and shut; then my eyelids flew open. "What the fuck happened?" Were the first words out of my mouth.

Dobbs's grin came into focus. "She's baaaack!"

I tried to sit up, but Mandy held me down gently. "Not yet, Mia. You had a nasty shock, so first take a few sips of this."

A glass of whiskey materialised before me and Chris held it to my lips while with the other hand he supported my head so I could take a drink. I did so and as the liquid burned its way down to my stomach, I coughed and spluttered. "Shit!" I exclaimed and waved away the glass as I shook Mandy's hand off my own. "Let me up!"

"Okay, she's definitely back!" Dobbs declared in a happy tone of voice. "She's her dear, gentle, old self again," he teased.

"Fuck off, Dobbs," I said dryly, but the look I threw him was one of warmth. He knew I hated it when people made a fuss. I always wanted to look cool in any situation. This time, however, I had failed miserably. I sat up on the sofa, where I had been lying, ran my fingers through my short hair, and glanced at Chris. "Some cold water would be good." Chris scurried off to the kitchen while Mandy stayed seated next to me and Dobbs took a seat opposite us. "What happened?" I asked.

"Smythe brought you back from the scene. You were out like a light," Dobbs answered.

Chris returned and handed me the water. I took a big swig. "Man, trust me to faint when Smythe was around. I'd much rather be chewed up and swallowed by Godzilla." I shook my head.

"But it was so romantic," Mandy piped in, and we all stared at her. "What did I say? That man is—"

"That man is an arsehole!" I interrupted her with a look of irritation on my face.

Chris and Dobbs laughed at Mandy's confused look. "Never mind, Mandy. It's a long story," Dobbs explained.

Mandy shrugged her shoulders and stood up. "How about I go and make coffee while you talk?" she suggested. "Chris, will you show me to the kitchen?"

Chris walked off with her and I turned to Dobbs. "I must apologise to Mandy. She doesn't know about my history with Smythe."

Dobbs nodded. "I'm sure she'll understand. Now, how do you feel?"

"I'm fine. Just mortified that I fainted and Smythe was the one who carried me," I confessed. "If it had been his partner, Sean, I wouldn't have complained." I threw him a wicked look.

Dobbs laughed. "You do beat all, girl! So what did you think of him?"

"I only met him briefly," I replied. "He's got an attitude and he's rather sexy."

Dobbs winked at me. "You never give up."

"No, I don't," I agreed, and then turned to business. "So tell me what we're doing about the guests to protect them from the scene."

"Luckily, Suite 1009 is at the end of the hallway, so we taped it off and in the morning we can move all the guests off the tenth floor, except for Jim Casey and his impersonators. They can stay in their present rooms."

"Good God, I'd forgotten about them!" I exclaimed. "Do they already know? And how come you're still around here in uniform? I would've thought you'd gone home and were fast asleep when the call came in."

"No," Dobbs replied. "I got delayed by a few things that came up at the last minute and was still on duty when Casey came running into the lobby screaming like a banshee. We had to call the doctor to sedate him."

"So he found the body?" I could just imagine Casey's reaction when he saw what was in that bathtub.

"He was incoherent," Dobbs explained. "As far as I know, he was the first to discover the body. The three impersonators were allegedly asleep, but of course Casey's screams woke up the whole tenth floor and we had to go into damage control and tell the guests the guy had suffered a panic attack."

I shook my head while I mentally visualised a scene right out of bedlam. "And then what happened?" I noticed how tired Dobbs looked. The shock of it all had worn him out.

Chris came back with cups, milk and sugar, and sat down next to me. "Mandy's bringing the coffee in a minute," he announced.

"Good," Dobbs sighed, "I could use a cup."

"Go on, Dobbs," I prompted him.

"Then, I called the cops and had the night manager call a doctor for Casey. I sent one of my guys up to the tenth floor to reassure the guests that all was well, and to ensure the impersonators stayed in their own rooms until notified."

Mandy walked in with a large pot of coffee and poured for all of us while Dobbs went on with the story. "We kept Casey in the first aid room until the doctor arrived and sedated him. Then we took him up to his suite. By this time, the police arrived and they called Smythe when they saw the crime scene."

Dobbs had a sip of black coffee and relaxed back in his seat.

I said, "So up to that point you didn't see exactly what had happened in the room?"

"No," Dobbs replied. "I told the cops we had a death in the hotel and waited until they arrived before I entered the room with them." He paused and took another sip of coffee. "It was horrible." He shuddered.

That's for sure, I thought. The scene in that bathroom was something I would never forget for as long as I lived.

# CHAPTER 5

Mandy and I made our way home just before seven, when the morning shift was starting to come in. By this time, the police had pretty much finished with the crime scene. Clee's suite was blocked off and guests reallocated to rooms on the ninth floor. Only Jim Casey and the female impersonators remained in their original rooms.

Just before leaving Dobbs informed me that Smythe was going to question Casey and his crew later in the day, after they'd had a chance to get over the shock of what had happened. I wanted to get to Casey and the drag queens before Smythe did, but I was so tired I had to put it off. I didn't inform Dobbs that it was my intention to make my own inquiries, but I did ask him if he had someone read the lock to see who had been in the room the day of the murder.

"Only the room attendant that cleaned the room in the morning and turned down the bed later in the evening," Dobbs reported. "The only other key used to gain access to the room belonged to the victim."

"Do you think she knew the murderer, and let him in?" I had a feeling this was the case.

"Either that or someone came in through the balcony door. But the police checked the lock and it looked fine, so unless we have a master 'picklock' with a liking for heights I don't know how the hell the killer got in." Dobbs rubbed his eyes. "I'm going to wrap up here and go home for some shuteye. You should do the same."

I nodded and once we said our goodbyes, Mandy and I headed for the car park. At home, we crashed on our beds and fell asleep almost immediately.

I was back on duty at three that afternoon and felt guilty that I didn't have time to show Mandy around. "I'll make it up to you,

Mandy," I said while I got ready for work.

"No worries," she replied, still looking sleepy, "I think the jetlag, plus all the excitement, is catching up with me. I feel like I could sleep for another twenty-four hours."

I smiled and patted her arm. "You do that. Tomorrow I have the day off, so I'll take you sightseeing."

"Mia." Mandy regarded me with concern in her eyes. "Don't feel you have to drop everything just because I'm here. I know you're busy with work, and now this murder. It can't be good for the hotel's image, either; so I really don't mind going out on my own."

"You're very sweet," I answered, "but the whole idea of your coming over was to catch up with me and have a break from Phil. And so far, we haven't even had a chance to talk about anything personal."

Mandy smiled. "Who cares about Phil with so much going on? At least there's plenty happening around here and I haven't had a single thought about him since I arrived."

Phil was Mandy's husband and, much as she put on a brave front, I knew she had a few decisions to make about her flagging marriage. I felt terrible that we didn't yet have a chance to even broach the subject. Even so, I made sure to roster myself off for the following day so I could devote the whole of that time to my friend.

"You have a good rest, and tomorrow we'll enjoy ourselves," I replied, picked up my keys, and headed for the door. "See you tonight." Mandy waved at me and put her head back on the pillow.

When I arrived at the hotel, I headed straight for Dobbs's office and found him at his computer. I came in carrying two cappuccinos I picked up on the way to work. Dobbs looked up from the keyboard with relief as I handed him one of the coffees. "Thank God!" he exclaimed, still looking rather tired.

I sat down opposite him in one of the visitors' chairs. "I slept like a log until about an hour ago, so I didn't get a chance to grab any food yet."

"No problem." Dobbs picked up the phone for room service. "Burger and fries?" he asked, already knowing the answer. I nodded and he ordered two meals.

"I thought you were on a diet," I remarked teasingly when he finished the call.

"Hey, I also slept right through and missed out on both breakfast *and* lunch."

"Fair enough. I guess we both earned this after what happened," I replied. "How are things, anyway?"

Dobbs took a sip of his coffee before answering, "Smythe and his partner came in at around eleven to question Casey and his troop. Nat logged them leaving by two, just before I arrived."

"Did they question anyone else?"

"The room attendant that had access to the room and the night staff. No one seems to have reported seeing anything suspicious," he replied. "Nat also took them through the CCTV footage to see if something showed up that could be of help, but there were no findings."

I leaned forward and planted my elbows on his desk. "So what exactly happened, starting from last night?"

Dobbs looked at his computer screen briefly. "According to the security log, the entertainers went for a drink to the cocktail lounge after the show."

"Yes," I confirmed. "I saw them heading for the bar when we were helping Mandy across the lobby. Mark Meadows was with them."

Dobbs's eyebrows shot up. "Mark, as in our functions supervisor?"

I nodded. "I thought it a little strange seeing as staff's not meant to fraternise with guests, but it looked to me like Mark was on friendly terms with Clee. In fact, he was holding on to her arm rather intimately."

"Hmm." Dobbs looked thoughtful for a moment and then went on. "Anyway, it looks like they left at around midnight, as reported by the bar manager; and as far as anyone knows, they all went to bed."

"That's it?" I looked disappointed.

"That's it," he concurred.

"So when did Casey raise the alarm?"

Dobbs consulted the security log again. "Around two-thirty in the morning. That's when he came screaming into the lobby, and the night manager called me. The rest, you know."

A knock at the door startled us, and I turned to see one of the room service waiters with our lunch. I opened the glass door and let him in. He deposited a tray on Dobbs's desk and left us with a smile.

Dobbs and I attacked the food like ravenous beasts and ate in silence. When we finished, we sat back and sipped on a couple of Cokes he drew from a mini-bar fridge in his office.

"I'm going to talk to Casey and the queens," I announced suddenly, taking a swig of my drink.

Dobbs turned alarmed eyes on me. "Oh no! Please don't tell me you're going to get involved in this one, Ferrari."

I grinned. "Okay, I won't tell you."

"That's not funny," he protested.

I shrugged. "It doesn't hurt to make some inquiries, Dobbs. The police could've missed something or perhaps the people they questioned would much rather open up to little me instead of an arrogant pig like Smythe."

Dobbs shook his head. "You never give up, do you?"

I stood up and threw my empty Coke can in the office bin by his desk. "You know me, Dobbs. If there's something to be found out, I'm on the case."

"And you know Smythe, Ferrari," he called out after my retreating back. "If you meddle, he'll throw your *ass* in jail."

I waved at him over my shoulder and left his office. Then, I headed straight for Casey's suite. There was no answer when I knocked on his door, but the door opposite his opened and a young man's head popped out. "You won't find him in there, darling. Nobody knows where he is."

I turned and faced an effeminate youth with dark brown hair. "You are... um..." I searched for his name in my memory but couldn't come up with it.

The young man stepped out and shook my hand with a surprisingly firm grip. "I'm Ayna Liscious, dear; but my real name is Frank."

"Do you mind if I call you Frank? Easier to remember," I explained lest he take offence.

"Sure, darling. Come on in and join the rest of the group. We're all in here having coffee." Frank invited by holding the door open for me to walk in.

The boys were sitting around the suite, cups and cake plates resting on a coffee table, colourful costumes with stones and feathers scattered all over the place along with high-heeled shoes, wigs and other female paraphernalia. Frank motioned for me to sit with them and offered me coffee. "I just had one, thanks," I declined politely.

"You're that Ferrari person, aren't you, honey?" A young man with light brown hair and green eyes pointed at me with his finger, and I nodded. He smiled. "I just loooove a good Ferrari, that's why I remember your name," he confessed. "I'm Tony, by the way, although on stage I'm Zsa Zsa Lahore."

"I'm Mia Ferrari, senior duty manager," I replied, even though I had introduced myself to them upon check-in, but I didn't expect them to remember too much—not after what had transpired in between.

The third member of the group was an attractive Asian youth who looked about Chris's age. "I'm Felle Ashio, but my real name is Alan." We shook hands.

"So, Mia, why are you looking for Jim?" Frank, who seemed to be the leader of the three, asked.

"Well, I heard about what happened and I wanted to pay my condolences to him and all of you."

"Jim took off after the police finished questioning us. I think he needed some private time to grieve," Frank informed me.

I gazed at all three faces and decided they didn't look too sad under the circumstances. "What about you, how are you all holding up? Oh, and I also want to ask if you wish the hotel to cancel your performance for this evening. We're happy to refund the ticket money."

Tony's eyes grew wide with surprise. "No way, darling," he gushed in a camp manner. "The show must go on! Ophelia would have been the first to agree." The others nodded in confirmation.

"I just thought that seeing as Clee... I mean, Ophelia, was murdered you'd all be in shock." I wondered why the queens seemed so blasé about the whole thing.

"If you're trying to ask why we're not in mourning, it's because none of us cared much for her. She was a real bitch," Frank declared much to my astonishment.

I cleared my throat. "I think I will have that coffee after all." I needed my wits around me and coffee was the only way to keep me on the alert.

Alan, the Asian flower, poured me a cup and offered milk and sugar. He then sat next to me on the settee and fingered my short, almost white-blonde hair. "Darling, is this real or out of a bottle? I just love that colour."

The other queens leaned forward in their seats to have a closer look and I experienced a sense of the surreal. Here I was in a room with three drag queens who didn't give a toss that their colleague had been horribly murdered, and they were asking me about my hair colour. Chills ran up and down my spine as I wondered whether one of the queens was the murderer.

"It's... um... it's real. Northern Italian extraction," I explained.

"Aaaah, bellissima!" Frank kissed the tip of his fingers in the Italian fashion.

I sipped some coffee in order to regain my composure while my thoughts started to run wild with my latest theory: what if all three of them had ganged up on Ophelia and murdered her for some reason?

"Do you mind if I ask you to elaborate on that?" I asked Frank directly, trying to keep calm.

He glanced at me without understanding for a few seconds, and then, "Oh, you mean about Ophelia being a bitch?"

I nodded, and every one sat back to listen to Frank's response.

"Much as we're sorry that she lost her life there was never any love lost between us, darling," he disclosed. "You see, she was forever lording it over us because she was wildly rich and didn't have to be a working girl if she didn't want to."

"Yes," Alan chimed in, "plus she also made fun of us because we didn't have the courage to get the operation, even though we're just as much female as she is... or was."

I looked confused and Tony explained. "Ophelia was a transsexual. You know, she had a vagina and so on. We're transvestites—we dress as women but still have the real toolbox, if you catch my meaning." He threw me a knowing look.

Frank was blunt. "In other words, we still have our cocks, darling."

I thanked God that very little shocked me working in hotels, so I didn't blush. "But you feel like women, right?"

"Sure," Frank answered. "We started off cross-dressing, but deep down inside we always knew we should be women instead of men."

"Okay." I nodded. "I understand. But if this is how you feel, why not change your sex?"

"Too expensive—and painful," Tony stated. "We chose to start taking hormones to grow breasts and have less facial hair and such;

but right now, the tool stays."

"We talked about it hundreds of times with Ophelia," Frank added, "but she couldn't relate to us. In fact, she often made fun of us, calling us 'hybrids' and 'in-betweens', as in between genders; but we put up with it. Ophelia was the star of the show and we didn't want to break up the act, at least not until we became better known and could afford to do without her."

"And what was that about her boasting of being rich?" I asked.

"She claimed she was worth at least twenty million." Alan rolled his eyes. "So she obviously didn't need to work. She said she did it for the love of the art, and all that jazz."

The others laughed, and Frank stated, "I think there was more to it than that, but let's just say she was worth a lot of dosh, darling."

I was amazed at the amount of information I was gathering from this conversation, and it occurred to me to ask, "What did the detectives say when you told them all of this?"

More laughter from the group. "Those bitches?" Tony exclaimed with derision. "Why, we didn't tell them shit, honey. It's none of their business."

I knew all of a sudden that I was going to get on with the "girls" really well. Despite this, I warned them, "You could be obstructing an investigation by not divulging all this information."

"Darling, we don't give a rats; not even a little rat! That bitch, Smythe, was a real macho prick; not to mention his young sidekick," Frank said with a leer. "I mean, aside from his cute and tight arse, he was a bigger bitch to us than the Smythe prick."

My curiosity was aroused and I could just picture the scene in my head: Smythe and Webb surrounded by a bunch of queens sizing them up. I felt like laughing but didn't want to lose the thread of my thoughts. "How so?"

"They treated us like second class citizens," Alan protested.

"You mean they were arrogant to you," I clarified.

"Yes," Alan concurred. "So we told them nothing."

"What's there to tell aside from the fact that Ophelia boasted she was rich?" I hoped there would be a clue in all this. "I mean, money's always a motive for murder, but there would have to be beneficiaries who'd benefit from her will; and they would be the first suspects on the cops' list. Besides, it's not like she went around carrying twenty million on her person for someone to steal outright."

Frank suddenly stood up and went to a chest of drawers where he drew out the soldier's cap Ophelia had worn in the opening act the night before. "That's where you're wrong, darling," he said, and handed me the cap.

I looked at it, but didn't understand. "What's your point?"

"Look at the hat carefully and tell me what's missing," Frank instructed.

I turned the hat in my hands a couple of times and looked at all the beautiful stones that covered it. Then, I saw the empty space above the visor and my heart quickened. "There was a pink stone here, if memory serves me right."

Frank sat on the armrest of the settee, leaning over me. "That's right, sweets!"

"But what's this got to do with carrying twenty million with her?" I asked, starting to get a feeling that the motive for the murder was within my reach.

Frank grinned. "You think the stone was a fake like the rest, right? Well, not quite, Mia Ferrari," he declared triumphantly. "Ophelia's ego was such that she carried her millions with her in the shape of a cursed, eighty-carat pink diamond called 'The Eye of Krishna'." He paused for effect, and then, "*This* is why she was murdered."

# CHAPTER 6

"What is this 'Eye of Krishna'?" Mandy asked the next morning over coffee.

It was my day off and we were having breakfast at Puccini's in Woollahra. I forked a piece of Italian sausage and popped it in my mouth as one of the waiters delivered our second round of cappuccinos. "It's a famous diamond worth millions," I answered as soon as the waiter walked away. "And it seems to carry some kind of curse with it."

Mandy's eyes lit up. "This is getting better and better, Mia. Mind if I blog about it?"

I threw her a warning look. "Don't you even dare, Amanda Wilson! This whole thing is part of a murder investigation, and we can't have you blogging about it to all and sundry."

Mandy ran a blog called "Fortifying your fifties" that was mainly about her trips abroad, and where she also touched upon health and the dilemma of ageing. Now, it seemed, she wanted to add murder to her list of topics.

"Okay, okay." Mandy tried to pacify me. "It was just an idea."

I sighed. "Sorry, I didn't mean to snap. It's just that no one knows about the information the queens gave me, and right now I need to digest all this."

Mandy patted my arm in sympathy. "Well, I'm here if you want to use me as a sounding board."

I smiled. "Thank you for understanding, but today is about sightseeing and introducing you to the wonders of Sydney."

"I'd say what happened in the last forty-eight hours pretty much makes up for the whole trip." Mandy winked at me. "Of course, I don't mean to appear heartless about the murder of this Clee...

whatever her name was."

"Clee Torres," I reminded her, a touch too firmly. I still couldn't get that bathtub scene out of my head. "Her real name was Ophelia."

Mandy took a sip of her coffee and looked contrite. "I'm so sorry about Ophelia. No one should have to come to such a tragic end."

We ate in silence until finished and then I settled the bill. Mandy wanted to pay, but I insisted this was my treat. "You can buy lunch," I told her.

The day was sunny and warm; a great day for driving around in the Ferrari. Mandy and I climbed in the car, ignoring the admiring looks of passers-by, and the engine purred into life when I turned the key. "I think we'll drive north to Whale beach," I informed my excited guest as I pulled the car into the traffic.

"So tell me more about this Eye of Krishna business," Mandy prompted. "Aside from this whole unfortunate situation, I find cursed gems a fascinating topic."

I grinned. "It seems we're going to have to combine sightseeing with murder, and now curses." Mandy went to open her mouth to defend herself, but I added, "Don't worry, I'm not upset. If you don't mind being a sounding board, as you've said, then I'll make use of you."

"Excellent," she exclaimed and popped on her sunglasses.

I turned left at the bottom of Ocean Road to head toward the city, and then onto the Eastern distributor, which would take us over the Harbour Bridge and onto the northern suburbs of Sydney and its renowned beaches. "From what the queens told me," I explained, "the diamond is some kind of family heirloom from Ophelia's mother's side of the family. Apparently, the mother's great grandfather served in India as a cavalryman and he somehow acquired the diamond when it was looted in 1857 from some temple or other. Anyway, to cut a long story short, every member of Ophelia's family that had some sort of contact with the stone died relatively young."

"What happened to Ophelia's mother?"

"I don't really know. The queens told me that Ophelia was given the stone by her mother, who died when she was quite young."

"What a story," Mandy remarked. "But how true can this curse be?"

"Who knows," I replied, never having believed in curses myself.

"So what will you do now?"

I frowned. "This is what I have to figure out. I will, for one, tell Dobbs all I know; and then see what else I can find out."

"What about the police?"

I wrinkled my nose in distaste. "The police can wait. It's not like I can go to them and tell them that Ophelia was killed because of a curse," I argued.

"Yes, but the stolen gem is a motive," Mandy pointed out. "Plus the queens gave you Ophelia's hat, which is evidence."

I threw her a quick look. "Hey, you're starting to sound like Dobbs now. He's always at me to go to the cops."

Mandy smiled. "I just don't want you to get into trouble."

"Trouble is my constant companion, it seems," I remarked mysteriously and changed the subject. "Let's enjoy the drive and forget about this for a while."

This, we did. We spent the rest of the morning at Whale beach, sunning ourselves and taking a dip in the ocean. I warned Mandy about the strength of the Australian sun and urged her to use sun block on her skin. I pretty much covered myself from head to toe with it as my northern Italian complexion was susceptible to the sun's strong rays and I could easily burn within fifteen minutes of exposure. Mandy seemed to bear the sun better than I; but even so, she started to look a little like a lobster by the time we threw on clothes over our swimmers and drove to a local café for lunch.

The place was high up in the hills above the beach and we were fortunate to get a table on the sandstone terrace, which overlooked the Pacific Ocean in all its sparkling glory. Mandy was in ruptures. "You are so lucky to have such great weather in Sydney. All we get back home is fog and rain most times," she commented. "You know, I can see myself living here."

I gazed at her, looking so relaxed, sunburned and with her hair more blonde than when she had arrived. The sun in Australia worked fairly quickly to make anyone who loved the great outdoors look like a true blue Aussie.

A young girl brought us the menus. And after such a big breakfast, we opted for chicken Caesar salad with crusty French bread and cool sparkling water. "So what's going on with you and Phil?" I asked when the waitress went off to place our order.

Mandy's face suddenly wore a frown. "Who knows?" Her tone was full of frustration. "Why is it that when women go through menopause they have to put up with hot flushes, mood swings, water retention, and heaven knows what else; while men simply pooh-pooh it. But when it comes to them reaching middle age, they fall apart unless they can define themselves by their occupation or some kind of status, and no one raises a peep!"

"At least Phil didn't dump you for a younger woman," I pointed out bitterly, referring to my case with the ex.

"True, but sometimes I almost wish he would," Mandy confessed. She saw my look of surprise, and added, "You know the good, old 'better to be alone than in bad company'?"

I nodded.

"Well, even though Phil now has an occupation, plus his hobby of flying airplanes, it's like his life isn't full enough for him; and I'm beginning to wonder if it's something to do with me."

I felt rising anger at this statement, but not toward Mandy. It was the male of the species that got my hackles up. "These fucking men always make it so that we think it's our fault; and women fall for it! I tell you, Mandy, it's nothing you did. It's all Phil. It's just typical of males in general, really," I remarked, a feeling of real fury threatening to rear its ugly head. "You see, they just can't handle life the way we do. They fall apart if things don't go their way, but when things aren't going our way, we're accused of whinging, ranting, being menopausal, having the vapours, and whatever other phrase you care to use."

"Wow!" Mandy exclaimed. "Nathan really did a number on you."

"Yes, he did; but he also did me a huge favour," I replied, feeling rather philosophical. "He liberated me from thinking that I have to have a man in my life in order to define myself. I did everything for that bastard while we were married, and he repaid me with betrayal. Nowadays, I fly solo—and I don't trust any man!"

"Not even David?" Mandy threw me a knowing look.

I sighed just as our drinks arrived. Great timing, I thought when I took a long sip of the cool water. "David is in the past. I really wouldn't know what he'd be like now. The David I'm in love with is someone from almost twenty years ago; he doesn't exist anymore."

Mandy looked at me with doubt. "Yes, but you still feel for him."

"I confess I do to some extent. Aside from Dobbs, who's like a father to me, David is probably the only other man I trust. But as to whether I would ever consider getting together with him long term, I still have my doubts."

"You're a tough one, Mia. I wish I had your strength," Mandy lamented. "I love Phil, but sometimes I want to kill him for being so negative and grumpy about everything. He drags me down so much, but then he'll do something really sweet for me, and I melt. What can I tell you? I'm a weak female after all."

Our salads arrived and we put our conversation on hold until we sampled the fare and enjoyed the multi-million dollar view. This brought me back to a sense of peace and tranquillity once more. Unfortunately, the feeling didn't last too long.

"Fuck!" I whispered harshly.

Mandy regarded me with surprise in her eyes. "What's wrong, is there a bug in your salad?"

"No." I jerked my chin toward the entrance to the café. "There's a *bug* at the door."

Mandy turned slightly to see what I was talking about, and a strange light gleamed in her eyes when she looked back at me. "Isn't that your detective friend?"

"He's no friend of mine," I replied through clenched teeth. "Oh, shit," I added. "They've seen us and are coming this way."

Mandy seemed delighted when Smythe and Sean Webb reached our table. "Ladies," Smythe said, mainly addressing Mandy. "What a rare pleasure."

I rolled my eyes and wished I could push the prick over the terrace banister so he would go hurtling down the cliff and splatter all over the beach. "What are you doing here, Smythe?" I dispensed with the greetings. "You're a bit out of your jurisdiction." I saw from the corner of my eye that the attractive Sean was smirking, and even though I knew he had an attitude, I rather liked him.

"Some police business with the local department over here," Smythe offered by way of explanation. "So we thought we'd have something to eat before heading back."

"There's a McDonald's farther down the road." My voice dripped with sarcasm, but he chose to ignore it and addressed Mandy again.

"Mandy, right?"

She nodded with delight at his remembering her name, and I tried not to gnash my teeth with annoyance.

"This is my partner, Detective Sean Webb, but you can call him Sean." Mandy and Sean shook hands while Smythe stood there with a stupid-looking smile on his face.

I frowned and before the whole thing turned into a tête-à-tête, I decided to put an end to it. "Well, how nice to bump into you, boys." The sarcasm was still in my voice. "Why don't you run along now and get your food?"

Smythe glowered at me while Sean threw me an impish smile.

Then, Mandy spoke. "Better still, why don't you join us?"

The men didn't need a second invitation, and Mandy obviously didn't catch the thunderous look on my face, or perhaps she simply chose to ignore it. Whatever the case, I was stuck with Smythe; but the presence of his cute partner made it slightly worthwhile.

The waitress returned to take their order and Smythe chose Thai beef salad while his partner went for a steak sandwich. They also put in an order for a large bottle of Pellegrino to share.

Mandy and Smythe fell into conversation immediately, and I heard him ask about how she was enjoying her stay in Sydney. But that's all I heard because Sean turned to me with a grin and spoke close to my ear. "I see there's no love lost between you and Smythe."

"You should ask him about that," I replied tersely.

"Well, I hope you don't feel the same way about me." He treated me to a devastatingly sexy smile, and I tried not to laugh in his face. If this "babe in the woods" thought he could charm me, he had another think coming. I was older and wiser than him, and the only way anything could ever happen between us was if I chose for it to do so.

"I don't know you well enough to make a judgement," I delivered in a tone that wiped the smile from his face, though it seemed he was not put off altogether because his eyes devoured me. I prayed I wouldn't blush.

"In that case, I hope you'll give me the chance to get to know you better." His voice was smooth as a good red wine.

What a come on, I thought, now feeling somewhat excited at the prospect. I had to admit, the guy had guts. "I'll let you know," I replied in a non-committal manner.

The sound of laughter from Smythe and Mandy shifted my focus away from the exotic Sean and I tuned into their conversation.

"Phil's entertaining me with some of his police stories," Mandy informed me when she noticed me glancing their way.

Phil? Since when had Smythe become Phil to her? And how ironic that she was running from one Phil, only to meet another. Both idiots, in my opinion. I couldn't wait until this infernal lunch was over and we could leave.

The men's food arrived, and I glanced at my watch. It was almost two. "I think we should head back," I addressed Mandy. "I'm sure you'll want to rest before dinner."

She looked at me as if I'd lost my mind. "What's the hurry? I would like to order some coffee."

I sighed but didn't reply. I couldn't very well get into an argument in front of Smythe. Meanwhile, he took this as his cue to attract the attention of the waitress and order coffees all around. Then, he and Mandy fell back into conversation, and this left me with the enigmatic Sean for company.

"Say yes," he whispered.

His brown, almond-shaped eyes were difficult to ignore, but I stayed strong, at least for now. "Say yes to what?"

"Yes to having dinner with me."

My hormones, which I thought were extinct by now, went into overdrive and I found myself nodding at him. What harm could one dinner date do? I asked myself. I already knew he was the bad boy type to which I always gravitated, so it wasn't like there would be any great surprises in store.

Sean smiled with a look of triumph in his eyes. "I'll ring you at the hotel."

Another bout of laughter from the other two broke the spell and I was no longer drawn to his glance, which was a good thing as I didn't want to make a fool of myself and look like a sex-starved teenager. We joined in the general conversation until the coffees arrived and managed to finish off without any further smart comments between Smythe and me.

The men insisted on picking up the tab, and I didn't do anything to stop them. They had gatecrashed my lunch with Mandy so the least they could do was pay. While we waited for the waitress to come back with Smythe's credit card, we chitchatted about Mandy's visit.

"You must be sure to visit the Blue Mountains while you're here," Smythe suggested. "It's a magic place."

"Why do they call them 'blue'?" Mandy enquired.

"Because the eucalyptus oil from the vegetation that's all around reacts with the atmosphere, and this forms a kind of blue haze over them."

"How romantic!" Mandy gushed dreamily.

I rolled my eyes again and pursed my lips shut so I wouldn't spill any acid from my mouth.

"So what are you girls doing for dinner tonight?" Smythe was bold enough to ask.

Oh no! It was bad enough that he had spoiled my day, but I wasn't about to allow him to spoil my evening as well. Before I could say anything, however, his mobile phone rang and he excused himself to answer it.

The expression on his face suddenly changed from jovial to one of worrisome concern. He nodded and kept saying, "Right, right", and then, "She's here with me now. Just call the security manager and tell him we're on our way." He rang off and directed a serious look at me.

I asked with a feeling of trepidation, "What's wrong this time?"

He wore a frown on his face when he replied, "It's Jim Casey. One of the hotel staff just found him hanging by the neck in his room."

# CHAPTER 7

**I** put my foot down on the accelerator and smirked when Mandy held on to her seat for dear life. In the event that I got booked for speeding, I figured Smythe would get me off the hook seeing as we had a death on our hands.

We went straight to the hotel and met Dobbs in the lobby. "This is getting to be a habit," I remarked, taking in the serious look on his face. "We were at the beach when the call came through, so I didn't have time to drop Mandy off. Is Chris around?"

"Not again!" Mandy protested. "Why can't I stay here at least?"

"You want to stay in the lobby? That's boring, Mandy," I replied. "Go to Chris and keep him company."

"Chris is in," Dobbs confirmed. "Come on, Mandy, I'll take you up."

Mandy looked from Dobbs to me and shrugged in defeat. "Very well."

I felt bad as this entire day was supposed to have been ours. "Mandy!" I called out as she and Dobbs started to walk in the direction of the lifts. They halted and turned to me. "Why don't you go home and rest? I'm sure I'll be through by dinner time, and then we can still go out."

"True. I wouldn't mind a nap."

"I'll telephone and keep you updated."

"Okay." She grabbed my apartment keys, which I held out to her.

"I feel so bad," I confided in Dobbs after Mandy left with a wave of her hand and we made our way to the tenth floor. "This hasn't been much of a holiday for her so far."

"She seems to be enjoying all the murder and mayhem though!"

Dobbs commented sounding put off.

"Don't be too hard on her, she's got hubby trouble," I berated him. Then I added, "Although, she seems to have the hots for Smythe." I frowned.

Dobbs laughed heartily. "Jealous, are you, Ferrari?"

"Buzz off, Dobbs!"

Smythe arrived at the hotel just as Dobbs and I reached Jim Casey's suite and stood waiting while the police and the forensics team worked the scene.

"You have a lead foot, Ferrari," Smythe reprimanded me harshly. "If I ever catch you driving like that again, I'll book you myself."

I glared at him. "Shut up, Smythe. Isn't it enough that I had to put up with you, gatecrashing my lunch?"

Dobbs looked confused, I noted; and Sean smirked in the background. Smythe shook his head as if to dismiss what I had said and addressed Dobbs instead. "What happened?"

"A room attendant went to clean the room but couldn't push the door open. She said it felt like something heavy was keeping it closed from the inside," Dobbs related as Smythe took down notes in his small, leather-bound notebook. "She then knocked on the door, thinking that the first time she'd knocked the occupant hadn't heard; but there was still no reply. She became concerned that the guest might be too sick to answer, so she was about to call for help when one of the female impersonators stepped out from his room and seeing the girl trying to get into Casey's room, he helped push the door open."

"I'll need the names of the attendant and the impersonator," Smythe said, still scribbling in his notepad.

"Already got it all in the security log," Dobbs replied. "I'll give you a copy."

"So what happened next?" I jumped in and earned a scathing look from Smythe.

"It turns out Casey was hanging by the neck from the door closer on the other side of the door and his feet were dragging on the carpet. Looked like the noose stretched with his weight; that's why it was too heavy for the room attendant to push the door open."

"And then?" This from Sean.

Dobbs sighed, looking tired. "The room attendant fainted and Frank, the impersonator, took her to his room. Then, he alerted his two buddies about what had happened. Shortly thereafter, they put in a call to security."

"Were you the first one to come up here?" I asked, once again getting a dirty look from Smythe.

"Yes. I was on duty so I came up and secured the scene the best I could," Dobbs explained. "Casey was in his bathrobe, which was hanging open, since he used the belt to hang himself. The floor was a mess, too. He lost control of his bladder and bowel."

I wrinkled my nose at the thought; Smythe kept writing furiously in his notebook; and Sean simply stood by, silently.

"There was a suicide note," Dobbs added, and all three of us looked up. "I bagged it and gave it to the police upon arrival."

"What did it say?" I urged.

Dobbs drew out a photocopy of the note from his jacket pocket and went to hand it to Smythe, but I got in first and snatched it from his hand. The look of thunder on Smythe's face was almost comical. I read out aloud, "I'm sorry if I upset anybody, but I can't live any longer with what I have done." There was a moment of silence as I handed the note to Smythe, who practically tore it from my hand. Then I remarked, "What do you suppose he's done?"

"That's what we intend to find out," Smythe replied tersely, looking daggers at me. "And, Ferrari, let this be a warning to you: if you in any way interfere with this investigation I will personally throw your arse in jail and let you rot there."

"You just try it, Smythe!" I returned defiantly.

Smythe took a step in my direction, and it flashed through my mind that there might be another murder in front of two witnesses; but Sean's hand shot out and pulled his partner away from me.

"C'mon, Phil, they're waiting for us at the scene." He winked at me when no one was looking, and I silently smiled my thanks.

"Did you lose your marbles, Ferrari?" Dobbs reprimanded me when we took the lift back down to the lobby. "I don't know what you did to Smythe today, but he's got it in for you real bad."

I grinned. "So what else is new? He's always got it in for me, Dobbs; and if he finds out what I know, he'll kill me with his bare hands." The look of horror on Dobbs's face made me laugh. "I'm just kidding. Relax, will you?" I tried to reassure him, but he didn't look too convinced.

We arrived at the lobby and made our way through the back-of-house door and down the corridor that led to Dobbs's office. All the while, Dobbs kept shaking his head and mumbling something to himself.

"What is it?" We entered the office and closed the door behind us.

"One day you're going to push Smythe too far; and trust me when I tell you that he'll lock you up for real and throw away the key!"

"Let him try," I spat out, not caring. "He's just annoyed because he hasn't come up with anything yet."

"Oh, and like you have!" Dobbs challenged me. Then he regarded me with mounting concern when he saw me smile. "My God, I should've known you'd be up to no good!" He sat down in his chair before he fell down from further shock.

I went to his mini-bar fridge and pulled out two cans of Coke. "Here." I gave him one, and he popped it open. I sat on one of the visitors' chairs and took a swig of my drink before I went on. "Do you honestly believe this is a suicide?"

Dobbs went to answer, but then stopped and gazed across at me. "I think you'd better tell me," he stated in a tone of defeat.

I filled him in on what the queens had divulged during our little meeting, including the disappearance of the pink diamond. As I related the story, Dobbs's gaze went from curiosity to interest and concern, and finally to deep worry.

"I'm too afraid to ask if you're holding on to a piece of evidence that will land you in jail," he remarked with a frown.

"I have the cap in my possession. The queens gave it to me. But what's a cap with a missing diamond, anyway? It won't tell the cops anything, except that the diamond's gone."

"It tells them there's a motive," Dobbs barked, slamming the palm of his hand on the desk. "And now we have a concrete reason for why Casey might have killed Ophelia. He's taken the diamond for himself!"

I leaned forward on the desk and gazed straight into his eyes. "So why would he commit suicide then? Why not sell the diamond and disappear?" I challenged.

Dobbs took a moment to search for an answer. "Perhaps he became overwhelmed and really felt sorry for what he did," he observed at length.

"Or perhaps he's been framed," I suggested.

Dobbs nodded gravely. "Yes, of course. This occurred to me, too."

I rested my chin on one hand, a thoughtful look in my eyes. "Yet, something doesn't add up."

"Like what?"

"Like Casey's personality."

"And what do you know about his personality? You only met him briefly."

"Only this," I explained, "the guy was devastated when Ophelia was murdered."

"So? He could've just been faking grief."

"True. But I think Casey didn't have it in him to kill someone," I stated; and when I saw his questioning look, I added, "Dobbs, Ophelia's murder looked like it was committed by someone in a rage. Her was body dismembered, cut up in pieces, for God's sake! Do you really think someone would do this just to steal a diamond? The queens knew about the stone, so I'm going to presume that Casey also knew. In which case, why not just steal the diamond when Ophelia wasn't wearing the hat? Why murder her in such a grisly fashion?" Dobbs looked thoughtful and nodded. I went on, "I think whoever did this has a real issue with gay men, queens and transsexuals. I also think this person has such deep-seated rage in him that he's capable of anything. In my view, this is definitely more than a simple act of theft."

"I have to agree with your theory," Dobbs finally said. "So you need to share this with Smythe."

"All in good time," I replied. "First, I have to get a little more information about someone who's been in the picture all along."

"And who's that?"

"Mark Meadows," I announced. "Our friendly functions supervisor."

Dobbs looked intently at me. "You think he's involved?"

"I don't know, but I saw enough on the night of the opening act to make me suspect something was going on between him and Ophelia."

We finished our Cokes in silence, each of us processing the information in our heads. Then, I glanced at my watch. "If I'm no longer needed, I'll go now. Do you know if the queens are going to be performing tonight?"

"Better find out." Dobbs went to pick up the phone to ring them.

"Let me do it," I offered. "It seems they've taken me into their confidence. Besides, I want to sniff around some more."

Dobbs gave me a warning look. "You better hope Smythe doesn't see you talking to them."

I smiled reassuringly. "Don't fret, Dobbs. I'll invite them up to the penthouse and meet them inside. I'll use Rourke's private lift so the cops don't see me."

"I don't like this," he protested. But he must've protested to thin air because even before he finished what he was saying I was on my way to the penthouse from where I intended to telephone the queens.

Chris was thrilled when asked if I could invite the queens to his place, but I had to warn him. "Don't think just because I'm using your digs to talk to them, that you're involved in the case."

"You know I would never think that, Mia," he responded with an innocent look in his eyes.

"Smartarse," I remarked fondly. My pseudo-son resembled me in his tenaciousness.

"Go on, make the call," he said. "I'm going to mix some drinks for the party."

"Hey, hold on a minute. What makes you think this is a party?" I frowned at him.

Chris grinned. "Not a party as in *party*, but a *party of people*," he clarified.

"Well, make sure we only offer non-alcoholic drinks," I instructed.

The queens were pretty shaken up over Casey's death, and Chris and I ended up having to fortify them with brandy and sympathy.

"That bitch, Smythe!" Frank cried, wiping at his tears with a wad of tissues. "He questioned me like I was some kind of suspect; just because I'm gay doesn't mean I'm not a person."

I didn't believe Smythe to be homophobic, especially as he had worked the Cross for so long and seen just about everything, so I put it down to Frank exaggerating. "I'm sorry, Frank, but I'm sure he didn't mean to be surly. He's a cop and sometimes comes across as being a bit rough." I couldn't believe I was defending Smythe's behaviour, but I wanted to console the despondent Frank.

Tony and Alan were equally affected. "That's nothing. We had to deal with that other bitch, Sean," Alan informed us, also in tears, "and I say that boy has a real attitude on him, sexy as he is, and with his cute tush."

I raised my brows at Chris over the top of the queens' heads, and he took this to mean more drinks. He came back with the whole bottle of brandy and a new box of tissues. "Thank you, darling." Tony patted Chris's hand while he eyed him up and down admiringly.

Oh God! I thought. "Look, one of the reasons I invited you here is so I could ask if you want me to cancel the show for tonight," I told them. "I think under the circumstances no one would mind."

Frank shook his head vehemently. "Not at all, honey! Jim would've wanted us to go on; and go on we will. We'll do the show in his honour."

The others agreed with tears and watery smiles, but they seemed to perk up after a few more shots of brandy. I motioned with my head for Chris to take away the bottle, which he did. "Very well, then. I guess this is all I wanted to know, plus to make sure you're all holding up okay." I regarded them with sympathy in my eyes.

Alan put an arm around each of his companions. "At least they're together now." He sniffed the last of his tears.

"Yes, together at last!" Tony chimed in with eyes aglow. "In a way, tragic as it may seem, it's also rather romantic."

Chris and I looked questioningly from the queens' dreamy look to each other. "What is so romantic about this?" I asked, thinking the queens had had too much to drink.

"Darling, didn't you know?" Frank remarked, and I shook my head. "Jim and Ophelia were an item for a long time. This is before she got mixed up with that gimlet, Mark Meadows."

I was too stunned to reply and could only sit there with a wide-eyed look on my face; so Chris jumped in, "You're talking about the Mark Meadows who works in this hotel?"

"Yes, sweet cheeks," Frank nodded. "Before we went on tour overseas we were based in Sydney and had a regular gig at Stonewall, down in Oxford Street. Jim and Ophelia were lovers. But then, this gimlet, Mark, wormed his way into Ophelia's heart. And during the tour, she and Jim had some really big arguments about her infidelity. So much so that for the sake of the act, Jim had to accept it was all over between them." Frank let out a sigh of indignation. "The man was heartbroken, I tell you!"

I managed to find my voice. "So what happened?"

"Oh, it was fireworks for a while, darling," Frank answered, waving his arms about in a gesture symbolising a big drama. "In the end, when we came back to Sydney, Ophelia tried to break it off with Mark, but he wouldn't leave her alone. He was too besotted with her."

"And?" I prompted.

"Well, Ophelia had no intention to get back together with Jim; but she wanted to keep the peace all around, so she decided to be a single girl for a while. That's why she gave up Mark."

"Why do you call him a gimlet?" asked Chris.

"Because he has that piercing, calculating look about him; and he misses nothing," answered Tony. "Don't be misled by his boyish looks. The man's a manipulative snake."

"Yes." Alan agreed, and added, "And to think I used to tease Ophelia about him going after her money."

"You mean he knew what she was worth?" I couldn't keep down my excitement, thinking we might at last have a suspect.

"I'm sure it was part of their pillow talk, honey," Frank replied. "You know I told you Ophelia went on and on about being rich. So maybe she talked too much and this gimlet decided to kill her for the diamond."

"But what about Jim, why do you think he killed himself?" I asked, and noticed Chris's sudden surprise at the conversation. To date, he knew nothing about the diamond or the connection between the two deaths.

Frank sighed dramatically and picked up a bunch of fresh tissues to wipe away another bout of tears. "Jim started taking anti-depressants since the break up, so who knows what was on his mind. Maybe Ophelia's death was too much for him and it pushed him over the edge."

I glanced at Chris and recognised the look in his eyes that told me he was dying to get on his computer to do some research. I saw no harm in allowing him to get more background on the diamond and its origins.

# CHAPTER 8

I was scheduled to work the afternoon shift so I took Mandy on the ferry to Manly beach, and after a long walk along the shore we went for an early lunch at one of Manly's many cafés.

When I had arrived home after spending time with the queens at Chris's place the previous evening, I drove Mandy to Chinatown for Pekinese food at one of my favourite restaurants. Later, we walked around Dixon Street and explored a number of small shops and the night market with its many stalls and interesting wares. Mandy loved a good bargain and she came away with a copy-watch for her husband, a green silk cheongsam dress with splits on either side of a long, straight skirt for her, and a pair of jade drop earrings that she purchased for me as a gift. The jade was genuine and rather expensive.

"Mandy," I protested when she gave me the earrings, "they probably ripped you off. This part of town is mainly for tourists."

"Never mind. I want you to have them. They suit you, and I won't take no for an answer after the great time I'm having."

I smiled. "Well, thank you." I put on the earrings and checked myself in my compact mirror. The green of the jade brought out the colour of my eyes and made an attractive contrast to my hair colour.

Now, as we sat drinking coffee and waiting for our meals to arrive, I remembered the watch Mandy had purchased for her husband. "We never really got down to the nitty gritty of what's going on with you and Phil," I observed, and caught a hesitant look on her face.

Mandy took a while to respond, in the meantime watching the crowds of tourists and beachgoers walking past us while we sat in the cool shade of a tree in the outdoor area of the café. Finally, she said,

"I'm not really sure what it is, Mia. Perhaps, it's the fact that Phil has found something to keep him busy while I'm back to being 'the little housewife'." She sighed despondently and had a few sips of coffee.

"But what about your blog?" I reminded her. "Plus you said you were earning some money by writing magazine articles; and you started working on your first novel. These are all things that keep you busy."

"Yes, but they're not a career per se," she pointed out, looking unhappy. "What I mean is I don't make enough money to be independent, so in essence I'm still a housewife."

"Well, what's wrong with that? Look at you: you're vibrant, you've made a home for your family, you have a son, your mother's still alive and you have a husband who loves you, though he may not show it as much as you'd like. You're surrounded by blessings, Mandy." I felt rather empty when I compared my life to hers.

She must have picked up on this because she patted my arm and smiled reassuringly. "I guess it's a case of 'the grass is always greener on the other side'. I look at your lifestyle and think of your independence, your career, the interesting investigations you get involved in, the bad boys..." Her voice trailed off thoughtfully.

I looked at her in surprise. "What's the bad boys got to do with any of this? All the bad boys I've ever been involved with turned out to be bastards. So here I am, almost forty-nine years of age, and I don't have much to show for it, except a nasty divorce and the memory of a one-night affair with a younger man."

"You mean David, of course. But don't you think that things could change in the future? You guys might get together in the end."

I shrugged, suddenly feeling sad. "Who knows?" I felt uncomfortable talking about David right now, especially as I didn't know what was before us. He was ten years younger than I; and though in our youth we had enjoyed a brief interlude, in the present I was getting to the age of major decline while David was still in his prime. He could have any woman with his looks and money, so why would he pick me? "We were talking about you and Phil," I steered the conversation back to Mandy's situation. "So let's leave David and my situation out of it for the time being and tell me more about you."

"Well," Mandy replied, "the way I feel right now is that I want to explore."

"What do you mean, explore?" I was on the alert all of a sudden and took a few sips of my coffee to try and look casual about the whole thing.

A secret smile appeared on Mandy's lips. "I want to see what it's like with other men."

I broke into a coughing fit as the coffee went down the wrong way. Mandy poured me a glass of cold water. Tears streamed down my face as I tried to take a few sips of the soothing liquid. Mandy handed me a few tissues from her handbag and I wiped at my eyes while I gave myself time to recover. "Are you insane?" I managed to exclaim after a few moments. "It's Smythe, isn't it? You've got the hots for him!"

"No need to get so uptight about it," she replied, and added, "unless, you want him for yourself."

"Oh my God!" I made like I was retching. "You can't possibly be serious!"

She threw me a knowing look. "For someone who doesn't like Smythe, you certainly have a funny way of showing it."

I swallowed the rest of the water and felt much better as I fixed her with a serious look. "Get this: I'm not interested in Smythe. He's my enemy! My concern is for you and your admission that you actually want to have sex with him."

"I never said that!" Mandy looked shocked.

"Come, come," I gazed at her reprovingly, "you didn't have to spell it out."

"Well!" She sniffed.

I grinned at the miffed look on her face. "Don't go all British on me now," I teased. "You're wondering what it's like with someone like Smythe, and I don't blame you, really. He's a good looking man, much as I hate to admit it."

A dreamy smile appeared on her face, and I couldn't believe my ears when she said, "He does have that Tom Selleck look, doesn't he?"

I nodded, still feeling dumbfounded. "Yes, he looks like Magnum PI minus the moustache and the Ferrari. In other words, he's a bum!" I declared dryly.

Our food arrived and I was grateful for the break in the conversation, but as soon as the waiter left Mandy eyed me with a conspiratorial look and announced, "He's asked me out to dinner on Friday night, and I accepted."

It was a good thing I had to return home and get ready for work after we finished eating; otherwise, I was sure Mandy and I would have had an argument. After dropping the bombshell about her date with Smythe, we ate in silence and then took the ferry back into the city, where I had parked my car. We chitchatted about mundane things all the way home, each of us knowing that we had called a silent truce simply by not referring to the touchy subject.

I jumped into the shower as soon as we walked into the apartment and Mandy popped her head into my room a few minutes later while I was dressing. "I'm going to go and get some groceries this afternoon. Your cupboards are empty."

I buttoned up my suit jacket and picked up my bag. "I apologise for that," I replied. "It seems I'm always eating at the hotel these days, so I barely ever shop."

Mandy smiled. "Well, no matter. I'm going to get a few essentials, and tonight I'll stay in and have a home-cooked meal. All this restaurant food is well and good, but I don't want to start packing on the pounds."

A few moments of chatter followed about what groceries to get and the best place to shop for them, and I took off for the hotel feeling guilty at my reaction to Mandy's date with Smythe. So what if they wanted to go out? I had too much on my plate right now to worry about my friend's love life. Of course, even though I tried to dismiss thoughts of her and Smythe, I found myself in a foul mood by the time I reached work and chewed off a porter's head for placing some guest luggage in the wrong spot.

Dobbs happened to be in the lobby when I sent the porter scurrying for cover and he approached me. "What's with you, Ferrari?"

I threw him a warning look. "Don't get me started, Dobbs. How's things around here? No more murders, I hope." This last bit came out with sarcasm.

He regarded me as if I had horns growing out of my head. "Whatever or whoever put you in such a filthy mood has my deepest sympathies."

"Quit the crap," I lashed out at him. "I have a lot to do tonight and I don't need any bullshit."

"Okay, Ferrari," he said in an attempt to placate me. "Let's go to my office so we can talk."

We made our way to the back-of-house area and down the corridor leading to his department. "I heard from Smythe," was the first thing that came out of his mouth when we entered the office.

My hackles rose at the mention of the name. "What did *he* want?"

"Autopsy on Jim Casey showed nothing suspicious so, as far as the police are concerned, it was a bona fide case of suicide."

For a moment, echoes of another time when the police pronounced a straight case of suicide came back to haunt me and I thought of Linda Liu. I then sniffed at Dobbs's statement. "We both know the police can get it wrong."

"Sure," he agreed. "But there being no other circumstances to make them think otherwise, they believe it's a suicide."

"Well, they're idiots!" I stated savagely.

"Right, time out." Dobbs snapped his fingers in front of my face. "You'd better tell me what is going on, Ferrari. You look pissed off big time!"

I took a deep breath and asked for a Coke. He gave me one from his mini-bar fridge and sat at his desk, waiting for me to speak.

"Let's not worry about my mood right now," I told him, wanting to avoid talk of a personal nature. "There's something more important you need to know." I knew I had his full attention and I went on. "Yesterday evening, the queens told me that Jim Casey was Ophelia's lover until she got mixed up with Mark Meadows."

"Get out of town!" Dobbs exclaimed, his eyes wide with surprise.

I briefed him on what I had learned while he kept shaking his head in disbelief. "So you see," I concluded, "the Jim Casey death is not so clear cut after all. I personally don't believe, as the cops seem to, that he committed suicide because he felt remorse at killing Ophelia. He loved her too much to do that kind of thing. Besides, why take a twenty million dollar diamond and then kill yourself? I think someone else did this, and they planted the suicide note to make it look like Casey committed the crime. They probably held a gun to the poor bastard's head so he would write the note in his own hand. How easy is that, I ask you?"

"Well..." Dobbs looked thoughtful. "I know Smythe's suspicious of the whole thing, and he smells a rat."

"Really?" I couldn't help the sarcasm in my tone. "You mean for once Smythe is actually thinking?"

Dobbs sighed and looked squarely into my eyes. "Look, I know your mood has something to do with him," he stated, and kept talking before I could open my mouth to protest. "No, Ferrari, don't deny it. I've known you for years and I see how you get when he does something to piss you off. But don't underestimate him; the man is not in possession of the insider knowledge you have right now. Despite this, he's still trying to do his job."

I had to acknowledge Dobbs was correct, but I was never going to admit to him. "And I suppose you're going to tell me that I should tell Smythe all I know."

Dobbs nodded.

"Well, he's just going to have to wait a little longer," I added stubbornly. "First, I need to have a little chat with Mark Meadows."

Dobbs watched me with defeat in his eyes while I finished my Coke and left his office without saying another word. I made my way to the functions department and asked one of the boys for a copy of the roster. Mark Meadows had been on since three and would be working the female impersonator act this evening; so now was as good a time as any to grab him. I found him in the employee restaurant on a coffee break.

"Got a minute?" I asked when I approached the table. He nodded and regarded me with sharp eyes. Just like a gimlet, I remembered the way the queens had described him.

"Have a seat," he replied, finishing his coffee.

"Not here." I returned his gaze with my own version of a sharp look. I wanted him to be in no doubt that this was a serious talk. "Let's go to the boardroom where we can have some privacy."

I noticed his rigid stance as he stood, and I sensed he was on the defensive already. He must have known that I was going to question him about Ophelia; after all, he was well aware of my inquisitive nature. Most of the staff in the hotel knew how I had worked the Linda Liu case, and word had gone around that I was the in-house detective these days.

We made our way to the boardroom, which was located off the Lobby, without speaking. Once there, Mark draped his frame on a chair at one end of the long oval table as if he owned it. His insolent glare told me he was not afraid of me.

I took a seat next to him, hoping the invasion of his personal space would intimidate him. It seemed to work because he moved his chair back slightly even though he still maintained his air of patronising nonchalance.

"I'm going to dispense with the explanations, Mark," I began in a serious tone. "Needless to say, I'm aware of your past involvement with Ophelia and I want to ask you some quest—"

"I don't have to answer anything you ask!" he interrupted in a harsh voice as he banged his fist on the table. "Who do you think you are, anyway?"

His violent reaction took me off guard for a few moments. Then, I felt my temper rise but did everything in my power to keep it under control. It wouldn't do to lose my head right now and smash his gimlet face with my fist. "I'm working with security on the events that led to Ophelia's death," I informed him in a cold voice, my eyes throwing him a glacial look. "And as I'm in charge of the hotel in the absence of the GM, I have every right to ask."

"You're not a cop!" he challenged me, a sneer on his otherwise handsome face.

I took a deep breath to calm myself and squash the stubborn urge I had to put my hands around his neck and squeeze the life out of him. "No, I'm not the police, but I can tell them about your involvement with Ophelia; and then the questioning will take place down at the cop shop." I noticed the calculating look in his grey eyes. He was probably wondering why it hadn't yet come out that he had been Ophelia's lover. But now he knew I was in possession of the information and it was only a matter of time until I informed the police.

He stood up, and the look in his eyes as he gazed into mine was one of pure hatred. "Do what you like," he spat out savagely. "I don't give a fuck." He then turned and walked out of the room.

I was astounded at the intensity of his hate and the way he had reacted to the whole thing. It was difficult to say whether he was involved with Ophelia's death, but his explosive reaction to the whole matter left me wondering.

My mobile vibrated then, and I jumped. I had turned off the ringtone for my meeting with Mark so the vibration startled my already frayed nerves. I took the phone out of my pocket but didn't recognise the caller ID. I still answered the call. "Ferrari here."

"Ms Ferrari," a male voice savoured the pronunciation of my

name at the other end, and I felt butterflies in my stomach. "Switchboard was kind enough to put me through to your mobile."

I recognised Sean Webb's voice immediately and a feeling of excitement started to spread through me. "Mr Webb," I greeted him casually, not wanting him to pick up on my vibes.

"Are you free this Friday evening by any chance?" he asked in a confident tone.

I knew what was coming and I should tell him I was working, but the thought of Mandy going out with Smythe still stuck in my throat and I figured that if she could go out with one cop, I could go with another. "Yes, why do you ask?" I replied, and didn't feel one iota of guilt at my intention to use him. The fact that he was a bad boy justified my reason for accepting the date. A bad boy usually deserved a bit of a dressing down from an older and more experienced woman.

"How about dinner?" Sean suggested. "Say I pick you up at seven-thirty."

I agreed and gave him my home address. "I have to get back to work now," I informed him, wanting to avoid further chatter.

"No problem. I'm at work, too. I'll see you Friday," he said and rang off.

So, Mr Smythe and Mrs Wilson, I have a date, too! I thought smugly, and then berated myself for being so childish.

# CHAPTER 9

Sean took me to an upmarket Italian restaurant in Paddington with a quiet atmosphere that made it easy to talk intimately. I was glad of this as I hated noisy places where one had to shout in order to make oneself heard.

I wore a sleeveless black dress with a straight calf-length skirt that hugged my slim figure. On my feet, I wore my only pair of high-heeled shoes. Normally, I enjoyed a more casual look with low heels, but tonight I wanted to look sexy. My white-blonde, spiky-short hair stood out in contrast to my dark clothing and the jade earrings Mandy had given me. I wore very little make-up, just some mascara and bright red lipstick. It was fortunate for me I had been blessed with an excellent complexion, which made me look younger than I was.

Sean wore black tailored pants and a burgundy shirt open at the neck. He looked casual but elegant, and I noticed he turned a few female heads as we walked into the restaurant and were shown to our table by the host.

"Do you drink red?" Sean enquired when a wine waiter handed him the drinks menu. I nodded, and he selected a Barossa Valley cabernet sauvignon. The waiter bowed and left us with the dinner menu.

I started to scan through my menu, all the while aware that Sean's eyes were on me. I felt nervous. It had been something like twenty years since I'd gone out on a date. For eighteen of those years, I had been married; and during the last year and half, I had been too busy putting my life back together to even think about dating. Sure, I had gone out for dinner plenty of times with Dobbs or friends from the hotel; and even once with David, but none of those had been official dates. So now, I felt out of touch, rather like a young girl on her first date. I only hoped my companion couldn't tell how anxious I was.

"I highly recommend the veal in marsala sauce," Sean suggested. "It melts in your mouth."

I smiled in response and wondered how many dates he'd brought to this establishment. It was a good thing that even though I was nervous, my mouth still worked. "Well, I guess I'll have to take your word for it."

He returned my smile and I couldn't believe how suave he was. He was smoother than velvet and for a moment, I felt intoxicated by him and his exotic looks; but I had to keep my head.

"I'll order the veal as you suggest." I closed the menu and placed it back on the table.

The waiter came back with the wine and Sean tasted it before he nodded for the waiter to pour. "If you're ready to order, sir, I'll send the food waiter over." The man bowed and walked off. Sean raised his glass and we toasted to a pleasant dinner.

I tried to pace myself with the wine, but I needed fortification right now and almost finished the whole glass in a few gulps. Sean refilled my glass with a knowing smile. I didn't care. The wine was already working on my empty stomach and I enjoyed the feel of the soft alcoholic haze permeating my body.

"Thank you for coming out tonight. It's certainly a pleasure to dine with a beautiful lady." Sean's eyes regarded me enigmatically.

Now, he was laying it on a bit too thick for my taste and my nervousness went out the window. "So what's the story with you and Smythe?" I changed the subject abruptly, putting an end to his flirting.

He blinked in surprise but managed to keep up with the flow of the conversation without any sign as to what he thought of my behaviour. "You mean, why we are partners?" I nodded and had some more wine, now feeling relaxed. Sean went on, "The department needed an extra head seeing as there's always trouble at the Cross and, due to my seniority in the force, they decided to pair me up with Smythe."

"You mean you're more senior than him?" I was genuinely curious.

"No. I'm one level down from him, but I've had a lot of experience in both narcotics and homicide, just like him."

"But Smythe is in charge of the department," I remarked.

Sean shook his head and explained, "Not quite. He's in charge of whatever shift he's on. Anyway, the big boys decided to pair us up because they felt we'd make a good team."

"Makes sense, I guess," I responded, and drank some more wine.

The waiter came over to take our food order and Sean ordered for both of us, choosing the veal as well.

"How long have you known Smythe?" he asked when the waiter walked away and he proceeded to refill my glass.

"I think I've known him forever." I felt like laughing for some reason and decided to wait until the food arrived before I drank any more wine. In the meantime, I gave Sean a watered-down version of my run-in with Smythe and the part he played in the rejection of my application to the police force.

"But you said the height restrictions had just been abolished," he argued. "So why didn't you reapply?"

"Too long a story to go into right now, and much too complicated," I replied. "Perhaps, I'll tell you some other time."

"Well, at least this explains your enmity towards him," Sean observed.

"Let's not spoil the dinner by talking about Smythe anymore," I remarked, now regretting having brought up the subject in the first place. "I heard the police ruled suicide in the Jim Casey death."

Sean laughed, but then his face went serious after the look I gave him. "I apologise," he said, and added, "I wasn't laughing at Casey's suicide; it's you I'm laughing about. You really do have an inquiring mind."

I frowned. "You mean Smythe's been talking about me?"

"He didn't say too much, so you can calm down," he reassured me with merriment in his eyes. "Besides, what he said was good. He told me about the Linda Liu case and how the cops would never have solved it without your help."

I couldn't believe my ears. Either Sean was really putting it on to score with me or Smythe was on crack. Sean noted the disbelief in my eyes. "It's true, I tell you. I asked him what the problem was between the two of you, and he simply said sometimes you think you're the police." I went to say something in my defence, but he held up a hand to stop me. "No, let me finish. He wasn't being derogatory; he just said you had a fine and inquiring mind and that you would've made a good cop."

"Well, he should know about that!" I tried not to sound too bitter. "He was the one who stopped me from becoming one; so it's a bit late now. But as I've said, I don't want to talk about him anymore."

Just then, the food arrived and I was thankful because it gave me time to regain my composure. While we ate, we talked about other things and we left Smythe well out of it.

"I wanted to be a cop ever since I could remember," Sean replied to my question about why he picked the police force as a career. "My parents were against it, and sadly we had a bit of a falling out; but that's history now."

"My father was a cop, and that's all I ever wanted to be; but things didn't work out that way. So then I became involved in the exciting world of hotels and discovered it can be quite addictive," I remarked.

Sean finished his wine and refilled his glass. Mine was still full but, now that I had some food in my stomach, I felt safe in having another few sips. "I know it can be rather exciting," he responded. "It's never a dull day in hotels, just as it's never a dull day in the police force."

He was right, of course. The world of hotels was crazy at most times, dealing with a whole range of international guests and locals that were not always on business or holidays, but sometimes conducting drug deals, committing suicide or sneaking a prostitute into one of the rooms. When I thought about it, hotels were rather insidious; and one either loved or hated working in them.

Five glasses of wine later, plus an outstanding dinner, and I felt quite tipsy but glad I didn't have to drive. Sean suggested a walk by the waterfront and he drove us to Darling Harbour where we strolled past restaurants, bars and stores. The fresh breeze from the harbour invigorated me and after a while, I felt like myself again. It had been a long time since I'd drunk so much alcohol, at least not five glasses of wine in a row.

We walked all the way to the Maritime museum and when we turned to go back to the car, I espied from the corner of my eye a couple, standing across the road, kissing. It was a good thing Sean was standing next to me and was able to hold me up when I tripped as I recognised Smythe and Mandy, snogging away like two teenagers.

"Are you okay?" Sean seemed concerned while he propped me upright.

I faked a smile. "I'm sorry. I'm not used to walking for so long in high heels and I felt like my legs were giving way."

He kept a hold around my waist. "How insensitive of me; I made you walk all this way and never even thought about your heels. Please, forgive me."

I looked furtively over his shoulder and noticed that Smythe and Mandy had moved on. I was thankful Sean hadn't seen them. "That's okay," I said, "you weren't to know, but if you don't mind, I'd like to go home now."

"If you stay here, I'll run back and get the car. This way, you don't have to walk all the way back again," he suggested.

I regarded him with interest, thinking how thoughtful he was. "It's nice to be with a gentleman," I complimented him.

He gave me a wicked smile. "Maybe not too much of a gentleman," he retorted, and before I knew what he was up to, he drew me to him and kissed me.

I was too surprised to stop him, and what with the wine and seeing Mandy smooching away, I threw caution to the wind and let him have his way. His kiss was long and erotic, and I was so intoxicated with the touch and scent of him that I held nothing back. At the back of my mind, I knew if he suggested we go back to his place to finish this off, I wouldn't say no. Luckily, he turned out to be a gentleman after all and he disengaged from our embrace, putting an end to our kiss. He then made sure I was okay to wait and broke into a run to go and collect the car.

I replaced my lipstick while I waited for him and threw another look around to ensure Smythe and Mandy were nowhere near the place. Somehow, I still felt unsettled about what I had witnessed, but I couldn't understand why. Mandy was simply exploring other men, as she'd put it. Besides, I had been kissing a bad boy and had thoroughly enjoyed it; so who was I to judge?

Within minutes, Sean was back and I climbed into the car. What should have been a short trip, turned out to be longer than expected because we got stuck in traffic coming up to William Street, toward Potts Point, where I lived. The traffic was crawling.

"How's the investigation coming along regarding Ophelia and Casey?" I decided to take advantage of the situation and pump him for any information he was willing to give. He had evaded me quite skilfully when I had mentioned Casey earlier in the evening.

There was an almost imperceptible hardening in his gaze, but it disappeared almost instantly and I thought I had imagined it. "You know I can't divulge anything confidential," he replied, "but seeing as we don't have much to go on I can safely say that so far there are no real leads on Ophelia's murder. We're fairly sure Casey killed her, though, and then committed suicide out of remorse."

"So the case is closed?" I thought about the missing diamond and all the other information I had learned from the queens.

"Not quite. But unless we come up with something else, or someone comes forward with new information, we have nowhere left to go at present."

For a moment, I felt guilty that I hadn't shared all I knew with the police. I hated to have to go to Smythe with what I had so far, but perhaps I could throw a little morsel of information his way via Sean. "There is something I found out, but this may be something you guys already know," I commented casually and was rewarded with a keen look of interest from him. "It's nothing earth-shattering, of course; but I wondered whether the cops were aware that our functions supervisor, Mark Meadows, used to be involved with Ophelia."

Sean didn't show any reaction but asked, "How do you know about this?"

I decided to lie in order to protect the queens. "Hotel gossip; plus on opening night, I saw Mark hanging out with Ophelia after the show. At the time, I thought nothing of it. Then, when I started to hear the gossip, I thought it might be something worth looking into."

The look Sean threw my way told me he didn't entirely believe me and that I was holding back a lot more. He didn't push the point, however, and simply said, "Thanks for that, Mia. I'll discuss it with Smythe."

Good, I thought. This way, the information came out as a "by the way" kind of topic and the police could check out the vicious Mark Meadows. Moreover, I could rest assured Smythe wouldn't be breathing down my neck and threatening me with jail for interfering in an investigation.

We finally reached my place and Sean kissed me once more as soon as he parked outside my building. This time, his hands started to rove around my body. I didn't mind at first, but when one of them crept up my skirt all the way to my panties, I gently pushed him away, but not before I noticed the bulge in his pants. I was tempted to ask him in, but the last thing I wanted was for Mandy to walk in on us. Besides, I didn't feel quite right about having sex with him on a first date.

"Perhaps, next time," I whispered in his ear and was out of the car before I had the chance to change my mind.

It was past midnight by the time I got ready for bed and Mandy had not yet returned. She was obviously still sampling the delights Smythe had to offer. The thought threatened to put me in a bad mood again so I simply went to bed and was lucky to fall asleep almost immediately. The wine plus the long walk in high heels had taken their toll, not to mention the effort it took for me to resist Sean's advances.

I slept soundly and woke to the sound of the alarm at six the next morning. It wasn't surprising I hadn't heard Mandy come in; I had been so tired that not even a bomb could have woken me. I jumped in the shower and later dressed in my uniform, and by six-thirty I was ready for my first cup of coffee. It was a shock to my system, therefore, when I came out of my room to see that Mandy was not in her bed as I had thought. She was still out! I couldn't believe it and was about to pick up the phone to dial Smythe and ask for her in a very concerned tone of voice, when I heard the keys at the front door and she walked in.

At least, she had the good sense to look guilty as I threw her one of my icy glares. She was dressed in the green silk cheongsam she had purchased in Chinatown, and though Smythe had obviously manhandled her she still looked presentable. "Coffee?" I asked casually.

She nodded and went straight to the bathroom to change into her bathrobe. When she came back out, I was in the kitchen with a pot of coffee and toasted muffins waiting for us. Mandy joined me at the table.

"I'm sorry," she said as she sat down, "I should've called."

"Yes, you should have. I was quite worried and almost called Smythe to ask whether you'd been involved in some kind of crime." If my voice dripped with acid, she chose to ignore it.

"Well," she replied softly, "I did wrong in not telling you that I was going to stay over. The last thing I wanted was for you to worry."

I was about to tell her I had seen her the previous night, pashing off like a crazed teen, when suddenly the whole thing seemed comical. I wasn't sure why, but it dawned on me that it wasn't any of my business if she wanted to explore other men and in turn get to know herself better. I had to admit, I didn't approve of infidelity but then again, I figured if Mandy was over here to have a break from her husband, she must have a good reason. Besides, she was my friend, and whatever she chose to do with her life was something I intended to support. Whether she stayed with her hubby or not was her decision and this would be easier to bear if a good friend stood by her—and that friend was me.

Therefore, instead of the dressing down I had intended to give her, I turned a wicked glance her way and asked in a saucy tone, "So, how was it?" We both burst out laughing.

# CHAPTER 10

"**B**een living it up, have we? Dobbs sounded like a schoolmaster when I rolled into his office at seven in the morning, yawning and with cappuccinos and croissants.

I frowned. "It shows, does it? I thought I put on enough make-up to cover the dark circles under my eyes," I replied with concern and examined myself in his wall mirror. "Man, I'm getting old, Dobbs. I hate this!"

He laughed. "Welcome to the club, Ferrari. You think I like being sixty-one?"

I turned back to him. "It doesn't count for you; you're a man. Men always age better than women. Look at the likes of Sean Connery and Richard Gere, they're ageless."

"They also have the money to have cosmetic touch-ups," Dobbs reminded me. "So you shouldn't go comparing yourself with celebrities."

I felt agitated. The thought of ageing always did this to me, and it was something I hadn't yet learned to live with. "Okay, but look at you. You look like someone ten years younger, and you're not a celeb!"

"And so do you," he pointed out.

I smiled. "Dobsy, you always know what to say to make me feel better."

Dobbs started on his coffee and croissant, and motioned for me to sit. "Now, stop this nonsense and tell me what's really been going on."

I hesitated momentarily. I couldn't tell him about my date with Sean, nor did I want to say anything about Mandy and Smythe. There was one thing, though, that I wanted to discuss with him: Mark's reaction to my questioning. I related the full details. "So what do you think?"

"Perhaps he became upset with you because he didn't want someone from work to question him about his personal life; especially his affair with Ophelia," Dobbs suggested.

"Could be," I returned thoughtfully as I munched on my croissant. "But Dobbs, he was really savage, and his gaze was so full of hate."

He shook his head. "Who knows with people, Mia. You have to expect all sorts of reactions."

"Well, I'll see how the land lies when he comes in today. I checked his roster and he's doing a back-to-back shift. In fact, he should be in by now."

"I haven't seen him around."

"But he's supposed to do the breakfast function for the Japanese group," I remarked. "I'd better go and check on where he is. I tell you, Dobbs, he's probably sulking and decided to take a sickie."

Dobbs nodded. "That sounds like Mark."

"I'll let him have it if he does this. I'll issue him with a written warning!"

"Just finish your breakfast before you go anywhere," Dobbs advised. "I'll ring functions from here and see what's going on." While he made the call, I finished my croissant and sipped on my coffee. When he hung up, he turned to me. "Mark's not in and he didn't call in sick, either."

"What a prick!" I said scathingly. "I'll get him sacked for this."

"The functions manager is looking after the breakfast, by the way."

"Oh yes, thanks," I replied absentmindedly as another thought occurred to me. "Say, did they have a funeral service for Ophelia and Casey yet?"

"I'm not sure. Last I spoke with Smythe the bodies were in the morgue pending any further findings in the investigation." He looked pointedly at me.

I rolled my eyes. "Yes, I know. I have to tell Smythe about my findings. At least, I managed to send a message via Sean regarding Mark Meadows' relationship with Ophelia."

Dobbs's gaze became alert all of a sudden. "And when did this happen?"

I felt warm under my clothes; I hated to have to lie to him, but I wasn't yet ready for him to find out about my date with Sean. "I ran into him at Bill's and we got talking." Bill's was our regular hangout—a popular jazz bar in the heart of the Cross mainly frequented by navy personnel, cops and hotel staff.

"And?" he prompted.

"And I mentioned casually that Mark had a thing with Ophelia and that the cops might want to look into it." Dobbs didn't look too happy at my response. "What's wrong?"

"Girl, why are you doing this when you should be talking to Smythe? He's in charge of this investigation and has every right to know what you found out."

Dobbs sounded like a broken record sometimes, but I acknowledged that what he said was true. It was awkward, however, for me to contact Smythe now; not after he shagged my best friend. How could I face him knowing Mandy thought he was a great lay? I smiled secretly about our conversation of the night before, when Mandy gave me a fairly detailed account of Smythe's prowess in bed.

"What are you smirking about now, Ferrari?"

Dobbs's voice made me snap out of my reverie. "Nothing, just something Mandy said the other day." Again, another lie.

"That Mandy's a bit of a floozy if you ask me," he commented with a cocked eyebrow. "She's always making eyes at Smythe; and she's a married woman, too!"

Obviously, Dobbs didn't miss a thing, and I felt like laughing at his disapproval of her making eyes at Smythe even though she was married. Dobbs had been blessed with a happy marriage, so he didn't understand how other people sometimes looked elsewhere because they weren't happy with their lot.

"Well, I'm off to do my rounds," I announced, not wanting to pursue the thread of our conversation further. "Catch up for lunch?"

Dobbs eyed me as if he wanted to say something else, but only nodded. I waved and made my way out of his office. My intention was to follow up with Mark Meadows and ring him at home to let him have it. He might be sick, but not having called in had inconvenienced the operation, and it was in breach of hotel policy.

I got the answering machine when I called so I left a message to contact me as soon as possible. Meanwhile, my day turned out to be super busy and by the time I took a break, it was almost the end of my shift. Mark didn't return my call and I had a good mind to drive by his place, which was close by, and find out whether he really was at home feeling sick. First, I checked on Chris after I signed off the duty manager's log at 3.00pm and handed over my keys and pager to the evening DM. Then, I made my way to the penthouse.

Chris answered the door and seemed surprised to see me. There was a quite a lot of noise coming from inside the place, and I became instantly suspicious. "I hope you're not having a wild party in there."

"At three in the afternoon? I think not," was his casual response.

"For all I know, you could've been carrying on like this since last night." I made to come in, but he blocked my way; and I was just about to demand that he move aside when I heard a familiar voice from inside calling out: "Darling, hurry! It's your turn."

Chris's cheeks flushed red and I pushed my way into the lounge room to find the three queens sitting in front of a big TV screen, playing computer games.

"It's not what you think." Chris followed close on my heels.

The queens looked up from their game. "Oh, darling, get that look off your face, we're not after his tush," Frank addressed me, and the others laughed. "We found out we have computers in common, especially computer games; and Chris was kind enough to invite us over to play."

I glanced from face to face to see whether I was being told the truth and their candid looks reassured me. I sighed with relief. "Very well, but don't go getting any ideas. Chris is straight and I don't want you guys making a play for him," I warned tersely.

"Hey," Chris interceded, "I don't need you to protect me. I have heaps of gay friends, you know."

"Just making sure, that is all." I then reminded him, "I did promise your dad I'd keep an eye on you, so I have to make sure he won't find you wearing a skimpy bikini and feathers upon his return."

The queens laughed good-naturedly. "Don't worry, sweetie. It's not like that," Tony assured me.

"Would you like to join us?" Chris invited. "I was just about to make coffee."

"That'll be nice, thanks," I accepted. "But I'm not here to play computer games. I need to talk to you boys… girls… whatever."

I sat down on one of the sofas around the TV and when Chris brought in the coffee, I asked the queens to switch off the game for a moment. "I need your help," I began, and then I told them about my meeting with Mark Meadows. "Of course, I had to let the police know that he and Ophelia were involved since he wouldn't speak to me, but I want to find out more about him."

"Well, there isn't much more we can tell you, honey, except that he always hangs out at Stonewall, and lots of the people there know him," Frank said.

"Yes," Alan concurred. "They may have more information than what we gave you."

"Frank told me all he knows," Chris addressed me, "and I've been doing a bit more digging on the diamond among other things."

My voice held concern when I asked, "You haven't hacked into any computers, right?"

"I swear I haven't," he reassured me. "I simply did some research through the news archives." Chris had our attention and went on to explain, "Ophelia, whose male name was Oscar, was the son of real estate magnate, Robert Hart. Oscar was the only child of Rachel Hart, who also came from money. When Oscar made it known to his family at a rather early age that he really felt like a female and wanted to follow the lifestyle of Ophelia, Robert disinherited him and cut him off from the family altogether. Rachel died when Ophelia was around thirteen years old, but she managed to pass on the pink diamond to her. I guess the mother wanted Ophelia to have something for her future seeing as she'd been disinherited."

"That's right," Frank jumped in when Chris paused to take a sip of coffee. "Ophelia did say she was in her teens when her mother gave her the diamond to secure her financially later in life. Then, she took off after the mother's funeral."

"Anyway," Chris took up the story again, "it looks like Robert remarried shortly after Rachel's death, and there was a son born almost immediately. Ophelia had a half-brother she never got to meet because as Frank just said, she left home to stay with some friends as soon as her mother died."

"So this new son inherited?" I asked, trying to keep track of the story.

Chris shook his head. "The information is not too clear on this, but it looks like the second wife died in an accident of some kind and Robert changed his will and left his son nothing."

"Why would he do that? And what happened to the son?" This

all sounded very mysterious, and I hated it that we still had no real answers.

"No one knows," he replied. "The son just disappeared from the scene, and when Robert died all the money went to some charity. That's as far as I got with the research, but I'm still trying to dig deeper."

Frank shook his head and gushed, "It's all so *Days of our lives*, isn't it?"

"It's certainly dramatic enough," I agreed, and quickly formulated a plan of action in my mind. "Okay, this is what we'll do. Chris, you keep researching; legally, of course." Chris grinned and nodded. Then, I turned to the queens. "Girls, how would you like to accompany my friend Mandy and me to Stonewall?"

A wicked smile appeared on Frank's lips. "Oh you naughty girl, you! I thought you'd never ask!"

"Never ask what?" I wasn't sure what he meant.

"Ask us to help you solve one of your mysteries, of course," Frank answered with excitement in his eyes.

Tony added, "Chris told us all about the Linda Liu case. Oh, darling, you were just fab! Move over Charlie's Angels, I say. And to think you got to lord it over that bitch, Smythe."

I couldn't be angry with Chris for telling them, not when "the girls", as I thought of them now, had finally taken me into their fold with such admiration.

We discussed which night would be best for us to go to Stonewall. It would have to be after the girls' own show at the hotel, of course. I told them I'd get back to them to confirm the date after I discussed it with Mandy. These days, I didn't know whether she was hanging out with me or if she had plans with Smythe.

When I left the hotel, I walked home but didn't go into my apartment. Instead, I got in my car and drove out to Bondi Beach where Mark Meadows lived. The human resources department had given me his address seeing as they were also concerned that he hadn't called in sick, nor had he returned any of their calls.

On the way, I rehearsed what I was going to say to that piece of trash and by the time I pulled up outside his apartment building, I had worked myself up into a foul mood. Mark lived in an old federation-style building of dark brick and without security doors. His block held twelve apartments and I headed for number 8, which was on the second floor.

I knocked on the door loudly and listened for any sounds from within. Nothing. I knocked again, louder this time, but no one came to the door. Then, I called his number from my mobile and listened with my ear against the door to see if I could hear his mobile ring. Sure enough, it rang and then went to voicemail. I rang again in case Mark was in the bathroom and couldn't hear the ringing; but again, no response.

By this time, I started to grow concerned. It was possible that he'd gone out and forgotten his mobile, of course; or perhaps, he was in a deep sleep and didn't hear the knocking on the door or the ringing of his phone. I called his name a couple of times as a last resort; this didn't yield any results, either. Finally, I tried the doorknob on his front door and, much to my surprise, I was able to turn it and open the door. This was when the hair at the back of my neck stood on end.

I walked into a messy lounge room furnished with retro furniture and old burgundy-coloured carpet. The room was littered with fast-food cartons; empty drink cans and bottles; clothes thrown over a two-seater sofa with ripped cushion covers; and gay porn magazines that lay across a scratched coffee table. The place smelled of jasmine, however, and I noticed a few scented candles on a rickety bookshelf. One of the candles was still lit up but fast burning down to a stump. I thought Mark might be taking a bath, which explained why he hadn't heard the ringing of the phone.

"Mark?" I called softly. No answer.

To my right was a narrow corridor that led to a small kitchenette-cum-laundry room. The place was just as untidy as the lounge and full of dirty dishes in the sink, plus clothes had been thrown carelessly on top of a washing machine. At the end of the corridor was another door standing open and I could see the end of a bed frame and a chest of drawers. I made my way slowly to the bedroom and poked my head in, at the same time calling out Mark's name once more. No one was in the room.

I entered the bedroom, which was just as untidy as the rest of the place, and espied a half-open door. I realised this was the bathroom. From where I stood, I observed a chipped and cracked basin, a toilet with an off-white plastic seat, and a bathtub with a sickly-green shower curtain around it. The place was quiet and I turned to go, thinking I had wasted my time in coming here. It was obvious Mark had decided to throw a tantrum after our little talk, and he probably crashed at a friend's place. I shook my head at his carelessness in leaving a lit candle inside the apartment. He probably had a bath and then took off so no one could find him.

As I was about to walk out, I became aware of a faint noise like drops falling into a body of water. I looked at the sink, it was empty and the tap wasn't leaking. I listened again and after a few seconds, I heard the sound once more. I stood silently for a while longer and heard the same sound around three to four seconds apart. I made sure the toilet wasn't leaking and then turned to the bathtub with its hideous, penicillin-green curtain.

Visions of Ophelia's dismembered body flashed before my eyes and fear turned my legs to jelly, but this bathroom had no visible traces of blood and the wall and floor tiles were clear of unusual stains. The shower curtain looked clean enough, too. I therefore drew a breath of relief, telling myself I was being fanciful and with one sweep of my arm, I drew the curtain aside.

A scream got stuck in my throat when I took in the scene before me. Floating face down in a tub filled with murky water and with a dripping tap, the naked body of Mark Meadows ended in a stump, where his head had been cut off. The head floated face up with a horrid grin that sickened me to the core—it revealed the terror Mark must have felt when he faced his killer.

# CHAPTER 11

I waited outside the building for Smythe to arrive. Meanwhile, I rang Dobbs to tell him I had found Mark Meadows, both pieces of him. I felt sick to the stomach and could have done with some caffeine, but there was no time to go and get some; I had to stay put until Smythe arrived.

"Dear God," Dobbs said after I related what had occurred.

"I... I can't talk for long, Dobbs. I think I'm going to puke any minute, but I had to tell you what happened." My head swam and I sat on a low garden wall that bordered the apartment block and common garden. If I didn't sit, I was sure to fall where I was standing.

"Did you ring Smythe?"

"Yes," I replied. "And you're right, it's time I told him everything."

Dobbs sounded relieved. "Well, I'm sorry it was you who had to find the body, but I'm glad you came to your senses and called him."

"I really have to go now. I'll see you tomorrow." I rang off and sat quietly, trying to fight off waves of nausea.

The minute I discovered Mark's body, I ran out of the apartment and my first instinct had been to call Smythe. I could've called the police emergency number on triple-0 or I could have dialled Sean, but my fingers seemed to have a mind of their own and Smythe's number was the first one they chose.

"What is it, Ferrari?" Smythe had greeted me in his usual gruff manner. Despite my shocked state, I realised he had my number saved on his mobile and therefore could see my caller ID. I didn't know why this made me feel better just as I couldn't explain why I had called him before anyone else.

"Phil," I said in a voice that wasn't my own, "you have to get over here, right now!"

The fact that I called him by his first name didn't even register in my mind, but it did in his; and his voice was full of concern when he asked, "What is it? Are you okay? Where are you?"

"Just come to 58 Flood Street, Bondi, and call the forensics. I found Mark Meadows' dead body in the bathtub." This was all I could manage to say and Smythe didn't question me further.

"I'm on my way," he responded and rang off.

The waves of nausea eased a little though my legs were still shaky. I didn't trust myself to walk to my car yet, but at least I didn't feel like vomiting anymore. I glanced at my watch a few minutes after I had spoken with Smythe and though only ten minutes had elapsed, it seemed like an eternity. Just then, in the distance, I heard the siren of a police car and I sighed with relief. I was fairly sure it was him. I didn't know where he had been at the time of my call, but he must've floored it through the afternoon peak-hour traffic to get to me so quickly.

Within a couple of minutes, a black Ford Falcon GT pulled up and I regarded Smythe as he walked toward me with what looked like a take-away coffee cup. He placed it in my hand when he reached me. "I brought you a cappuccino," he said. His eyes showed concern, and since I had never seen him looking so worried, especially about me, I did the unthinkable and burst into tears.

He pulled me to my feet and held me quietly in his arms. The whole thing was so surreal that for a second I thought I was in one of those police shows where the hero saves the girl from a fate worse than death. I became conscious of the coffee cup I still held in my hand and the fact that Smythe's arms felt good around me. That's when my tears dried up instantly and I gently pulled away. "I'm so sorry," I apologised in a slightly uneven voice. "It's just the shock. Thanks for the coffee."

Smythe seemed relieved that he wasn't going to have to play nursemaid to me and I felt my strength come back as soon as I had a few sips of the cappuccino. I even managed a smile. "Who would've thought I'd get police room service in this manner," I joked and was glad to see that things were back in perspective. Smythe in the hero role just didn't fit into my reality. He was the anti-hero.

"You okay now?" He was still regarding me with concern.

I nodded and switched to business. "I don't know if Sean told you about Mark Meadows, but I recently found out he had a thing with Ophelia."

He nodded. "Yes, he mentioned it when he came on shift this morning. He said you told him last night."

I was grateful Smythe didn't make any reference to the fact that I had gone out with his partner. I searched his eyes to see if I could find anything to reflect what kind of a night he'd had with Mandy, but he looked himself. It was obvious that men didn't go around with a dreamy look in their eyes after a good shag like some females did.

"Where is he now?" I wondered why Sean wasn't tagging along if he was on duty.

"We had a call come through on another case we're investigating, so I asked him to follow up while I came over here," he informed me. "I called forensics and they should arrive any minute. So tell me what happened."

I filled him in on my talk with Mark and his rudeness to me, plus the fact that he didn't show up for work and hadn't called in sick. "Seeing as neither I nor the HR department could reach him, I decided to look in on him," I explained. "Then, when I got here, I couldn't get a response from him, though I knocked on his door and rang him several times. I could actually hear his phone ringing on the other side of the door, and that's when I knew something was not quite right. I turned the doorhandle and the door was unlocked, so I went in and found him. His body's face down in the bathtub; the head's been severed from the body and it's floating face up." I paused and sipped more coffee before the nausea came back; then, I went on. "I noticed there wasn't any blood in the bathroom. Even the water wasn't bloody, so the dismembering took place post mortem; probably hours ago, even last night, I'd say."

"Why didn't you place a triple 0 call?"

I sighed. "I don't know, I guess it was because I knew this was your case. But Smythe, there's a lot more you don't know about this situation, so we need to talk after you're done here."

The look he gave me told me he wasn't at all surprised about my suppressing information but fortunately, he didn't berate me for withholding it. In fact, he threw me a bit of smile, which shook me to the core as I would never have expected this reaction from him. "Don't tell me you already solved the case, Ferrari," his tone held a trace of amusement.

"No, of course not," I smirked, "but the queens think you're a 'bitch' so they didn't tell you everything when you questioned them. They found it easier to talk to me instead. We bonded, you see."

Smythe didn't seem annoyed by my comment. "I had a feeling they weren't being upfront with us; but then, why would they come and talk to you voluntarily? I think it was the other way around, and that *you* approached *them*."

I grinned, guilt written all over my face, and just then the forensics van pulled up followed by a couple of police cars and an ambulance. "I'm not going back in there," I told him, shivering momentarily at the scene in the bathtub. "He's in Unit 8."

Smythe patted my shoulder. "You did good, Ferrari," he said, and I felt warm all over. Praise from Smythe was unheard of. "Are you okay to drive home or would you like one of the boys to give you a lift and you can pick up your car later?"

"I'm all right." There was no way I was going to leave my car here. "I guess you'll want me in for a statement and all that?"

He nodded. "I'll call you. But for now, go home and rest. You've been through a nasty shock. When I see you, however, I'll expect you to give me *all* the information you've learned so far, okay?"

"Okay, but this is on the condition that you don't throw me in jail as you've threatened to do earlier." I thought I may as well cut myself a deal while I had him in a good mood. He didn't say anything but simply saw me to my car and bade me on my way.

When I arrived home and told Mandy what had happened, she clucked around me like a mother hen and insisted on preparing dinner while I had a nice, hot shower and relaxed. I followed her advice. I felt totally wiped out and didn't have a shred of energy left, so I was relieved that Mandy was taking charge. It was nice to have someone looking after you once in a while. This was the one thing I missed about being married.

Mandy made a healthy stir-fry with chicken and vegetables accompanied with fluffy jasmine rice. I came to the table in my bathrobe and we opened a bottle of sauvignon blanc.

"I'm famished," I announced. "Thank you for cooking. If I'd been alone I would've ordered a pizza and then gone straight to bed."

Mandy smiled. "I don't know how you manage to stay in shape with all the junk food you consume."

"It's the long hours of work I put in," I explained as I tucked into my meal. "You'd be surprised how much weight you can shed simply by walking around and being on your feet most of the time."

Mandy nodded. "You're right, of course. I remember when I was in France last year and dog sitting for a family. I walked everywhere with that dog, and I shed several pounds despite the fatty French food."

"Well, there you go."

"Of course, I imagine murder and mayhem also keep you trim," she added, taking a sip of the cool white wine.

I felt a sudden shiver. "If you see what I saw in the last week, you'd never eat again." I was referring to the horrible bodies I'd seen in two different bathtubs, but I didn't want to think about this now. "Of course, being the resilient person that I am, my appetite comes back fairly quickly. In fact, a strong cappuccino today saved me from puking my guts out."

"You have such a way with words, Mia." Mandy grinned. "But I thought you were stuck waiting for the police after you discovered the body."

"Smythe brought me a coffee. It was the strangest thing," I said wonderingly, and then noticed a serious look on her face. I added quickly, "I mean, the guy hates my guts, but I guess he wanted me awake instead of unconscious when he got there so he could get the details of what had happened. I don't think for a minute he went to all the trouble of stopping off for a cappuccino, when he was responding to a homicide call, just for my wellbeing."

Mandy's eyes told me she wasn't convinced this had been the reason why Smythe had brought me coffee, but she didn't pursue it. "So what happens now?"

"Oh, just before I forget," I added without answering her question, "how would you like to come to Stonewall with me and the queens?"

"What is Stonewall?"

"Only the best nightclub in gay city central," I responded.

"And where is that?"

"Oxford Street, daaahling!" I gushed in imitation of Frank.

This made her laugh. "So what are we going to do at Stonewall?"

"We are going to talk to lots of nice people to find out anything we can about Mark Meadows. He was a frequent visitor there, especially when Ophelia was performing at the club," I explained. "So are you in or out?"

"In, of course."

"Okay, I'll arrange it. It can't be tomorrow as I'm sure Smythe will need me to come in and give my statement; plus I have to tell him what I know so far about the case," I confessed. "It's time he knew what's been happening."

"What is it with you and Phil?" Mandy asked in a rather suspicious tone of voice.

"In what way?" I almost sounded defensive at having to explain myself. "If you mean why the enmity between us, it goes back to the time he was responsible for having my application rejected by the police department. It's a long story that I never went into with you, but let's just say I've always hated his guts because I never got into the force."

"It's not that," Mandy replied, searching my eyes. "There's something else."

I felt the underlying tension behind her statement, but I didn't want to go there. "Nothing's going on between us, if that's what you're trying to find out," I reassured her. "Smythe's not my type; he reminds me too much of my ex. David's more for me." This seemed to do the job and Mandy looked more relaxed. I asked, "Is this because you're developing feelings for him after a one-night stand?"

"What makes you think it's only a one-nighter?" Her tone sounded abrasive all of a sudden.

"Don't get me wrong; but you're going back home soon. So what else could it be? Besides, you still have a husband," I reminded her, trying to remain patient. "Even if things take off with Smythe, you're a long way off from coming to live with him here in Australia."

Our eyes met across the table like two cats sizing each other up before a fight. Then, I shook my head to dispel my mounting frustration with her. "This is ridiculous. You're here on holidays and if this fling of yours works out, then you'll have to make a decision about your husband and changing your whole life. But I refuse to further justify my relationship with Smythe to you, Mandy. I've known the man for approximately twenty years and, though we were never friends, we are adversaries of sorts; and nothing's going to change between us. Certainly not a cup of coffee that he was kind enough to bring to me at a murder scene!" I stood up from the table, having lost my appetite. "I'm going to bed," I announced. "I've had a really bad day and I'm not about to end it by having an argument regarding someone who's nothing to me, except a colleague I occasionally deal with on police matters."

Before Mandy could respond, I went to my room and shut the door behind me. I couldn't understand what had come over her, and I was far too tired to try to analyse it now.

# CHAPTER 12

**I** left for work in the morning before Mandy woke up. It was bad enough we had quarrelled the previous evening, and I didn't want to spoil our friendship by having more words over breakfast. Therefore, even though I wasn't on shift until early afternoon, I rose at six, showered and put a call through to Smythe so we could meet up to go over the information. He suggested we have breakfast at Bill's, the pub-jazz club we often frequented, and which operated 24/7.

I walked in wearing a tight pair of faded jeans and a black T-shirt. The day was cool, but I found it invigorating and didn't need a jacket. I was glad, however, I had taken the trouble to put on make-up and wear lipstick because as I approached Smythe's table, I espied Sean Webb coming out of the "Gents". My heart skipped with excitement and this brought a smile to my face.

"Good to see you're feeling better," Smythe commented when I took a seat at the table.

"I had a long sleep," I replied, "and now, I'm ravenous. So how about we order first?"

Sean motioned to the waiter for menus and we ordered coffee to start with. "I'm going for the big breakfast," I announced, snapping my menu shut.

"Well, it seems murder makes you hungry," Sean observed. "I'll go for the big breakfast, too."

Smythe glanced at the two of us and nodded his head. "Sounds like a plan. Let's make it three."

"How did it go yesterday?" I addressed Smythe while we waited for our coffees.

"The forensics confirmed that the head was severed post mortem. Once I went over the scene, I left them to get on with their work. I'm not sure yet what they found. I'm still waiting for their report to come through."

"Well, whoever did this must have a secret spot where they cut up the corpse before they brought it back to Mark's place. What I don't understand is why they would go to all that trouble," I remarked. "Why not do the same thing they did at the hotel with Ophelia?"

Sean raised a querying eyebrow. "What makes you think this is the same killer?"

"Call it women's intuition, but I know the killings are connected."

"But in Casey's case, he committed suicide," Sean stated.

"I don't think so," I declared with confidence.

Sean was about to argue, but the coffees arrived and we took the opportunity to place our breakfast order. I noticed Smythe had said nothing during my discussion with Sean, and I wondered what he was thinking.

"I don't know how you came to this conclusion," Sean continued after the waiter left.

"Never you mind." I stirred one sugar into my cappuccino while I tuned in on his energy. For some reason, he wasn't happy with my comment. I figured perhaps, like Smythe, he didn't like to be told he was wrong. Well, he had another think coming if he wanted to get involved with me, I thought with a secret smile.

Smythe finally spoke. "Let's focus on the information you have for the time being."

I told them what I had found out to date, and all through breakfast the men listened attentively. Smythe even scribbled some notes in his little notebook. The only thing I didn't tell them was that I had every intention of going to Stonewall to get any information I could on Mark Meadows. When I finished recounting my story, we ordered another round of coffees when the waiter came to take away our empty plates.

"You'll need to give me the hat," Smythe said. "We need it as evidence."

"Yeah, yeah," I replied. "I'll drop it off at the station tomorrow."

"We also need to question the queens again," he added.

I grinned. "Well, good luck on that one. They think you're both *bitches*." I enjoyed the look of annoyance on their faces.

"Why do they think that?" Sean looked none too happy.

"Because you guys don't know how to handle people," I answered; and added when I saw Sean about to say something, "I meant to say the police in general, not just the two of you. So don't go getting on your high horse."

There was a smirk on Smythe's lips. "And how are we supposed to handle our witnesses, *Miss Marple*?"

I ignored his patronising tone. "With compassion and understanding," I threw back at him with a serious look. "You'd be amazed at the stuff people will tell you if you show them you genuinely care."

"Oh, so you're saying we should make them afternoon tea and crumpets?" Sean quipped in a rather harsh tone.

I shook my head. "I'm giving you guys a bit of advice, and you're taking it as a personal attack. Well, let the results speak for themselves, and you two do as you like."

"Ferrari, don't get us wrong," Smythe said with amusement in his eyes. "We appreciate your coming forward with all this information; in fact, we are honoured. Oh, and I'll keep my promise not to lock you up for withholding it in the first place."

"Fuck off, Smythe," I threw at him. "If you guys can't learn to question a witness, it's not my fault if they later talk to me." I dug in my pocket for a few dollar bills and slapped them on the table. "That's for my share of the meal." I went to stand up, but Smythe reached out and grabbed my wrist.

"Not so fast," he said. "We're not finished yet."

I pulled my arm free of his grasp. "Oh, yes, we are. It's about time you guys did your job! And if you can't solve this by yourselves, my consulting rates are very reasonable."

The amazement on Smythe's face was comical, while Sean's look of admiration made my day. I smiled sweetly, and added, "*Arrivederci*, boys." Then I walked out of the café without looking back, but I caught the one word Smythe called out after me. "Smartarse!"

It was almost one by the time I returned home. After my breakfast meeting with Smythe and Sean, I ran some errands and then stopped off for lunch at a noodle bar. I hoped that by now Mandy had gone out somewhere so I could get ready for work and not have to see her until either late this evening or even tomorrow.

All was quiet when I entered the apartment and I found a note from her on the kitchen table. It read: *Gone sightseeing and staying with Phil tonight. See you tomorrow. Mandy.* Well, I thought, that takes care of that. Smythe had been a dark horse, not mentioning that he was seeing my friend this evening. But then, he was hardly going to confide in me after the way I treated him over breakfast. I shrugged my shoulders, not caring what he thought, and made coffee. At least I could relax for a while before it was time to go to work.

It was a shame things had become strained between Mandy and me, but when I saw her next I would insist we talk about it and hopefully return our friendship to the way it had been before Smythe entered her life. I couldn't believe it that the man had not only spoiled my potential police career, but now he was coming between my friend and me.

As soon as I took over from the morning DM, I went in search of Chris. He was alone, playing computer games. "Don't you have anything better to do with your time?" I asked when he let me in. "What about your studies?"

"I skipped a semester since I completed extra units last year, so I'm free until after the July break," he explained.

"Well, some people are lucky," I remarked sardonically. "What about work? I thought you were doing casual work in the functions department."

"Yes, but things are a bit slow at the moment, and I'm not needed."

"So you'd rather play computer games."

"Hey, is this an inquisition or what?" Chris protested. "Dad's happy for me to hang around."

"Your father doesn't even know what's going on right now. He's too busy with the project in Hawaii," I scolded him.

Chris threw me a sheepish look. "Since you won't let me hack into any computers to get more information on the case, and you won't let me take your friend sightseeing in the Ferrari, what else am I supposed to do?"

I shook my head in disbelief. "You really know how to try someone's patience, don't you? I suggest you find something constructive to do. For instance, did you continue with your research on Ophelia's background?"

"I went through the archives of most newspapers and found nothing. If you want to know anything else you'll have to let me get creative," he stated with hope in his eyes.

"I'll let you know." My tone soon quelled his enthusiasm. "Keep out of trouble, okay?"

He nodded and walked me to the door. "Do you wanna have dinner tonight?"

"That'll be nice," I replied. "I'll come up around eight." I bade him goodbye and made for my next port of call—Dobbs's office.

"There you are, Ferrari," he greeted me as I walked in. "I see you gave Smythe and his mate, Sean, a little 'whatfor' this morning."

I plopped down on one of the visitors' chairs. "Does nothing escape you? Don't tell me I've hurt Smythe's sensibilities and he called you to have a good cry. After all, he can dish it out himself pretty well, you know."

Dobbs laughed. "Yes, but no one can beat these hot-tempered Italians."

I frowned with anger. "These guys are not grateful, Dobbs. I give them all the information I learned, and they don't even thank me."

Dobbs said with a knowing look, "I hear that someone actually did appreciate the way you handled yourself."

I rolled my eyes. "You mean Sean? I'm not sure he appreciates me as much as he makes out. He just likes it when I stick it to Smythe. Besides, I have a feeling he believes himself superior to all of us."

"Why do you say that?" He gave me a curious look.

"It's a feeling I have."

"I never liked that young rookie."

I gazed at him with surprise. "Where does this come from? Sean hasn't done anything to you."

"I guess when you've been around as long as I have you get a feeling about people, just as you have your female intuition."

"Hmm," I mused. "Well, I just put it down to the fact that he's a bad boy and likes to show off."

"How did it go with the Mark Meadows thing?" Dobbs changed the subject.

I gave him a detailed account of everything, right up until my meeting with Smythe this morning. "What I don't understand is how Mark was involved in all of this and why the killer needed to silence him. After all, it's obvious Casey was killed so he'd take the fall for Ophelia's murder. So where does Mark fit into it?"

"Smythe mentioned you thought it was the same killer."

My eyes grew wide with annoyance. "Since when is Smythe sharing so much information with you? He's probably testing the waters to see if I told you anything differently from what I told him."

"Well, Miss Uppity," Dobbs said as if to a spoiled child, "if you must know, he rang me around half an hour ago and gave me a run down on the forensic report on Meadows."

I half leaned across his desk to get a closer look at him. "He did?"

"Hey, sit back." He shooed me away and turned his attention to a piece of paper on his desk. "I wrote it all down so I wouldn't forget anything."

"Yes?" I prompted impatiently.

"They found flutitrazepam in his system. You know, Rohypnol."

"The date rape drug."

"Well, yes. They call it the date rape drug, but it's not as common as everyone thinks, and not easy to get a hold of unless you're well connected," he explained. "In any case, Meadows was drugged; a fatal overdose from what they can tell. Then the killer severed his head post mortem."

I felt a wave of nausea in my stomach and asked Dobbs for a Coke. "The thing I don't understand is why the killer would bring the victim's body back to the apartment and risk being seen by someone." I popped open the drink can and had a few sips.

"Smythe has a theory. He said Mark's place was really messy, so he believes the killer was searching for something."

This had never occurred to me, but when I thought about it, it was possible. The place had looked like a bomb hit it, but I had simply put it down to Mark being a messy person. "Can they prove this?"

"Not exactly. But there were items lying about everywhere, some that even a messy person wouldn't disturb."

"Such as?"

"A cutlery drawer in the kitchen was lying open with cutlery spread all over the kitchen bench, but the cutlery was clean. A messy person would've only taken out whatever they needed to use and left only dirty cutlery lying about," Dobbs pointed out.

"Makes sense," I replied. "I must say, I didn't pay much attention to this because I was only there a short time, and once I found the body I fled outside to ring Smythe."

"Anyway," Dobbs added, "it's just a theory at this time. Other than this, they didn't find anything else."

"Oh my God!" I cried out, startling Dobbs. "What if the killer was looking for the diamond?"

Dobbs looked at me with doubt. "Why would Meadows have the diamond in the first place unless it was he who killed Ophelia?"

"I don't know, Dobbs. But what if Ophelia knew the killer was after the diamond and she gave it to Mark for safekeeping?"

"You think?" Dobbs stated with doubt. "If Ophelia cared so much for the diamond, she would have put it in the hotel safe and not wear it in her hat."

I shrugged. "Who's to know what she thought. She seemed to have the same arrogant self-confidence you find in people with big egos—people who think nothing bad ever happens to them."

"True."

"Did Smythe say anything about the bodies being given a service yet?"

"No," Dobbs answered. "I'd say until the police get more answers those bodies aren't going anywhere."

"I just think how terrible it is that they're lying in some drawer in the morgue," I observed.

"At least no one's disturbing them."

"Mark's killing is still so baffling," I remarked, somewhat puzzled. "Even if the killer was looking for something in the apartment, why bring the body back with him?"

"Why indeed? But don't discount the fact that perhaps your hunch is wrong, and the murders are not connected after all," he suggested. "So far, the MO for all three killings is different: Ophelia dismembered in her suite; Casey found hanging; and Meadows dismembered off-site somewhere and brought back to his apartment."

"Dobbs, while my intuition about men is shocking, it never lets me down when it comes to murder," I informed him. "I say the murders are connected and I'm fairly sure we're looking for one killer."

I left him to chew on this while I did my rounds and then joined Chris for pizza at the penthouse. Later, I looked in on the girls while they were getting ready for the show. They seemed to be in good spirits.

"Darling, are you joining the audience this evening?" Frank called when I stuck my head in their dressing room.

"Too busy. I stopped by to wish you good luck and to let you know we can do Stonewall tomorrow night." The girls and I agreed on what time to meet up for our outing. Then they blew kisses at me when I left them to finish dressing.

By the time eleven o'clock rolled around, I had finished my work and logged off my computer after updating the DM's log. I then handed over my keys and pager to the night manager and left for home.

The Cross was busy with people going to bars and nightclubs that were hosting drag queen shows and gay acts leading up to the gay mardi gras, which was now almost a week away. Usually, thousands of tourists descended upon Sydney around this time, and Kings Cross, Oxford Street and other inner city suburbs were the main locations that hosted events during the mardi gras festival.

I made my way home walking past tourists, prostitutes, exotic dancers, druggies and police, all co-existing in a seedy and often dangerous world of its own. When I reached the end of the main drag, I turned into the side street that led to my block of apartments in Potts Point. I drew out my house keys in preparation to enter the building and just then, I heard a wolf whistle coming from across the road and I turned to find Sean Webb leaning against a silver grey Porsche Boxster S.

He wore tight faded jeans and a white shirt, open at the neck and accentuating his tawny skin. "I heard a sexy lady lived in this building," he said in his smooth voice.

"Nice car," I returned, wondering how much it had cost him.

"You're not the only one with a sports car, Ferrari," he remarked, almost reading my thoughts. "You don't mind if I call you Ferrari, do you? I kind of like it."

I shook my head. "No, I don't mind. What are you doing here, anyway? Come to show me your new toy?" I looked pointedly at his car.

He laughed. "This is my private car; the one I had the night we went for dinner was a police issue."

"Is that right?"

"As to what I'm doing here; well, after this morning's roasting against the cops I thought I would come over to get some of your *consulting* services."

The way he delivered this line, while he swallowed me with his eyes, left nothing to the imagination. It was my choice—I could either send him packing or invite him in and shag him silly.

# CHAPTER 13

It's not every day that a woman of my age gets to shag a young man in his prime, and I suddenly felt like Mrs Robinson as Sean started to undress me the moment we entered my apartment and shut the door behind us. I was proud of my petite and slim figure, still in excellent shape due to the physical nature of my work and the fact that when young, I used to do martial arts. So those bits that start to sag and drop at a certain age didn't show as much as they would have on someone who didn't keep fit. I was one of those lucky individuals who could eat almost anything and still lose weight by walking and keeping actively busy. Just in case, though, I didn't switch on the lights.

Sean's body was to die for—typical bad boy looks—young, firm, athletic, smooth to the touch and with barely any hair on his chest. One thing that turned me off was an overly hairy chest and most of all, a man with hair on his back. I fleetingly remembered Nathan had been rather hairy, and this might explain why our sex life wasn't great. Failing this, Nathan had been a rather boring lover.

Thoughts of my ex went scurrying out of my mind as soon as Sean's hands started to caress my body. He had me against the lounge room wall, naked as the day I was born and somehow, he had managed to shed his own clothes without my noticing. I found myself pressed to his body with not a millimetre of space between us.

His mouth devoured mine while his hands touched me all over, and I turned to putty. Sean pulled back for a moment to look into my eyes and then his hands were back, kneading my breasts, his mouth sucking at my nipples. I was sure I was going to climax at any moment, but I held back with all my willpower. One of his hands reached down to that magic place, which had been out of service for so long, and he inserted two fingers inside me. I arched back against him and moaned with pleasure. He played me like a finely tuned instrument but stopped just before I could orgasm.

I didn't want him to stop, but he withdrew his fingers and before I knew it, he plunged inside me, his thrusts making me gasp. They hurt at first, but when I got used to his delicious invasion, I relaxed and started to climb toward that sublime moment of release. Then he withdrew abruptly and looked into my eyes again, his gaze one of exultation. He knew he could control my body in any way he chose, but even though I was in the middle of an amazing experience, I wasn't about to let this happen. Nobody controlled Mia Ferrari!

Much to his surprise, I pushed him away from me and wiped the perspiration from my forehead with one hand while I caught hold of his wrist with the other and pulled him into my bedroom, where I pushed him rather roughly onto my bed. His self-confident smile goaded me on and I straddled him, guiding his hard cock into me with one hand. He gasped with surprise as I started to move on top of him while I held his arms above his head. He was now my captive and I was in control, and every time I felt he was about to come, I withdrew.

This went on for quite a while until I must've driven him over the edge. When I went to withdraw once again, he pushed me off with his superior strength and I found myself lying on my back. Sean then entered me once again, and this time I gasped with pain for his thrust was very deep; but before I could push him away, I climaxed in a series of orgasms that brought tears to my eyes. Sean came immediately after me.

A few moments later, he raised himself on his elbows and gazed into my eyes with a satisfied smile. He was still on top, and inside me, but I could already feel him growing softer.

"You're one piece of work, Ferrari," he said before he rolled away and headed for the bathroom.

I sat up, feeling raw and rather sore between my legs; and though this hurt, it also felt good. My equipment had been out of commission for a while and Sean's onslaught had made it go into overdrive too quickly. I felt luxuriously sated but exhausted.

I heard the flushing of the toilet and the tap running for a few moments before Sean came out of the bathroom and walked straight to the lounge room to retrieve his clothes. I quickly threw on a robe and followed him.

"What are you doing?" I asked as I watched him dress.

"What does it look like?" he returned, his tone patronising. "I'm on the graveyard shift tonight, so I have to go."

"Just like that?" My temper began to fire up. How dared he treat me like a cheap fuck!

"Babe," he said, almost sneering at me, "there's crime out there and someone has to fight it."

I felt like puking at his macho-shit, chauvinistic behaviour, but I controlled my rising nausea and flaming temper. "Okay, off you go then," I replied nonchalantly. "Thanks for the fuck, it was rather enlightening." I made to turn away, but he grabbed hold of my wrist and pulled me around to face him.

"What's that supposed to mean?" He drew me close to his face.

I disengaged myself from his grasp. "Don't flatter yourself about your sexual skills. It was a good shag, I grant you that; but as far as lovemaking is concerned, you have a lot to learn. Now, get the hell out of my place. And next time, go fuck someone who doesn't know much about skilful lovemaking, like some hot babe in her twenties."

He looked like he wanted to hit me, but my glacial gaze must've made him have second thoughts, so he finished buttoning his shirt and then left without a word.

I had a bath after his departure and sat soaking in the warm water while I drank a glass of red to calm my nerves. I'd had my fair share of one-night stands with bad boys prior to my marriage, but not once had I run across a man who turned it into a cheap, prostitute-like transaction sans the money. My one-nighters had always been playful and fun, and though there had never been any intentions of an on-going relationship, I had remained friends with several of the men with whom I had been involved.

The episode with Sean shook me to a large extent. It was obvious we were both sexually dominant, and there was nothing wrong with that; but what made it weird was the fact that he seemed to want to prove it every step of the way. I replayed the whole thing in my mind from the time he turned up at my door in his expensive car, and his boasting of it, to the look of victory in his eyes when he thought he was dominating me; and finally, his atrocious behaviour after it was all over. It was like he disliked having the tables turned on him by my sexual assertiveness; therefore, he had to belittle me. So once he satisfied himself, he left as one would leave a prostitute after services rendered. Plus his excuse for leaving, "to fight crime" as he put it—I mean, could he get more narcissistic than this?

I gulped the rest of my wine and got out of the bath. Bloody men! They liked the chase, but when the woman showed any kind of assertiveness, they weren't man enough to handle it. God forbid a woman should bruise their fragile egos. My only regret was that I had succumbed to Sean's charms like an idiot, only to end up feeling degraded by his behaviour.

I slept the sleep of the exhausted and didn't even hear my alarm go off in the morning; however, Mandy awakened me when she popped her head into my room at around six-thirty and called out my name. I took one look at the bedside clock and jumped up.

"I made coffee," Mandy said. "Do you want some toast?"

"Sure, thanks," I replied and started to get ready for work.

I was ready in fifteen minutes and joined Mandy in the kitchen for some breakfast despite the fact that I was going to be late. I made a quick call to the night manager at the hotel, letting him know I would be there in half an hour, and he reassured me that all was fine and he didn't mind waiting for me.

"What time did you get in?" I asked Mandy while buttering my toast. "I must've slept like a log."

She blushed. "I came in just now."

"Oh." I added strawberry jam to the toast.

"I... um... I came to get some extra clothes and to let you know I'll be out all day and will return tomorrow. Phil's taking me to the Blue Mountains." She buried her face in her coffee cup, avoiding my gaze.

I didn't say anything but made a mental note that we would have to talk soon. I didn't like the underlying tension between us, and it was about time we cleared the air.

I changed the subject. "I'm going to Stonewall tonight, so I guess you won't be coming along after all."

Mandy shook her head. "Sorry, I guess I'll miss out."

"Well, maybe next time," I replied, and we finished breakfast in silence.

I left Mandy to her own devices while I hurried to work. In the end, I was only fifteen minutes late, and I took over the keys and pager from the night manager.

"Thanks for waiting, Paul. Anything I should know about?"

Paul shook his head. "Slow night. Only news is that Mr Rourke's back. He walked in around ten minutes ago.

"Okay, thanks." I tried to keep a calm countenance despite the excitement coursing through me. I had missed David and wanted to see him plus update him face to face on what had happened at the hotel during his absence. Dobbs had placed a call to him in Hawaii when the first murder occurred; and since then, I had been corresponding with David on a daily basis. He had been too busy to take everything in, however, and I now wanted to brief him personally.

I gave him a while to settle in and then put a call through to book a meeting, but just as I decided on this, my mobile rang. It was David.

"Are you in the hotel?" he asked after greeting me.

"Yes, I was going to call you to hook up for a meeting."

"No need. Just come up when you're ready," he responded. "I slept on the plane, so I'm not tired."

We rang off and I did my morning rounds before I went up to the penthouse. David was alone, Chris having gone to play tennis with friends. "Coffee?" he offered.

"Yes, thanks," I replied, watching him pour coffee in two cups.

"Please," he said, "have a seat. I won't be long."

I sat on a three-seater sofa by a large coffee table and he joined me, handing me my cup and asking if I wanted milk and sugar. I added a splash of milk from the milk jug he brought over. "Thanks."

"So it's been a very eventful time for us, I see," he observed as he spooned one sugar into his black coffee.

"That's an understatement," I answered, thinking of all that had transpired since he had left on his latest trip. "Thankfully, we managed to keep the hotel's name out of the paper; and the guests were none the wiser when we moved them to the ninth floor after the first murder."

"The first?" David queried. "I thought there was only one; the other being a suicide."

"Well, the cops thought it was a suicide, but I have reason to believe that—"

"You're not at it again, are you?" he interrupted.

"What do you mean?" I played the innocent.

"Mia, this is me you're talking to." He gave me a knowing look.

"You're investigating this thing, aren't you?"

I nodded. "You're right, of course. But I couldn't help it seeing as the female impersonators decided to give me more information than they gave the police," I stated in my defence.

David shook his head. "Last time you became involved in an investigation you had me worried no end. And this sounds a lot more serious than the last time. I think you should let the police handle it."

A feeling of warmth spread through me at his concern, and I thought of the poor victims who had lost their lives for what seemed to be a pink diamond. The whole situation had been horrid and traumatising. Added to this, was the tension between Mandy and me, plus the episode with Sean. All of a sudden, I felt I couldn't take any more stress and I burst into tears like a helpless female. David put down his cup and took me in his arms.

"What's wrong, Mia? How can I help? You take so much on your shoulders that I don't know what to do with you at times." His soothing voice and the protective feel of his strong arms were my undoing; and before I knew it, we were kissing passionately, our bodies reclining back on the sofa. My heart beat so wildly that the pounding sound of it in my ears made me deaf to anything David might have said. All I knew was that I needed his tenderness and passion to erase the horrible events of the past few days.

We kissed for a long time while our hands explored each other's body. David's fingers ran lightly over me and started to unbutton my shirt while I did the same to his, and we shifted our bodies into a supine position on the three-seater. I longed to feel him inside me, after all these years, and couldn't wait until we were naked.

My passion started to mount and it was all I could do not to rip off his clothes. David was trying to undo my bra while he kissed me deeply, his tongue exploring my mouth. Then, I felt cold, and I opened my eyes to see him sitting up and readjusting his clothes.

"What is it?" My voice was drunk with desire.

"I'm sorry," he said, regret in his tone. "It shouldn't be like this."

I shook my head to clear my thoughts and sat up, buttoning my shirt and throwing my jacket over my shoulders. I felt chilled and needed more coffee to warm me up. David must have read my thoughts and he took our cups away momentarily only to bring them back replenished.

"Thanks." I gave him a weak smile when he handed me mine.

He sat down next to me. "You must think me a fool for what just happened," he explained, "but the fact is things are still quite fresh with our respective marriage break ups; and though I never really had what I would call a genuine relationship with Elena, I'm still going through a period of readjustment."

I nodded, indicating I understood. "It's okay, you don't need to explain."

"But I do, Mia. The time never seemed to be right for us all those years ago; and now that we're single again there's the possibility that things might progress. But not until we're both over the hurt and sorrow."

"I'm not asking for anything, David," I reassured him.

"That's not what I meant," he persisted. "I know the passion between us never died, but it's more than passion I want to offer you. And right now I don't think I can do that."

I stood up. "Please, you don't have to explain. We agreed we're both getting over the past and we're not in a position yet to commit to anything. I certainly don't want you just for a shag—you mean more to me than that. So I think we should forget what happened."

David ran his fingers through his hair. "It would be so easy to simply marry you," he stated.

"But you didn't ask me, and we're not at that stage," I replied and cleared my throat of the emotions that threatened more tears. "I'd better get back to work."

He nodded but remained silent, and I made my way out of the room, feeling disappointed.

Dobbs was on a day off so I never had a chance to catch up with him, which was a good thing lest I be tempted to tell him about David or even Sean. Not that I could ever confide in him about my sex life; he was like a father to me and I wouldn't even know how to broach the subject without shocking him. Still, thoughts of what had happened with Sean, and how he had behaved, bothered me; and unfortunately, there was no one I could share this with. For a moment, I thought of Mandy, but we still had to work on our fragile friendship. So it seemed I would have to bear this all alone.

The rest of the day went quickly and by three-thirty, I was home and ready for a nap. Tonight, the queens and I were going to Stonewall. I got out of my uniform and slid in between the bed sheets; I was asleep in no time.

# CHAPTER 14

Chris decided to tag along with us; so we all climbed into a taxi at around eleven that evening and were deposited outside Stonewall within ten minutes. The historical building with sandstone walls and classical arches and columns welcomed us as the queens walked straight in with Chris and me, not too far behind.

A scream of delight from the bar and shrieks from the queens, which could be heard above the loud music, alerted us to the fact that already the girls had found an old work mate. There were hugs and kisses galore with the bar and floor staff; even the DJ threw a wave salute our way.

I spotted a couple of gorgeous young men, dancing topless on top of the bar counter to the beat of the music, and I noticed the place was mainly packed with males, although there were a few females here and there. Some of the men were in drag while others wore nothing but tight jeans, showing off their bare well-built torsos; yet others, had on body-tight T-shirts and very skimpy shorts that left nothing to the imagination. Some wore leather jerkins with a G-string underneath and their bare upper bodies were criss-crossed with leather straps, very reminiscent of the Village People's biker. The females opted for a butch look, though I spotted a few lipstick lesbians wearing skimpy dresses and outrageously high heels.

Chris and I exchanged a look of resignation, which pretty much made us stand out as one of the few straight people in the place. Of course, Chris attracted many looks from the young males around him, and I was sure they would be more than happy to convert him given half the chance. On the other hand, I noticed a lipstick lesbian giving me the eye and I felt flattered that I still had the power to attract both males and females.

"Darling!" Frank materialised next to me after much hugging and kissing with his friends. "Come out back where we can talk to some of the boys and girls. Too noisy in here," he yelled in my ear.

I caught hold of Chris's hand and followed Frank's lead as he headed toward a passageway that took us to a small room, which looked like some kind of storage area.

Aside from our group, two bare-chested young men in their twenties followed us in. They wore tight white jeans and looked fresh-faced, with short jelled spiky hair and a sprinkle of glitter on their faces. In my opinion, they were absolutely drop-dead gorgeous and I had to stop myself from drooling. It didn't matter they were gay; they were a feast for my jaded eyes.

"These are James and Damien." Frank introduced them. James was blond and Damien, dark-haired.

The boys nodded to me, but their eyes went to Chris, who actually blushed and tightened his grip on my hand. I shook his hand loose and smiled at the handsome young men. "I'm Mia Ferrari."

"I'll let you lovelies talk," Frank interjected. "I might have someone else you may want to talk to later." With this said, he withdrew from the room leaving behind the heavy aroma of jasmine, which he must have acquired on arrival as he didn't wear any scent on the way in. Chris and I were left alone with James and Damien.

"Frank told us what this is about," James, the blond God, spoke. "I used to do Clee's make-up when she worked here. Aside from being a make-up artist, I'm an exotic dancer."

I visualised him in a G-string and had to force my mind to focus back on our conversation. "Did you ever know Mark Meadows or did Clee say anything about him to either of you?"

James glanced quickly at his friend, who nodded, and then back at us. "Mark and I had a thing, but it didn't last long once Clee came on the scene," he informed us.

I swallowed uneasily. "Um... I hope you don't mind my asking, but if Mark had a thing with Clee, does this make him bi-sexual or did they do it... well, you know..."

Damien smiled at my confusion. "Clee was a double-adaptor," he stated bluntly.

Charming! I thought. "Okay, thanks for clarifying that one," I remarked casually as if I heard this kind of talk every day. "So did either of you notice anything unusual about Mark's behaviour toward

Clee?"

James answered, "Mark was possessive to the point of obsession and seemed to have some kind of hold over her. None of us could get close since he became her lover. Clee hated exclusivity, but she and Mark were a hot item; and she wasn't ready to let him go."

"Anything else?"

"No, that's about it. When Mark broke it off with me, I stopped being Clee's make-up artist. I didn't feel too friendly towards her, but we still had to work together so we maintained a surface civility," James replied.

"And you?" I turned to Damien.

"I was also Mark's lover, before he left me for Clee," his tone was resentful. "As James said, Mark and Clee were exclusive, and Mark made sure we all knew it."

"Hmm," I responded thoughtfully. I was still trying to figure out if all this bed-hopping activity would reveal anything of importance.

"Yes, but remember the other guy?" James said suddenly to Damien, and my ears pricked up.

"What other guy?" I jumped in before Damien could reply.

"There was this young guy who came here once or twice," James explained. "I heard that he and Clee had a huge argument."

"Who was this guy?" Chris finally decided to speak.

"That's all we know. We never actually met him. But at one stage, Clee complained to Mark that her young half-brother was bothering her. This was some time ago, though."

Chris and I looked at each other with wide eyes. "That's all the information we have," Damien stated.

I shook their hands. "Thank you, boys; you've been very helpful."

"Any time, doll." Damien hugged me to him, much to my surprise, followed by the sexy James, who did the same thing. They then hugged Chris, who looked very uncomfortable, and left us.

"Relax," I grinned. "Your tush is still intact." Chris didn't appreciate my teasing and threw me a warning look. "Hey," I protested innocently, "you're the one who wanted to tag along."

Before he could reply, Frank walked in with a tall and very flamboyant drag queen wearing a bright pink wig and extremely heavy make-up. She had on an off-the-shoulder, silver sequined dress that clung to her shapely body. "There you are, darlings," Frank greeted us. "This is Holly Goheavily. She worked closely with Clee."

I tried to keep a straight face at Holly's last name. Chris said nothing and simply stood a few feet behind me. "What a beautiful dress," I remarked in order to cover my amusement at her name.

Holly hugged and kissed me on both cheeks, European style. "Thank you, daaaaahling. I just love petite girls like you."

This time, it was Chris who couldn't keep a straight face as Holly hugged me to her again, and I threw a quick peek at his smirking face. I made a note to make him suffer for his impudence when I had the chance.

"I'll leave you girls," said Frank. "When you're finished, come out to the bar for a drink. We're catching up with the old crowd, darlings." He waved at us and disappeared.

"I heard about my dear friend's murder," Holly sobbed, dabbing at her heavily made up eyes with a wad of tissues. "She was practically my best friend." She took a few moments to sniff into the tissues while Chris and I stood quietly, giving her time to regain her composure. "Apologies, my sweets," she spoke after she blew her nose. "It's just that I can't believe she's gone."

"So sorry for your loss, Miss Go... Go...," Chris started to say, and Holly reached out and caressed his face lightly.

"You're a sweet boy to say that. Thank you." Then, she turned to me. "You have a wonderful son, love. Not many young people would care about an old queen like me."

I didn't correct her about Chris's relationship to me. "You're not old, Holly. You look no more than someone in their mid-thirties," I observed.

"Oh, darling, I could kiss you!" Holly exclaimed, and I braced myself for another hug and kiss. Fortunately, she didn't reach out for me. "I'm actually forty-five, love. It's amazing what a little nip and tuck can do." She smiled. "Now, what would you like to know?"

"Anything you can think of," I replied. "James and Damien told us about Clee and Mark Meadows."

"Oh, that manipulative devil," Holly hissed. "He was so rough with her at times. Once, they had a huge row about something or other, and Clee came away with a terrible bruise on her beautiful face where he had slapped her really hard. I really don't know what she saw in him. He was skinny as a reed and not all that attractive."

"Did Clee ever comment about their arguments?" I fervently

hoped something about the pink diamond would come out, which would pretty much link Mark's murder to Clee's.

"Not really. He was just possessive and very jealous. And then there was her half-brother."

The half-brother again! According to the research Chris had done, Clee had never met her half-brother because she had left home before he was born; and yet, the world was full of surprises. "What about him?"

"Oh, he was always at her for money, darling. It seemed he was broke all the time."

"Did you ever meet him?" I wished someone had seen this guy so I could track him down.

"No. Mind you, this was some time ago and I can't remember much about it."

"What happened to him?"

Holly shrugged. "Who knows and who cares. All I remember is Clee telling me how glad she was that he'd gone from her life. She was relieved she didn't have to give him any more money. The last time she saw him, though, he left her with a black eye. What a shit!"

"Did you ever learn his name?" This from Chris.

"No, sweetie. Clee just referred to him as 'the half-brother'."

"What about his age and looks? Did she or anyone ever comment on this?" I was fast running out of hope.

Holly paused thoughtfully for a moment. "Well, she did say he was a lot younger than her and quite good looking because he took after his mother. But that's about all I can tell you."

"Was he gay?" Something started to bother me at the back of my mind, but I couldn't quite put my finger on it.

"I always assumed so seeing as Clee talked about his sexy tight arse and athletic body, but who knows." She looked at Chris. "Darling, what time is it?"

Chris glanced at his watch, "Almost midnight."

Holly let out a little scream. "Sorry to be rude, my loves, but I have a show on in a couple of minutes. You two are gorgeous, absolutely fab, my dears," she exclaimed, blowing us a kiss, and then she left.

"Well, that was interesting," Chris remarked, and went on when he saw the query in my eyes, "about the brother being younger."

"Yes, that's what I've been trying to work out." I frowned. "You said Clee ran away from home at age thirteen and that her brother was born shortly thereafter. So this makes him at least thirteen years younger than she. But you saw Clee at the hotel; she looked in her late twenties."

Chris nodded. "This would make the brother around fifteen years old now, but Holly said she knew of the brother coming to see Clee some time ago, which would have made him even younger at the time."

"Exactly!" I exclaimed. "Depending how long ago we're talking about, he would've been almost a child then. This doesn't make any sense. Let's get out of here, I have to think."

We went back out to the bar and found Frank and the others drinking with a group of young men and queens. They invited us for a drink and we had a quick one out of politeness. All I wanted, however, was to get away as soon as possible.

The queens stayed on to party, and Chris and I caught a taxi. "I'll drop you off at the hotel and continue on home," I said, and turned to the driver to give him our destination.

"You're going to have to let me do some more research," Chris stated.

I glanced at him and noted the seriousness on his face. "If you mean what I think you mean, I don't want to know anything about it. In fact, I don't think you should even entertain the idea. If Smythe gets wind that you're, well, you know what; he'll have us both for breakfast." I didn't want to mention the word "hacking" in front of the taxi driver.

Chris sighed. "I don't see any other way of finding out about this, but I'll take your advice for now and stick to more research through the news forums and such."

"Good boy," I replied, looking thoughtful. "You know, one other thing that bothers me is when Holly said Clee remarked on her half-brother's good looks, and how he took after his mother. This would mean Clee must've known her step-mother as well."

"Or maybe she saw a photo of her," Chris suggested.

"True. Anyway, I'll touch base with you in the next couple of days. I'm taking some time off seeing as I've been working so many shifts lately."

"How's it going with your friend?" Chris didn't know that Mandy had a thing with Smythe, and I wasn't about to tell him.

"This is the reason I'm taking a couple of days off," I replied. "I haven't had a chance to take her sightseeing all that much."

"What about the mardi gras?" he asked.

"We're going, if that's what you mean."

"None of my friends want to come along, so is it okay if I tag along with you girls?"

I shrugged. "I don't see why not. I'll have to make sure I roster myself off on Saturday though," I said more to myself than to him. The mardi gras parade was on this coming Saturday.

The taxi pulled up outside the hotel and Chris jumped out. He offered to pay for his fare, but I waved him away. "I'll get this one. You go and do your research, and call me if you find anything."

We bade each other good night and the taxi pulled back out into the traffic to take me home. The going was slow as we rode along Macleay Street, the Cross's main drag, which was packed with cars and people crossing in front of moving vehicles, even at this time of night.

My head was full of the information I had learned from my visit to Stonewall and I needed time to process it. The first thing to do was to find out how old Clee had been at the time of her death. This should be easy, I thought. The queens would be able to shed some light on her age. She had looked so young when I'd met her. Then I thought of what Holly's response had been when I complimented her on her looks—she'd said she kept herself looking younger with a nip and tuck. It was possible that Clee, or Ophelia, as I thought of her, was older than she looked, in which case this would make it easier to work out how old her half-brother was. Without a name, however, it was going to be very difficult to track him down even if he was still living in Sydney.

I was so engrossed in my thoughts that I jumped when I felt the mobile vibrate in the back pocket of my jeans. I drew it out and answered it without checking the caller ID. "Ferrari."

"Smythe here."

I was surprised Smythe should call at such a late hour, especially as he was supposed to be with Mandy. Suddenly, my heart was in my mouth. What if something had happened to my friend?

"Smythe, what's going on?" I didn't bother to hide the enmity in my voice as I remembered his attitude toward me at our last meeting.

"I need to meet with you tomorrow morning," he informed me,

and I interrupted before he could go on to explain.

"Well, this is a fine time to let me know! Besides, where the hell is Mandy?"

"She's asleep and I'm in the bathroom," he answered, clearing his throat.

"Eeew! Spare me the details, will you? I'm not interested in your sex life." I expected him to make a snappy remark at my insolence, but he didn't.

"Will you meet me? We need to talk."

I sighed, wondering what this was all about. "Fine, but I'm not getting up at six," I warned him. "I just got off my shift and I'm dead tired." I lied of course, not wanting him to know what I had been up to.

"How about we do brunch at Puccini's in Woollahra at ten thirty?" he suggested.

"You're paying?" I asked, wanting to get a reaction out of him, but he didn't bite.

"My treat," he replied. "Be there."

I felt annoyed. "I just agreed to meet you, so why wouldn't I be there? What's with this cloak and dagger shit, anyway?"

"Just be there," he repeated and hung up.

# CHAPTER 15

Puccini's was rather quiet when I walked in the next morning and saw Smythe sitting at one of the tables toward the back of the room. He wore jeans and a T-shirt, and he looked younger than his forty-something years. Normally, he would be in a suit or a smart pair of pants and shirt if on duty. For an undercover cop, he was rather stylish.

I took a seat opposite him and couldn't help but notice the tired look on his face and something like sadness or regret in his blue-green eyes. "So what's up?" I said by way of greeting.

"Let's order first," he suggested, and motioned for the waiter to bring us a couple of menus.

I was relieved Sean wasn't around, but just to make sure I asked, "Are we expecting anyone else?"

Smythe shook his head, and when the waiter arrived with our menus, we ordered a couple of cappuccinos.

"It's my day off today," Smythe replied, looking through his menu.

"Well," I gazed at him, "I can see Sean's not joining us, but where's Mandy?"

He looked up from his menu, his eyes alert. "She's not with you?"

I felt concern suddenly mounting up. "No, she's not. Did you lose her or something?" I threw him an accusatory look.

He rolled his eyes. "How could I lose a person, Ferrari? She's not an object, you know." He sounded upset, and I wondered whether the two had had an argument, and Mandy was now waiting for me at my place.

I didn't say anything but glanced through the menu until I found something I liked. "You ready to order?"

He nodded, and when the waiter brought our coffees, we ordered our food. Smythe went with the big breakfast and I opted for the Italian sausage omelette. The waiter brought a bottle of cold water and two glasses before he left us.

"Okay, I'm here now, and we ordered the food. So what is it that you want? I hope I didn't somehow interfere with your investigation and you're going to give me one of your lectures," I remarked rather impatiently.

He cocked an eyebrow at me, looking annoyed. "You're a little spitfire sometimes, Ferrari; but I wish you'd just shut up for a moment and let me get this off my chest."

I stared at him in mock astonishment. "Are you sure you're the Smythe I know? Good God, whatever it is, you're having trouble putting it into words! This must mean you're developing a little sensitivity. Unheard of really." I shook my head as if wonders never ceased to amaze me.

Smythe gave me a warning look that told me he didn't appreciate my sarcasm, and I shrugged my shoulders and sat back enjoying my coffee, waiting for him to begin.

He was silent and frowned for a few moments as if doing battle with his thoughts. Then, he drank some coffee before turning his gaze on me. "The thing with Mandy, it's not working out." He sounded unsure.

I almost choked on my coffee. Of all the things I thought he would say, this was the last one; and why confide in me? I had never known Smythe in this way, and I wasn't sure how to proceed. I decided to veer on the side of caution. "I'm sorry to hear it," I said quietly, repressing my desire to pepper him with all kinds of questions.

My serious countenance seemed to encourage him to keep talking. "You know Mandy better than I do," he stated. "The thing is I find her head's still full of her husband. She may not realise it, but she's still very much in love with him. And I have a code about these things. I don't start up something with someone who's vulnerable. I really think she needs to sort herself out, and I know this'll take time." He waited for my reaction.

"Well," I declared, trying to take it all in. I thought it very perceptive of him to tune into Mandy's feelings; but then, he was a cop and trained to detect behaviour. "I must say I didn't see this coming. It's very decent of you to bring it up and not go on using her like most men would." I grudgingly acknowledged that the man was not a complete bastard after all. "Mandy came on this trip in order to have a break from her husband," I informed him. "I'm sure she told you this."

Smythe nodded. "Yes. She mentioned she was at a crossroads, but the way she became involved with me so quickly told me more than words could say. I think she's trying to obliterate thoughts of her marriage by having an affair rather than face the issue square in the face."

Our meals arrived and we kept talking while we ate. "I think you're right," I agreed with him. Mandy had been so confused of late about her situation that I thought going off with another man was the wrong thing to do; but she was an adult, and I couldn't very well keep her locked up. She had to find out for herself what it was she wanted. Now, looking at Smythe, it occurred to me she had hurt his feelings. I wondered whether he had begun to fall in love with her and his heart was broken at the discovery that she didn't know what she wanted. "So what happened this morning?" I simply asked.

"We had a talk and I told her she needs to spend some time on her own," he replied, looking somewhat despondent. "I think it's best this way, don't you?"

He was asking for my advice and I felt flattered that he actually wanted to know what I thought. "I agree with you," I stated. "By not knowing what she wants she's not only hurting herself, but she's also hurting her husband, and you. I'm sure Mandy didn't set out to hurt anyone's feelings, but she can be a little impulsive and I can see how meeting you would have turned her head."

My admission brought the first smile of the day to his face. "Are you saying you think I'm attractive, Ferrari?"

Well, I walked into that one! I gave him a serious look so he wouldn't think I was trying to flirt. "Smythe, just because I hate your guts doesn't mean I think you're ugly," I responded with some of my old spirit. It was unsettling to think that by taking me into his confidence, he had changed the footing of our own relationship. I just wasn't ready for the shift of going from archenemy to friend. "All I'm trying to say is Mandy found you attractive and probably thought that by getting involved with you her other problems would go away. Amazing how people always do this and never stop to think how their actions will affect others." I was referring to my ex when I said this. He had simply jumped from one relationship to another without any thought in his head other than himself. In a way, he had behaved like Mandy. "I'll have a chat with Mandy when I return home and see how she's doing," I reassured him. "Thanks for trusting me with this."

Smythe sighed and looked as if a weight had been lifted from his shoulders. He obviously wanted to ensure Mandy was okay even though she was the one who had hurt his feelings. I was impressed by his consideration despite his broken heart, and the unthinkable happened—I felt envious. Envious that Smythe should feel like this about Mandy instead of me. God, I was losing it! I gulped down the rest of my coffee and signalled the waiter for more. "Another one for you?" I asked my companion. He nodded and I held up two fingers for the waiter and pointed to my coffee cup.

"Thanks for listening, Ferrari," Smythe said with sincerity. "I can see Mandy has a great friend in you," he added, sounding a bit gruff.

I thought it was high time we moved on before this scene turned into something out of *Sense and Sensibility*. "So where's Sean today?" I changed the subject abruptly, and this seemed to suit him as well. He sat back, looking rather relieved after having divulged his feelings to me, and waited for the second coffee to arrive.

"He's working another case. We're a little short-staffed at present."

"Besides, you work better alone, isn't that so?" I gave him an inquisitive look.

"Yes, I do," he admitted. "Too long on the force working on my own. Besides, I find young Sean a bit gung-ho in his methods. Somehow, I don't think we make a very good team."

I could certainly relate to Sean being gung-ho, and not only in his work. Of course, I wasn't about to open up to Smythe about my one-night stand with that self-centred bastard. "Any progress on the case?" Then I added quickly, "If I'm allowed to ask, that is."

Smythe treated me to a second smile. "I shouldn't be discussing police business with you, you know that. But seeing as you've been very supportive lately, I think I can trust you on this one."

Wow! Smythe was really forthcoming today, I thought. If I tried any harder, he'd tell me the size of his jocks, too!

"You know I won't repeat what I learn from you to anybody except Dobbs," I assured him. "I trust the man with my life."

"So do I," Smythe affirmed. He was referring to the time, years ago, when Dobbs had saved him from being stabbed by a druggie. Our coffees arrived and he remained silent until the waiter cleared our table; then, he went on. "We're trying to trace the diamond at the moment," he informed me. "It's probably going to be sold on the black market, and it may even be cut into smaller pieces and sold separately."

"That'll lessen its value."

"Yes, but a large diamond like this one can be easily traced," he replied.

"Not if it's sold to a private collector," I observed.

"I know. In any case, whichever way you look at it, it's a long shot. Even so, we have to cover every angle."

I debated whether I should tell him about Ophelia's half-brother, but decided against it for the time being. First, I wanted to see if I could dig up the information myself. "Do you agree the murders are connected?" I asked instead.

"Yes, I think so," he replied. "Right now, though, it's like a big jigsaw puzzle with scattered pieces all over the place, so I need more information before I can fit the pieces."

"Well, it doesn't take an Einstein, does it?" I snapped in frustration, not so much at him but at myself for not having all the pieces by now. "We know Ophelia was involved with both Casey and Mark Meadows; and now, all three are dead. Of course the friggin' murders are connected!"

Smythe shook his head and sighed. "You're too impetuous, Ferrari. It doesn't matter what we know, it's finding the proof so we can cement it all and solve the case."

I could see we were fast reaching our old footing of enmity and I liked it better this way, so I replied in my usual smartarse manner. "Whatever." This brought our meeting to a close.

Mandy was at home, a half empty bottle of red wine by her side while she sat on the sofa bed, legs crossed, staring into thin air.

"Oh, Mandy, thank God you're okay," I exclaimed when I saw her.

"You've been fraternising with the enemy, I see." She scowled at me and proceeded to pour herself another glass of wine.

I moved closer and sat on the edge of the bed. "That's not true! Smythe wanted to explain what had happened because I'm your friend; and he cares very much for you," I assured her. "The man's heartbroken."

A hopeful look sprung to her eyes. "He is?"

I nodded. "Yes, he is. But Mandy, you played shamefully with his affections," I admonished gently. "You must admit you're confused about things with your marriage; and I think you still love your husband. Smythe was simply a diversion."

Mandy started to say something; then, she thought better of it and looked down at her drink, crestfallen. "You're right." She nodded, not meeting my eyes. "He must be a good cop, Mia, because he saw right through me. He knew I was on the rebound." She added, "But I do care for him. He's a dear man, and such a caring lover."

I cleared my throat. "Well, I wouldn't know about that, but he does have genuine feelings for you, and he's proved that at least he's not a total bastard. By the way, how did you know I was with him?"

"He told me this morning during our little talk that he was meeting you, but I thought it was about police business."

"Well, perhaps, he felt awkward admitting he was going to pour his heart out to me of all people."

Mandy looked up then and we smiled at each other. I patted her shoulder and said encouragingly, "You'll be okay, Mandy; you'll see. Just take this visit simply as a sightseeing trip and relax. I'm sure when you go back to the UK things will look different to you."

She sighed but already started to look more cheerful. "You're right, of course. And Mia, the last thing I wanted was to have tension between us. Our friendship comes first."

I dismissed what she said by shaking my head. "Forget about all that. I guess I was envious that you could attract a man the minute you got here, while I've been celibate since things went bad with the ex."

"But you have David," she reminded me. "I'm sure he loves you."

It was my turn to look sad now. "David's in two minds about everything at present. We talked, you know, but he's not clear about the way he feels."

Mandy sipped some more wine. "Well, he doesn't know what

he's got!"

I didn't want to talk about David or what had transpired between us, so I turned the conversation in a different direction. "Mandy, I've a confession to make."

Mandy looked straight into my eyes with trepidation. "Don't tell me you had sex with Smythe!

"No, no! How could you even think that? No. I'm afraid it's much worse," I announced gravely. "I guess because I saw you and Smythe having such a time of it, I allowed myself to succumb to the charms of Sean Webb."

Mandy shrieked with excitement and almost upset her wine glass. She took a hold of it and rested it on the night table. "He must've been a good lay." Her eyes were full of wickedness. "Imagine; he's like twenty years younger than you. Way to go, girl!" Then she noticed the look of regret in my eyes. "What happened?"

"It was horrible," I answered. "The sex was good, if a little rough; but the whole thing was so sordid." I then went on to relate what had happened between Sean and me, and how I felt after he'd ended things so abruptly.

Mandy was horrified. "What a bastard! How could he treat you this way? Oh, but I'm so glad you gave him a dressing down, if you pardon the pun." She grinned.

"Yes, I kicked him out, insulting him as best I could," I replied. "But there was something about him that was so distasteful, kind of putrid, you know? Like someone with a rotten soul."

"Sounds like your ex," Mandy pointed out.

"My ex was a bastard all right," I acknowledged. "But he never made me feel like a prostitute."

"Did you tell Smythe?"

I glared at her. "Have you lost your mind completely? Why would I tell him?"

"I don't know. It's just that Sean deserves to be told off severely by someone."

"Well, trust me, Mandy; if I'd had a gun at the time, I would have blown off his balls. Besides, I don't need Smythe to get involved in my personal affairs."

"So it looks like we're both back to where we started," Mandy commented, refilling her wine glass.

"Hey, take it easy with that. We're going out sightseeing and then to dinner at the Casino."

She smiled and put the glass back on the table. "We are? Oh, thank you, Mia. I wasn't sure what to do with myself today."

"I'm sorry I neglected you so. Perhaps, if I'd been with you every day, you wouldn't have become involved with Smythe."

Mandy smiled wickedly. "No, Phil's too cute for me not to go for him. Sorry, my friend, but while your company's compelling, his is... well, let us say... very stimulating."

I laughed. "Okay. I see you're back in fine form, Amanda Wilson! And good thing, too, because I'm taking a couple of days off to spend with you, and on Saturday we're going to the mardi gras parade."

"Can't wait!" Her eyes lit up with excitement.

# CHAPTER 16

After taking in a few famous Sydney landmarks from my Ferrari, Mandy and I stopped off at a waterfront restaurant in Birkenhead Point, an inner west suburb near the city, which was renowned for its shops and factory-direct fashion outlets. We enjoyed a late lunch, then went shopping and gave our credit cards a good airing. I purchased a pair of red, patent leather Diana Ferrari moccasins—no relation to me, by the way. Mandy went crazy on dresses, skirts, blouses and pants from various outlets, and I knew she was healing from her liaison with Smythe through retail therapy.

We returned home in the late afternoon and had a rest before we got ready for dinner at The Star, Sydney's luxury casino at Darling Harbour. I had made reservations at Balla, an Italian restaurant with signature dishes that promised to be delicious.

Mandy wore one of her new purchases, an off-white outfit consisting of a sleeveless top and wide, bell-bottom pants that suited her beautifully because of her height. She put on white strappy high-heeled sandals and gold drop earrings, which set off her outfit to perfection. I decided on a chic little black dress with black high heels, and I wore the jade earrings Mandy had given me, plus a jade and gold bracelet I picked up years ago in Singapore. After applying make-up and a dab of perfume, we were ready to take on the world.

When we pulled up at the casino valet parking in my car, we attracted looks from everyone, including a very warm smile from the valet, who was a good looking young man with an athletic build. I handed him the keys. "Take good care of it," I told him.

He winked at me. "Don't you worry, Miss."

I warmed to him straight away for not calling me "Madam",

126

which made me feel like I was eighty, and handed him a five-dollar tip for his efforts. He gave me an effusive smile this time and ran ahead of us to open the door that led into the casino.

"Honestly, Mia," Mandy commented once we were inside, "don't you ever give up on the younger men?"

"I will one day."

"And when will that be?"

"When I die." I grinned.

"You're a shocker," she returned with a smile.

Once seated in the luxurious restaurant, we ordered a couple of antipasto dishes to start with, *olive miste e giardiniera di stagione,* mixed olives with seasonal pickled vegetables, and *mozzarella di bufala e carciofi,* buffalo mozzarella with marinated artichokes, and sprinkled with sun-dried tomatoes. The waiter suggested a light white wine from the north of Italy to accompany our starter dishes, and we let him select one for us.

Mandy and I toasted to our friendship when the wine arrived and then took in the harbour lights while we waited for the antipasto. "Sydney's so beautiful," Mandy mused, "that it's hard to believe there could be so many murders in one place."

I smiled cynically. "All great cities have their fair share of crime. Of course, I wasn't counting on three murders at our doorstep this time around. Although," I added, "technically, Mark Meadows was killed outside the hotel."

"But you still think the murders are connected."

"Yes, I do."

"Do you think it's the curse?"

I eyed her with incredulity. "Don't tell me you really believe in curses."

She nodded. "I must admit, I do."

"Well, I don't know what to tell you," I replied, savouring the delicious wine the waiter had picked for us. "All three victims came into contact with the diamond, or so I presume. We know Ophelia definitely did, and she was involved with both Casey and Mark Meadows, so it's very probable that they also came into contact with it."

"But it's obvious neither Casey nor Meadows killed her for it. After all, they wound up dead themselves."

I gazed at the harbour lights in deep thought. The whole thing was one big puzzle, as Smythe had put it, and we were still missing a number of pieces. "Let's not talk murder tonight, Mandy; let's enjoy our meal," I suggested with a smile.

"Very well," she replied. "And I look forward to a little after-dinner gambling."

We finished our meal with espressos rather than dessert as we were too full after the mains. I had ordered pan-fried veal cutlet with butter and sage, and Mandy chose roast swordfish roll with asparagus and cherry tomatoes. The food went well with the fruity white wine the waiter had brought us with our antipasto, and we finished the bottle between us.

Mandy insisted on picking up the bill; and then, we made our way to the casino area and headed straight for the roulette tables.

"I love roulette," Mandy stated, her eyes taking in the multitude of tables.

"As long as it's not the Russian kind," I jested.

We played for a while, but I stopped after about an hour, having lost most of my winnings. Mandy, on the other hand, was on a winning streak, and she had now amassed close to a thousand dollars worth of chips.

"I think you should stop while the going's good," I advised.

"Don't be a killjoy." She reprimanded me with a smile. "I'm unstoppable!"

I laughed. "You'll be very *stoppable* once you lose all your gains." It seemed my comment turned her luck and after a few losses, she ended up with five hundred dollars.

"Not bad for a night's work," she declared with satisfaction as we made our way to the cashier's window to collect her winnings. "I may have lost half of it, but at least I had—"

She didn't finish what she was going to say because I grasped her arm and whispered harshly in her ear, "Oh my God! Look over there."

"Over where?" She cast me a look as if I had taken leave of my senses. "And why are you whispering in a crowded and noisy casino?"

I grabbed both her arms from behind and shifted her body to shield my own. "I don't want to be seen," I said in her ear. "Look over the first three roulette tables in the first row and see who's at the fourth one."

Mandy took a few moments to gaze in the direction I gave her; and then she saw him. "Sean Webb with a twenty-something blonde bimbette on his arm," she spat out in disgust. "These bloody men! I told you, Mia, the younger ones don't go for older women like us. What you need—"

"Never mind what I need!" I replied through gritted teeth. "Walk backwards. We have to get the hell out of here before he sees me."

Mandy shook herself loose and turned to face me. "Oh, and you think that by walking backwards we'll remain inconspicuous."

I looked over her shoulder and saw that Sean seemed occupied with his young babe. She had wrapped herself around him like a limpet, and the chances of him spotting me right now were slim. I was surprised he didn't throw the babe on top of the roulette table to shag her right there and then.

"You're right; too conspicuous," I agreed. "Look, just stand here while I walk away; then, go to cash in your chips and I'll meet you at the car." Before she could reply, I took off like the very devil was in hot pursuit.

I went down to the valet and handed my ticket to an old man, noting the young valet must have finished for the day. While I waited, it came to me that the table where I had spotted Sean was a $20 dollar minimum betting table. I couldn't believe he'd show off like that. He was betting high stakes for the benefit of his bimbo—either this or he had a gambling problem.

Smythe had said Sean was gung ho about things, and after experiencing his mega ego, I had to agree. He must feel so insecure inside that he had to validate himself through expensive cars, fine clothes and high gambling stakes. It made me wonder why he even got involved with me; but he had given me the answer to this. He had found my exchange with him and Smythe a turn-on, and secretly he probably wanted to put me in my place. His enormous ego obviously couldn't stand it that a woman was ahead of the cops in the investigation.

My car arrived and I jumped in after tipping the valet and within moments, Mandy joined me. She got into the car and we drove off.

"I'm so tired," she remarked. "I need to sleep."

"We should be home in fifteen minutes," I informed her. "I take it you had a good time?"

"Wonderful, thank you," she sounded contented. "What was that all about with Sean, anyway? So what if he saw you?"

"After the way we parted, I didn't want to give him the satisfaction of showing off his new babe to me."

"He probably has lots of babes, Mia," Mandy commented. "You don't think that type would stick to just one woman, do you?"

"No, of course not. But just the same, I didn't want him to see me."

"Something's on your mind. I can sense it."

"Well," I replied, "it just rankles that he treats women like they're playthings, and he's a smug bastard to boot."

"At least you no longer have to see him. Just remember you're the one who kicked him out of your place, and he's not bound to forget it either."

I glanced at her with curiosity. "What makes you say that?"

"You mean about him not forgetting?"

I nodded.

"Well, it's his personality type: ego-maniac, self-centred, in love with himself. So by kicking him out of your place, you might say you made an enemy out of him."

"Food for thought," I remarked in a serious tone.

Saturday morning rolled around in no time and the queens made arrangements to stay an extra two nights at the hotel.

The show had come to an end on Friday evening, and Saturday was the big day of the mardi gras. The queens were invited to a private function at Stonewall, a great place from which to watch the parade. After this, they were going to a big "after-parade" party and on Sunday, they were attending a "recovery" party. This information, I received from Frank, who telephoned to let me know they wouldn't be checking out until Monday.

"And darling," he said, "in gratitude for being so supportive, you and your cute friend, Chris, are invited to the Stonewall function so you can watch the parade with us."

"Frank, that's wonderful, but unfortunately I have to decline. I have my friend, Mandy, and—"

"Not another word, sweetie," he interrupted, "I'll make sure there are three tickets waiting for you at the door."

I thanked him profusely and turned to Mandy, who was making breakfast for us. "Well, it seems we're watching the parade in style tonight," I announced when the call ended. Then, I told her about

Frank's invitation.

Mandy replied excitedly, "That's wonderful! I'm going to charge my camera after breakfast. I promised Mum I'd send her heaps of photos, so she can have a look at all the costumes."

"I'm sure you'll be able to purchase the DVD of the parade soon enough," I laughed. "I can send it onto her."

"Oh, that'll be fab," Mandy exclaimed. "I'm sure she'll love it!"

"Leave it to me."

That evening, Chris, Mandy and I arrived at Stonewall for a pre-parade cocktail party before the actual parade kicked off at around 8.00pm. I wore black jeans, a rainbow-coloured, see-through top worn with a black bra underneath and flat black canvas shoes for comfort. Mandy was similarly attired, only she wore white jeans and a sleeveless white knitted top with flat sandals. Chris opted for the usual jeans and a well-worn black T-shirt.

The party was on the top floor of the venue, where a huge plasma screen was mounted in order to watch the parade, but we could also see out through the windows, even though they were rather narrow. Someone mentioned that a select group of special guests, including Frank and his friends, would be able to make their way to the rooftop to watch the parade. I hoped this was the case as I was already feeling rather warm despite the air-conditioning.

The room was full of gay men, lesbians, drag queens, transsexuals, bisexuals; you name it, and they were there. We weren't the only straight people, either. After all, everyone was welcome at the venue.

Frank, Tony and Alan greeted us with big hugs and kisses upon arrival and they went out of their way to introduce us to several "hot, young things", as they referred to their gay friends. It was all Mandy and I could do to keep our eyes from popping out of our heads at so many good looking, young men.

"Oh, Mia," Mandy confided, "I'm in heaven!"

I laughed, knowing she felt the same way I did. I loved attractive and young gay men because they were beautiful to look at and safe to be with. One of my sexual fantasies was to be able to convert one of them, at least for a night; but I wasn't going to share this with anybody. After seeing Mandy's face, however, I could tell by her drooling look that she probably shared the same fantasy.

"When you're through staring like hungry guppies at all this

131

flesh, let me know what kind of drinks you'd like," Chris spoke dryly in my ear.

I sensed his discomfort but didn't care. He was the one who had wanted to attend the mardi gras. "Get me a vodka and orange."

He nodded and moved off to try and catch Mandy, who was talking to two delicious young men in black G-strings.

A few drinks later, and we were all dancing with one another, including Chris. This went on until around eight, when a few of us navigated our way up to the rooftop of the building.

The fresh breeze cooled our flushed cheeks, and I was grateful to be out of the stuffy room. I'd had fun dancing, but now it was time to watch the parade. I noticed Mandy was ready with her camera, snapping photos of the guests on the roof, including the queens and the boys with the G-strings.

When the parade started, we leaned over the parapet and peeked down at all the fantastic floats. The costumes were lavish, wild with colour and the brilliance of sequins, feathers and all sorts of paraphernalia including quite a lot of nudity. In addition to the private floats, there were floats representing all sectors of the community such as the lifeguards, fire service, coast guard, the police and others.

I espied a member of the police float wearing nothing but a black leather bikini brief with his police badge attached at the crotch. His athletic body was otherwise naked, except for a police whistle hanging on a string around his neck and a silver Mohawk hat intermingled with the police force colours of blue and white. An image of Smythe wearing something similar popped into my head and I burst into a fit of laughter. Smythe would die rather than be caught in something like that.

The streets below were jam-packed with onlookers, and I was glad we had been lucky to be invited to Stonewall. Had we ended up at street level, I doubted Mandy would have been able to shoot any good photos. She was now snapping away madly at anything that moved.

Someone brought drinks to the rooftop and a couple of boys went around serving the guests. One of the boys approached me with a tray full of drinks and I was pleasantly surprised to recognise James, the young blond God I had questioned last time I had been at Stonewall. He smiled as he stopped in front of me, wearing nothing but a silver bikini brief and Roman sandals.

"Mia; isn't it?" he asked, and his smile made my knees grow weak.

"Yes, hi," I replied, trying to control my fantasies. "Any soft drinks? I've had enough alcohol for one night."

"Coke?" he suggested. I nodded, and he handed me a glass and took one for himself. "Give me a moment," he said, "there's something I want to tell you. I'll be right back."

He walked off and I watched as he handed the tray to another young man, and then returned. "Come with me." He took hold of my hand and led me back inside the building. I fleetingly wondered where we were going but didn't exactly care; he was so good looking, that I would've gone anywhere with him.

We made our way down a dark passageway and turned a couple of times. The place was rather eerie and I could hear the "thump, thump" of the music from the floor below us and the chatter coming from the rooftop. Finally, we reached the end of another passageway and James opened a door and flipped on a light switch. I found myself inside what looked like a small dressing room.

"We use these rooms when we have a show," he explained, closing the door behind us.

I took in a large mirror with the customary make-up lights and a long dresser with its tabletop covered in pots, jars and brushes. There were a few chairs with outlandish costumes carelessly thrown over them, and the floor was full of shoes of all kinds.

"Wow!" I exclaimed.

"Excuse the mess." James cleared a couple of chairs so we could sit. I had a sip of my cool drink and waited for him to speak. "After our last chat, I remembered something."

I instantly began to feel the mounting excitement I usually experienced just before a clue came my way. "Yes?" I barely dared to breathe.

"You know how I said I was involved with Mark until Clee came along?"

I nodded.

"Well, it never occurred for me to tell you that Mark had a half-brother who was also involved with Clee. Sometimes, the three of them slept together," James informed me, and I marvelled while trying to keep up with Clee's promiscuity.

"So what are you saying?" I prompted, trying to digest this new bit of information and how it fitted into the puzzle.

James took a few sips of his drink before he answered, "I was once walking past this very dressing room, after one of Clee's shows, and there were raised voices. I couldn't hear too clearly because it was rather noisy with a show going on below, but I recognised Mark's voice and that of his half-brother. They were yelling at Clee. All I caught was something about 'the diamond'. Then, there seemed to be a lot of noise, like someone was throwing things around the room. Lastly, I heard Clee shouting, 'You and Shane get out of here'."

I was floored. Finally, a name! My mind suddenly flooded with thoughts coming from all directions, but I was brought back to the present by James's hand on my shoulder, tapping me gently to attract my attention. "I'm sorry," I said and refocused. "I was trying to take all of this in. Tell me; did you ever meet this Shane?"

James paused to think and then answered, "Only once, at a party. It was a long time ago, so I can't recall much of it, plus I was a bit under the weather at the time."

"What can you tell me?"

"I can't picture him clearly, but I know he had dark, good looks. Clee always liked her men like that."

"So what was she doing with Mark? He was rather fair and not so very good looking; at least, not in the way you say Clee liked her men." I also thought about Jim Casey; middle-aged, average looks. What had Clee been up to with so many men?

James's voice broke into my thoughts. "She liked variety," he sounded resentful. "And she never valued Mark, either. Even so, she took him away from Damien and me. She had to have anyone and everyone. Not many of us liked her, you know. We called her 'the vamp'."

I noted the dislike in his tone but didn't want to lose the thread of my thoughts. "What about Clee's own half-brother; are you sure you never saw him? You mentioned him last time I was here," I asked in the hope that someone would be able to give me a clue on him.

James shook his head. "No, I don't recall him. I only know he came here a couple of times; like I told you before."

"And what about Damien; does he recall anything about Shane

or Clee's half-brother?"

"Not to my knowledge," James answered. "All I know is not long after that particular argument Clee finally broke it off with both Mark and Shane." He then added, "And this, I remember. A few weeks later, Clee was crying in Jim Casey's arms. I came into the dressing room to borrow an outfit, but they didn't see me at first; and Clee was saying to him something about how she was afraid Shane wanted to kill her for it."

# CHAPTER 17

"**W**ell, you've certainly been keeping busy!" Dobbs sounded miffed.

I was back at work after my days off, and Dobbs and I were having a late lunch in the staff restaurant.

"I was going to invite you to the mardi gras, Dobbs," I explained. "But I didn't think you'd want to go to Stonewall on parade night. What would you have told Eileen?"

Dobbs harrumphed and said, "It doesn't matter now, does it?"

I glanced at him pointedly and smiled. "You're not fooling anybody, you know? You would've felt like a fish out of water, trust me."

"Fair enough," he conceded grudgingly. "But at least you could've phoned me during your days off to keep me updated."

I felt guilty about that. Dobbs and I always discussed everything, and he was right; I should have at least phoned. "I have no excuse, so I apologise," I admitted. "These past couple of days have been fairly full with Mandy being down and out about her marriage; and then all the information I found out about Ophelia's case." Dobbs was unaware that Mandy had had a fling with Smythe and it was not my business to tell him about it. Smythe could talk, if he wished, at the boys' poker night; but somehow, I didn't think he would.

"I know you didn't hold back the information intentionally," Dobbs remarked gently, my apology obviously disarming him. "And now you've filled me in, I understand how everything was so confusing to the point that it was perhaps too complicated to discuss over the phone. It's best to discuss it face to face."

"Exactly what I thought," I concurred and looked around the almost empty restaurant, noting the time was just after two in the afternoon. "Let's get some coffee," I suggested.

We went to the service counter, ordered two cappuccinos from the restaurant attendant, and waited quietly while he made them. Then we took our cups to a corner table and sat down to go over the information in more detail. I took a pen out of my jacket pocket along with a small notebook I kept for making notes during my rounds.

"It looks like we have two half-brothers," I told him, and wrote down the information in point form. "Mark's half-brother is supposedly called Shane; we don't have a name for Ophelia's half-brother yet."

"What about the age factor?" Dobbs reminded me.

"Yes, that's very important." I wrote down "age factor" in my notebook. "We'll work on the premise that Ophelia was older, like say in her mid to late thirties or even early forties." I remembered how Holly Goheavily, the drag queen friend of Ophelia's, had admitted to being in her forties even though she looked like a thirty-something. "This would then make it possible to have a half-brother who's already a young man, like say late twenties and even up to thirty or so."

Dobbs nodded. "Did you ask the queens how old Ophelia was?"

"Believe it or not; no. There were so many other things happening around me, but I'll fix that in a jiffy." I drew out my phone, fast-dialling Frank.

"Darling," he sounded chirpy when he answered, "how great to hear from you so soon."

"How was your recovery party?" I asked with laughter in my voice.

"Disaster, sweets, disaster!" Frank announced with the voice of doom. "Poor Tony threw up, and Alan had a horrid headache." He then expelled a sigh. "Oh, well, they should've taken the vitamin pack I take every day. I'm fit as a fiddle and tight as a drum."

I chuckled. "Good on you, Frank. Listen, I just wanted to ask you a quick question."

"Shoot, darling."

"Do you know how old Ophelia was?"

There was a pause at the other end as if Frank was searching his mind. "Well, I'm not exactly sure," he said, much to my disappointment. "I thought she was in her twenties."

"But if she was," I argued, "how can she have a half-brother thirteen years younger than her, who was described as a young man by those that vaguely remembered him?"

Silence at the other end, and then, "Good question, my darling Sherlock, but I couldn't say. Perhaps, the young man was an early bloomer," he suggested. "I'll ask around Stonewall, though, and get back to you. You know, we got our old gig back, and we start in a few days after we rehearse some new numbers. Darling, I'm on cloud nine!"

"How wonderful for you. Congratulations."

Frank gushed, "Oh, darling, we are so happy to be back with the Stonewall family. Anyway, must dash, gorgeous. I'll get back to you if I find out anything. Please send my regards to that cutie, Chris. He was a little shy the other night, especially when Alan tried to pat his sexy tush. You must bring him back to visit us soon."

I rolled my eyes and gazed at Dobbs, who had a questioning look on his face. "Stay away from my boy, Frank. Catch you soon." I rang off and declared with an "I told you so" look at Dobbs, "Aren't you glad you didn't come with us? They tried to touch Chris's tu... I mean, arse."

Dobbs looked horrified and I couldn't help but laugh at the look on his face. "Frank said he'll ask around about Ophelia's age."

"Call me old-fashioned," Dobbs stated, shaking his head, "but I can't relate to all this 'ass-touching' thing."

I grinned and threw him a wicked look. "Then you should be thanking me I didn't ask you along after all. Imagine what these queens would do to a sexy black man from Hawaii who used to be a detective with Five-O." Then I made out to sound like Frank, "Why, daaaaaahling, they would've asked to touch your gun." I guffawed at the terror in his eyes.

Dobbs cleared his throat. "Let's get back to business, shall we?"

"That's right," I said, recovering from my fit of laughter. "Now, where were we? Oh yes, Ophelia's age. Okay, we can assume she was somewhere in her late thirties or early forties and that she had plastic surgery."

"So this leaves us with a half-brother who's around thirty, and who had a few arguments with her about money and eventually gave her a black eye," he summed up.

I nodded. "That's right. And then, there's this Shane person who was supposedly trying to get his hands on the diamond or at least, this is what young James told me when he overhead Ophelia crying in Casey's arms in her dressing room."

Dobbs looked thoughtful. "I think we can pretty much rule out that Casey committed suicide or that he was going after the diamond for himself."

"I would say so," I agreed. "I think whoever killed Ophelia definitely did it for the diamond. Then he killed Casey and made it look like he committed the crime, but was so remorseful about it, he ended up killing himself."

"So far it makes sense. Though I don't see why the killer would think we'd believe Casey committed suicide after stealing a diamond. It's strange," Dobbs observed.

"True, but more importantly, we still have the question as to why he would kill for the diamond—the real killer, I mean. Why not just take it by stealing the cap? It wasn't like Ophelia locked it up anywhere secure." This had been bugging me from the beginning. Both the murders of Ophelia and Mark Meadows reflected a rage killing rather than simply killing to steal an object of value.

"It has to be someone close to Ophelia; someone who hated her for some reason," Dobbs remarked.

"Yes. I think Ophelia made a lot of enemies with her ways of 'lording it over people' and stealing other men's boyfriends. So chances are that whoever killed her did it because he hated her, in addition to wanting the diamond."

"We have two suspects then: Shane and Ophelia's own half-brother."

I eyed him with doubt. "I tell you, Dobbs, when taking into consideration the number of men Ophelia was involved with I think half the gay population are suspect. However, let's work with the most likely people who would've had a motive to kill her." I wrote out a few names in my notebook.

"Who did you put down?" Dobbs tried to peek at my notes but couldn't see properly from where he was sitting.

"There's Shane; Ophelia's own half-brother, who is currently nameless; James and Damien."

"You mean the men that were dumped by Mark Meadows when he took up with Ophelia?"

"That's right," I answered. "And God knows there could be

others we know nothing about. This whole thing is so messy!"

"And what about Mark Meadows? Why would the killer go after him?"

I thought for a moment before replying, "For one, Mark was unfaithful to his lovers, James, Damien, and even Shane." Dobbs threw me a querying look, and I went on. "At one stage, Ophelia was having threesomes with Mark and Shane," I pointed out. "The second thing that comes to mind is Mark might have known Ophelia's killer or at least could identify him, and so he had to be silenced."

Dobbs stood up abruptly. "I think I need another coffee. How about you?"

I nodded and went on making notes while Dobbs walked off to get two more cappuccinos. When he returned, I said, "Do you think Shane would kill his own half-brother; that is, assuming Shane is the killer?"

Dobbs remarked, "In a world where families kill each other for the smallest of reasons, I wouldn't discount anything."

I took a sip of my fresh cappuccino and followed a different train of thought. "Here's another thing; according to the research Chris dug up in the news archives, Ophelia left home as a young teen. Therefore, we assume she never met her half-brother. But so far, everyone I spoke to that was connected with Ophelia confirmed her half-brother was always at her for money. The question here is: when do you suppose Ophelia met this half-brother of hers?"

"Who knows," Dobbs replied. "Perhaps, he tracked her down. Don't forget the news research stated that the half-brother didn't inherit when the father died."

I wrote this down, feeling excitement growing within me. "Yes. I wonder why that is. And let's suppose, somehow, the half-brother found out about the diamond Ophelia's mother gave to her, and that's why he tracked her down, to steal it."

"Possibly."

"So until we find this half-brother, we'll never know. I have to admit his is the biggest motive of all, although it doesn't explain why he hated Ophelia enough to kill her."

"My suggestion is you bring Smythe up to date with what you've learned recently. He's in a position to get Ophelia's age and the name of her half-brother through birth records."

I frowned. "I would rather get Chris to hack into the birth registry."

"Stop this crazy competitive thing you have with Smythe," Dobbs berated me. "You two need to co-operate for once."

I sighed, feeling defeated. I couldn't really ask Chris to compromise himself by hacking into a government computer system. Besides, I had promised myself I wouldn't have him exposed to danger. The only way to get this information, then, was the legit way—and that meant going through the police.

"Oh, all right. I'll do it!" I protested like a spoiled child. "I don't like it, but I'll do it."

The smile on Dobbs's face told me that for once I had made him a happy man.

Before I left for home that afternoon, I placed a call to Smythe to give him the latest on the two half-brothers. I was surprised when he didn't chew me out, as he normally did, for having held back information. In fact, he sounded preoccupied with other things, but I didn't want to ask him if this had something to do with his break from Mandy.

"I'll come back to you," was all he said.

Mandy and I ate in for dinner and she prepared a pasta dish and salad. The evening was warm and we sat out on the balcony, eating our food and sipping on a lovely Shiraz while we enjoyed the landscaped gardens around my apartment block.

I went through all the facts of the case with her, as she was now pretty much "in the know", but we couldn't come up with anything new at present. When I mentioned I had to leave the whole thing with Smythe, I saw the frown on her face reflected by the candlelight at our table.

"I called Phil this morning," she confessed suddenly. "I just didn't want us to end things in this way; so abruptly, you know?"

This explained Smythe's state of mind when I had talked to him earlier. "So what happened?"

"It's my fault, really," she admitted. "I know I caught him on the rebound, but it never occurred to me at the time that I was going to develop strong feelings for him."

I was astonished. "Are you telling me after all that's happened, you truly love him and you're going to end your marriage?"

Mandy didn't reply straight away. She sipped her wine for a few moments, deep in thought, while I felt sorry for Smythe. I still believed he had been right in ending things; and judging by Mandy's frame of mind right now, it seemed she believed herself to be in love with him when in actual fact she lacked the courage to do anything about it. In my book, this meant her love for Smythe wasn't deep enough, and that she still had unresolved issues about her husband.

Ironically, this was reminiscent of what had happened with David and me. He had expressed certain feelings towards me, but then had pulled back because he wasn't ready. He hadn't stopped to ask me if I was ready, however; and though I loved him, I'd had the strength to walk away and leave him to it—just as Smythe had done with Mandy. Blimey! I thought, I had more in common with Smythe than I thought possible. We were both of a strong turn of mind and it seemed that, like me, when he made up his mind about something, he did it and didn't procrastinate like some.

"I'm pretty sure I love him." Mandy's voice brought me out of my reverie.

"Did you tell him?" I thought I'd test her resolve.

"Not in so many words," she answered, avoiding my eyes, and drank some more wine.

I sighed and said gently, "Mandy, I think what Smythe did was right. You really do need time for yourself in order to sort things out. You're not a whole person right now; not to your hubby and not to Smythe. You're somewhere in the middle and therefore cannot offer anything to either of them."

She nodded as if agreeing with me and then kept drinking her wine. I went on, "As your friend, and someone who's going through something similar with David, I think you need to give this thing time."

"What about David?" Mandy jumped on this in order to steer the conversation away from Smythe.

"He's free to love again," I explained, "and says he loves me, but he's not taking any action. It's a little like what you're doing with Smythe, really. I believe the reason you're not taking action is because you're not ready; just as David isn't ready to do something about me."

"You're right, you're right," she exclaimed and hugged herself in angst. "When I think of going back to the UK, I feel terrified. I don't want to face Phil and all that's going wrong with our marriage. At the same time, I can't commit to this Phil because we've been together for a short time and I'm not yet free of my feelings for the Phil back home. Oh, why do they both have to have the same first name?" She became teary-eyed and wiped at her eyes with a serviette.

I patted her arm. "Give yourself time, Mandy," I advised. "Go home when you're ready and face what you have over there first. If things are not meant to be with Phil, then you'll know in time. And when you're ready, you can come back to Smythe. I'm sure he's not going to stop loving you if you go away for a while."

"Yes, but I don't want to keep him hanging on, either," she sniffed. "Oh, how can I be such a wicked person? I never set out to hurt anybody." She then started to sob, and I popped inside to bring her a box of tissues.

"Mandy, you're not a wicked person." I tried to reason with her when I returned. "You're just a little confused at the moment. Be kind by giving yourself the time to sort things out; and in this way, you'll end up being kind to the two men in your life."

Mandy wiped at her tears and had some more wine. "Thank you, Mia. Please don't take any notice of a crying fool."

I gave her a comforting smile. "Come on, let's go back inside. The mosquitoes are feasting on us."

Mandy nodded, more in control of her emotions, and we cleared the table.

# CHAPTER 18

Smythe dropped by the hotel a couple of days after I put the call through to him, and Dobbs and I joined him in the hotel's lobby café. His face wore a tired look, like he wasn't getting enough sleep, and I attributed this to his issues with Mandy. I sighed and wished relationships didn't have to be so complicated.

We sat around having coffee in one of the more private booths of the café while he filled us in on the latest. "We tracked down Mark Meadows' half-brother through the birth registry records." I went to open my mouth to say something, but he didn't let me speak and went on, glancing my way, "His name's not *Shane*, but Tim."

"How can this be?" I was surprised. "James distinctly told me I heard the name 'Shane' when he overhead Ophelia crying."

Dobbs observed, "Maybe he got it wrong. Remember, he said it was a long time ago."

"Yes, but how do you get Shane mixed up with Tim? They have two totally different sounds," I argued.

"Never mind," Smythe interjected. "His name's Tim and he's twenty-eight years old."

"Did you locate him?" I asked.

"Not yet. We're checking to see if he has a passport. This way, we can get an idea if he's overseas or still in the country, plus we can get a photo of him through the passport office."

"What I wouldn't give to have the power to be able to have these resources at my fingertips." I sighed wistfully.

"You'd be a bloody liability, that's what, Ferrari," Smythe snapped at me. "Thank God you don't have access to these things; otherwise, you'd land yourself in all sorts of trouble."

Mandy or no Mandy, Smythe got my back up and I flew at him

in a harsh tone. "Listen, Smythe, don't forget that you got as far as you did in the investigation because of me."

He threw me a dismissive look. "How could I forget when you never let me?" He then turned to Dobbs. "Mate, can you do something about her?"

Dobbs shook his head, opting to stay out of it. I, on the other hand, pinned Smythe with one of my icy glares. "I'll remember that when you next need to talk about more personal things."

He suddenly fiddled with his collar and tie as Dobbs shot an enquiring look at both of us. "Am I missing something here?"

"Don't worry, Dobbs," I said before Smythe had a chance to reply. "Mr Wonder Cop doesn't appreciate the help he sometimes gets from me."

"Enough!" Smythe uttered. "Let's get back to business."

I looked at him pointedly. "Yes, let's," I replied coldly; any shred of sympathy I might have had for him, evaporating into thin air.

Smythe consulted his little notebook and spoke mainly in my direction as if this would put me in my place. "There is a Shane, after all; but he turns out to be Ophelia's own half-brother. He's aged thirty and the son of Robert and Lana Hart—Lana being Hart's second wife."

I glanced at Dobbs. "This puts Ophelia's age at forty-three," I stated. "Man, whoever her plastic surgeon is, he deserves a medal. The guy did a fabulous job on her!" I then addressed Smythe in my enthusiasm, forgetting my animosity towards him. "You never got to see her perform. But I can tell you, she had the most perfect breasts."

Dobbs cleared his throat. "I don't think Phil wants to know about her breasts."

I said with incredulity, "Dobbs, have you been under a rock all this time? All friggin' men want to know about breasts! But," I toned it down a little, "I agree this isn't the time to talk about them."

This conversation was getting crazy. Whatever made me mention Ophelia's breasts? I put it down to Smythe and his "official cop" manner. The whole thing was his fault for rubbing me up the wrong way.

"Do you have a location on Shane Hart?" Dobbs asked.

"Not yet," Smythe responded, but his eyes were still on me; and I was sure he was thinking murder. "We're going through the passport office for him, too."

"Okay, so that brings us back to a big, fat nothing," I noted with asperity. "Except now we have the names of the two half-brothers."

"That's pretty much right," Smythe agreed, and then glanced at his watch. "I have to go. Thanks for the coffee; and I'll keep you posted." He addressed his comment to Dobbs.

We stood and as Dobbs walked him to the front door, I threw daggers at Smythe's back, wondering how Mandy could have fallen for the insensitive oaf. I then remembered what she had said about his sexual prowess and flushed at the thought.

"What's the matter with you, Ferrari?" Dobbs's voice startled me. "Are you trying to sever the relationship we've managed to build with the police?"

I sat back down and motioned the waiter for another round of coffees. "Jesus Christ, Dobbs, if this is a relationship then I'm the Queen of England!"

"Listen to yourself," he chided me, "you'd better get that bee in your bonnet out of there before Smythe stops helping us."

My eyes almost bulged out of my head at what I was hearing. "Are you fucking kidding me? Trust me when I tell you that Chris could've found out the same information for me in a second if I'd given him permission to hack into those damn computers!" My tone was on crescendo mode. "Furthermore, where does that bastard get off telling me I'd be a liability if I had such resources? I'll show him!"

Dobbs shook his head and drank his coffee quietly, giving me time to calm down.

I threw myself into my work and spent the rest of my shift running around attending to guest issues, and when I finished work at three, I ran into David on the way out.

"Oh, I didn't know you were still here." I smiled hesitantly. "At the ops meeting this morning, they said you were off to Hawaii again."

Since our last meeting, when things had become extremely cosy between us, I'd stayed out of his way. Bumping into him had not been in my plans, especially as they announced at the operations meeting that the big boss was leaving today for Hawaii. I had secretly hoped I wouldn't have to lay eyes on him for a while seeing as in this situation, I pretty much felt as Smythe did about Mandy.

David seemed glad to see me, however; and we stood outside the service lift that went down to the back-of-house area, where I had been heading before he came out of it. "I'm afraid it's going to be a bit like this for the next few months until construction starts. I'm going to appoint an operations manager over there who can oversee the day to day things so I don't have to fly out quite so often."

"Well, I wish you a safe trip," I kept up a businesslike manner. "You must excuse me; I'm running rather late for an appointment." This was a lie of course, but I didn't want to linger with him.

He looked as if he wanted to say something, but smiled instead and bade me goodbye. I rushed down to housekeeping to pick up my dry-cleaned uniform for the next day and then went home where I found Mandy with an upset stomach.

"It must be all the eating out," she explained as she sipped on chamomile tea.

"That, and all the stress," I added. "Well, we'll definitely eat in tonight. I'll run down to Woollahra to get a few groceries, and tonight I'll cook something light."

Mandy sighed with relief. "Thanks, Mia, you're the best."

"Hey, you cook for me, too, remember?" I commented. "So it's now my turn." I changed into jeans and T-shirt, picked up my wallet, mobile and keys. "I'll see you soon," I called from the door and bade her adieu.

I intended to drive to Giorgio's, my favourite deli in Woollahra. As I drove along Edgecliff Road, I hoped I wouldn't run into Smythe, who also liked to cook Italian food and who frequented Giorgio's as much as I did. After today's tumultuous meeting, the last thing I wanted was to see him once again.

The traffic was slow going toward Ocean Street, where I had to turn right to head into Queen Street, and where Giorgio's was located. Once I turned, however, the road cleared up and I was able to give Mia a little more leeway. Living in Sydney was probably boring for a Ferrari car as there was too much stopping in city traffic and not enough empty road to simply put one's foot down on the accelerator and fly like the wind. As I thought about this, I noted I was speeding, and I put my foot on the brake to slow down. Heaven forbid that I should get a speeding ticket and never hear the end of it from Smythe!

I pressed softly on the brake pedal, but nothing happened. I pressed again, this time with mounting anxiety, and the car still failed to slow down. "Fuck!" I swore aloud. The brakes were gone, and just ahead of me was a small truck waiting for the lights to turn green. If I didn't slow down now, I was going to plunge straight into it.

Fortunately, Ocean Street ran uphill heading toward Woollahra from the direction I was travelling, so I managed to regain control of the car by slowing down through the gears and using the handbrake. I manoeuvred the car toward the left just before I reached the truck and stopped by the kerb, where I killed the engine and applied the handbrake. Only then did I allow myself to take a deep breath, and I noticed my legs had turned to jelly. It had been a close one.

I didn't understand why the brakes should suddenly give way. I'd had the car serviced just before Mandy arrived in Sydney and my mechanic told me the brake pads were in excellent condition considering I usually liked to speed and often had to brake suddenly when in city traffic.

I popped the bonnet with the intention of checking the brake fluid, when another Ferrari pulled up behind me and a middle-aged man approached me. "Car trouble?" he enquired with a kindly smile. "Please allow me. I always stop when I see another Ferrari enthusiast in need of assistance."

I returned his smile. "Thank you."

"What happened?" The man raised the bonnet lid.

"The brakes just went on me," I reported. "I don't understand it as I recently had the car serviced."

The man took a look under the bonnet. "Well, you seem to be rather low on brake fluid, but the brakes should still be working. You'll need to get it checked by a mechanic who'll have to look under the car to determine what's wrong."

I thanked the man, and he wished me luck and went on his way. I then rang Mandy to let her know I was going to be delayed due to car trouble and then contacted the road service who advised they would have someone out within the hour.

While I waited, I ran across the road to get a coffee from a small café I espied and then sat in the car to wait for the road service mechanic. I could have rung Dobbs to come and collect me and have the car looked at the following day, but I didn't want to leave the Ferrari on the road overnight. Luckily, the road service mechanic arrived fairly quickly.

"I was just around the corner finishing off with another car when the call came through," he explained.

I told him what happened and after checking under the bonnet, he slid an arm under the car and felt around for a while before he stood up, wiping greasy hands on a rag. "I can't get fully under the car because it's too low; but I have a feeling the brake line has either come loose or perhaps it somehow sprung a leak. You'll need to have the car towed to your mechanic who can have a proper look. In the meantime, you won't be able to drive it."

I sighed, feeling frustrated. This was the last thing I needed.

"I can arrange for a tow truck for you if you like," the mechanic offered.

"Yes, thank you. I'll give my mechanic a call now to let him know the car is on its way."

The tow truck arrived within half an hour and I hopped into a taxi to take me back home. I would get the groceries for dinner from the local market in Potts Point.

"What is it exactly that you want to do?" Mandy asked over a dinner of chicken broth, salad, cheese and French baguettes.

"I need to get into Mark Meadows' apartment," I replied, breaking off a piece of bread and helping myself to a slice of Swiss cheese.

"But that's breaking and entering," she exclaimed.

"Trust me, Mandy; it never stopped me before." I popped the cheese in my mouth and stood from the table. "You finish eating; I need to make a phone call."

I dialled Chris from my bedroom and asked him to lend me his car. I explained mine was out of commission and told him about my little plan. "I'm coming, too," he exclaimed. "I'm not letting you go alone, Mia."

I didn't see any harm in letting him come along; after all, no one knew what I was up to. "Very well. Be here in half an hour." I rang off and returned to the kitchen where I saw Mandy clearing the table.

"What are you doing? You're not feeling well. You're supposed to be in bed."

She looked at me with determination. "No way, Ms Ferrari! If you're going snooping, I'm there, too."

"But how..."

"How did I hear you? It comes from the long practise of listening in to my son's phone conversations during his teens to ensure he stayed out of trouble." She smiled.

"You're very clever, Amanda Wilson." I regarded her with admiration in my eyes.

"I'm going to get changed." She made for the lounge room.

"Are you well enough to come with us, you think?"

"Lady, your soup had healing powers," she replied. "Now, get ready."

I went to my room for a bag and threw in a couple of small flashlights, a Swiss army knife and three pairs of surgical gloves. I changed into black jeans and a long-sleeved black body shirt.

"You look like a cat burglar," Mandy remarked when I came back out.

"We're breaking and entering, remember?" I grinned.

"You're right," she said and peeled off her white jeans and T-shirt while she rummaged through her things for dark clothing.

Chris texted me upon arrival and we met him out in the street. We jumped into his car, with me sitting in the passenger seat and Mandy in the back. "Flood Street, Bondi," I instructed and he headed toward Edgecliff Road.

I filled them in on the half-brother findings, but left Smythe's name out of it for the sake of Mandy.

"Man," protested Chris, "I could've found that out in two minutes, let alone two days. You should've come to me instead of the police."

"I didn't want to involve you, Chris," I replied firmly. "You know I don't want you in danger."

"Who's going to know, for God's sake?"

"Never mind," I said. "Just drive."

Chris sighed and drove on while I finished updating them on everything I knew to date.

"So what exactly are we looking for at Mark's flat?" Mandy asked.

"I'm not sure yet, but something that might indicate why he was murdered. We know the killer searched his place, but he could've missed something."

"True," Chris agreed. "If he brought in the body, he wouldn't have wanted to risk sticking around for too long, just in case."

"Exactly," I concurred.

"And how do you intend to get in?" Mandy asked from the back.

I turned to her. "When I went there and found his body, the

door was unlocked. The killer didn't even bother to lock it. We might get lucky and find it still like that."

"You're kidding, right?" Chris glanced at me. "You think the cops are going to leave the door unlocked?"

I threw him an enigmatic smile. "It doesn't matter. Even if the door's locked, I'll be able to open it."

"And how, pray?" This from the back seat.

I turned again to Mandy. "You don't grow up with a cop father without learning a trick or two."

# CHAPTER 19

The door to Mark Meadows' apartment was locked, so I put on a pair of the latex gloves I had in my bag, took out my Swiss army knife and pulled out a long, thin, metal toothpick-like tool with a small hooked head at the end.

"What the hell is that?" whispered Mandy in my ear.

I didn't want to make any noise in case one of the neighbours poked their head out to see what was going on. For this very reason, we had also left the passage light off, which in an old building such as this had to be switched on by pushing a timer button. "Shhhhh! Stay quiet for a moment and give me some light with this flashlight," I whispered back and handed her one of the small flashlights I had packed. "Cup your hand around the light so we only have the beam on the lock. Chris, you keep a lookout and above all, don't touch anything!"

Mandy cupped the end of the flashlight with her hand, hence directing a small beam of light to the keyhole and I went to work. I inserted the tool from my knife into the lock and twisted and turned very carefully until I heard a "click" and was able to open the lock.

I asked Mandy to switch off the light, and I turned the doorknob. "Follow me, and remember not to touch anything," I whispered when I opened the door and walked in with the other two following close on my heels. Once we shut the door behind us, I asked Mandy to switch on the flashlight again while I handed the other flashlight to Chris. Then, I gave them each a pair of latex gloves. "Put these on before you touch anything. I don't want any of our fingerprints left behind."

Chris put on his gloves and then directed his light beam around the messy lounge room. The thing in our favour was that the windows had blackout curtains, which were drawn, and we were able to switch on a couple of small table lamps. I didn't want the main lights on just in case the bright light seeped out from the edge of the curtains, but I figured the table lamps were safe.

"Okay, so what now?" Mandy asked, putting on her gloves.

"Now, we search," I said, placing my bag on the floor. "Be sure not to move anything out of place in case the cops come back and realise someone else has been in here. They take photos of everything, so anything you pick up to examine must be put back exactly where you found it. Got it?"

The two nodded, and Chris spoke. "I suggest we split up. I'll do the bedroom. Mandy, the bathroom and kitchen; and Mia, the lounge room."

I agreed and we set off to our tasks. "Just ensure you don't switch on any big lights," I reminded them in a low voice.

We searched for the next hour or so, but came up with nothing. There were no documents, photos or computer disks; nothing that could give us relevant information. I felt disappointed but not surprised. I figured the police had been fairly thorough in their search of the apartment. Chris had even managed to lift parts of the linoleum, which covered the kitchen floor, and corners of the carpet in the bedroom and lounge, in case something had been hidden underneath; but still nothing.

"Well, that was a waste of time," Chris remarked when we left and were safely back in the car.

"We had to be sure the police or the killer didn't miss anything," I replied. Just then, I felt the hair at the back of my neck stand on end. I turned and looked out through the rear window.

"What's wrong?" Mandy asked, looking out behind her.

"I don't know," I said thoughtfully. "For a moment, I had the feeling we were being watched."

We stayed silent in the dark for a few minutes and looked all around us. There were a number of cars parked in the street, but they seemed to be empty as far as we could tell.

"We could always go and check the cars," Chris suggested and went to open the car door.

I stopped him by grabbing hold of his arm. "No. It's too dangerous. Let's just get out of here. This place gives me the creeps."

"Where to now?" He glanced at me as he started the engine.

"Home to bed," Mandy answered.

"Not yet," I interjected. "Let's go to Stonewall."

"Stonewall?" Chris queried, a touch of dismay in his voice. "What for?"

"My sweet golden boy, James, showed me Ophelia's old dressing room the other day. This is where we should be searching."

"My God, why didn't you think of this earlier?" Mandy protested as she yawned.

"Because even God can make a mistake," I replied with a grin.

Chris smirked at my little joke and steered the car out onto the street while I put a call through to Frank.

"Darling, you're becoming rather attached to me," was his comment when he answered the phone.

"Are you at Stonewall right now?"

"Where else would I be, sweets? We have a show on in half an hour—it's karaoke night with The Tit Elating Follies!"

"You don't mind if I poke around the dressing rooms with my friends, do you?"

"Oh, daaaaahhhhhling, not if you bring that precious, young thing with you," Frank gushed and let out a wolf whistle.

"You mean Chris," I said dryly.

"Who else?" Frank laughed and rang off.

"What's that about me?" Chris asked, glancing my way for a moment.

"Trust me, you don't want to know."

We made Stonewall in fifteen minutes and spent almost half an hour looking for a parking spot around busy Oxford Street. When we walked into the place, we spotted the queens on top of the bar counter, wearing Ziegfeld Follies-style costumes with feathers and covered in fake diamonds. Alan had a microphone in his hand, which he shared with a dark-haired, sexy young man in skimpy denim shorts and a tight, white T-shirt, hugging his well-developed muscular body. They were signing Helen Reddy's *I am woman,* and the crowd joined in every time they hit the chorus.

Frank spotted us, climbed down from the counter and made his way toward us. He was dressed in a gold-tissue bikini with yellow-dyed ostrich feathers forming a fan from his behind and with a yellow diamante tiara set on his golden, longhaired wig. He had sprinkled his body with gold glitter and his make-up consisted of golden eye shadow and lipstick plus very long false eyelashes, also in gold.

He threw himself into Chris's arms and hugged the poor boy until Chris blushed to the roots of his hair. "Oh, darling, you came!" He then looked pointedly at Chris's crotch. "Well, not quite yet." He laughed at his own joke, and Chris looked like he wanted to die. I rescued him by pushing my way in between them and gave Frank a hug and kiss.

"Frank, dear," I reminded him, "don't forget your other admirers."

Frank gave me a dazzling smile. "But of course, Mia, my precious; how rude of me." He kissed me back and then went onto hug and kiss Mandy.

"Frank, the dressing room?" I spoke in his ear, above the loud music.

"Of course, dear." He responded by letting go of Mandy and grabbing hold of my hand. "Follow me, toots."

We made our way across the floor and toward the back stairs while the show went on with Alan and Tony picking on another member of the audience and starting to sing *I'm so excited*, by the Pointer Sisters.

When we reached the top floor, Frank made his way along the dark passage through which James had taken me on the night of the mardi gras parade, and he stopped outside the dressing room that had belonged to Ophelia.

"We don't use this room anymore, except for storage. There are a lot of costumes in there, so try not to ruin anything, my dears—oh, not that you would!" he exclaimed smiling. "And darling," he now addressed Chris, "feel free to try on anything you like, sugar puff." He blew us a kiss with both hands and left us to it.

Chris was finally able to speak. "Good God, this is the last time I'm coming here."

Mandy laughed. "That Frank is so witty; and you so shy, Chris!"

Chris threw her a look of annoyance. "Don't you even dare tell anyone what happened here tonight. I'm mortified!"

Mandy and I looked at each other and grinned. I commented, "The queens are harmless, Chris. Frank was just having a bit of fun."

"Well, I didn't see it that way," he protested. "And I didn't like his sexual innuendos either."

"Just put this down as part of your civic duty to help me solve a series of murders," I comforted him. "That way, you'll feel better about Frank having a crush on you." I laughed, and Mandy smirked.

Chris threw us a stony look. "Can we get on with it now?" His tone was surly.

I nodded, all business. "Of course. I want you two to look in every nook and cranny. Remember, the police don't know about this place, so if Ophelia was hiding anything of value it might be here, waiting for us to find it."

We searched for close on two hours and looked through every costume, inside and under the insole of each shoe, through every drawer in the dressers, under the drawers, behind all pieces of furniture and under them; we even took the mirror apart to see if there was something hidden in between the mirror and its frame.

Finally, we hit pay dirt. At around one in the morning, looking exhausted and dirty from all the dust around us, we extracted a photo that was hidden in between the theatrical mirror and the wall frame it was screwed onto.

It was a small photo taken by an instant Polaroid camera. The picture quality was poor, the image rather faded; but what we saw made the whole search worthwhile.

In the photo, a naked Ophelia sat astride a young, naked male with an athletic body. He looked tanned in contrast to Ophelia's fair skin and had short black hair. Ophelia's face was visible in profile, but the man's face was looking directly at the camera. Unfortunately, we could only see half his face; even so, it was so faded that it was difficult to make out the features properly. The other half of the face seemed to have been scratched off with something sharp, such as the point of a knife or a nail file. I turned the photo over and on the back, I read the words: "My lovely Shane" in blue pen.

"Does anyone recognise this guy?" Chris asked.

Mandy and I shook our heads. "If this is Shane, Ophelia's step-brother, then she could have been blackmailing him," I offered.

"But I thought he was broke and always after money," Mandy pointed out.

"Yes, he was," I answered, looking intently at the photo. "But Holly, Ophelia's drag queen friend, told me that after a while Shane stopped coming round. So now I wonder if Ophelia seduced him in order to blackmail him into leaving her alone."

"You think? In this day and age, incest is so common, especially amongst two consenting adults, that it wouldn't surprise me if these two were really having an affair," Chris observed.

"True," I agreed. "But just think if one of these adults didn't want word to get out about it because they couldn't afford this kind of information to become public."

"You mean like they're famous or in an important occupation, and they can't afford the scandal?" Mandy asked.

"Exactly! Whatever this Shane is hiding might be big enough to give him the motive to kill off his half-sister," I suggested.

"True!" Chris and Mandy exclaimed at the same time. Then, Mandy added, "What about the diamond, though? Do you think he stole it?"

"Who knows? We'll think about that one later." I wrapped the Polaroid in tissue paper to protect it and put it carefully in my backpack. "Let's get out of here."

The others didn't need a second prompting and after refixing the mirror back in place, we left the club. Once out in the street, I couldn't help but feel there were eyes following our every move while we walked back to Chris's car. Though I turned around several times, however, I couldn't see anybody suspicious.

Chris dropped us off at my place, and Mandy and I fell asleep in our beds fully clothed. Neither of us had bothered with changing; we were that exhausted.

It was almost ten-thirty the next morning before we were both showered and dressed, but as I had an afternoon shift, so I could afford to take my time. The sleep-in had been great and we felt refreshed and ready to face the world.

Mandy made breakfast while I brewed coffee, and every few minutes I went over the Polaroid photo with a magnifying glass. It was such a shame the quality of the picture was so bad.

"It's a pity about the fading colour," Mandy remarked, taking a quick peek at the photo while I examined it for the umpteenth time. "How can you tell the guy is tanned, anyway? His body looks yellow to me."

"I know, but if you look at his skin colour in contrast to Ophelia's, I'd say he has a tan or a darker complexion because her skin is not yellow, it's more like an off-white colour. So I'm making the assumption the guy's darker than she."

"Okay, we know he's tanned or whatever." Mandy served a cup of freshly brewed coffee and handed it to me with a plate of ham, eggs and grilled tomatoes. We sat to eat at the table and she went on thoughtfully while she buttered her toast. "Unfortunately, his features are unclear, and the quality of the picture is so poor, this person could be anyone of hundreds of the boys who frequent Stonewall."

I nodded. "You're right, of course; except that Ophelia presumably wrote those words on the back of the photo, identifying the guy as Shane."

"Then we need to get another photo of Shane to compare. Surely, there must be a driver's licence or a passport photo somewhere."

"You would think," I replied, knowing Smythe was trying to get a photo of Shane through the passport office. He hadn't mentioned a driver's licence, but I was sure he would try this as well.

Just then, my mobile rang. "It's Justin from Motorsports," said my mechanic when I answered.

"Hi Justin, how's my baby?"

Justin's tone was serious when he replied, "I think you need to call the cops, Mia. Someone's been tampering with your car and they cut the brake line."

# CHAPTER 20

I hightailed it back to Stonewall the following day and caught up with the queens and James in the early afternoon.

"Darling, you're lucky to find us in." Frank kissed me on each cheek in greeting. "We dropped by to try on some new costumes for the act, so it's a good thing you rang to say you were coming." His eyes wondered to the door. "But where is that cute boy who always follows you around?"

I smiled. "Probably recovering from his last shock when he was accosted by you, my dear."

Frank winked at me with a grin. "Ah, young flesh... I love it!"

"Now, boys and girls." I drew out the Polaroid photo from my bag. "I need you to tell me if any of you recognise the guy in this photo with Clee."

Frank took hold of the photo and looked at it for a few moments, then passed it around. "I don't know who the man is under her, but he doesn't look too happy," he commented. "I mean, who would? Clee was a ferocious man-eater. I'm surprised she didn't bite off their cocks and had them for breakfast!"

Alan and Tony grinned at his comment. "Never seen this person," Alan said, with Tony agreeing.

"This is poor quality, of course," James stated when he gazed at the photo. "But I'm almost sure this is Mark's half-brother, Shane. I remember him being kind of dark and good looking like this guy in the photo."

"The police checked up on Mark's half-brother, and his name is Tim. Shane came up as Clee's own half-brother," I informed them. "Perhaps, James, you got their identities mixed up?"

James looked unsure. "Could be. I really couldn't say as I only heard a snippet of the conversation that time, and I simply assumed

Clee meant Mark's half-brother."

"Oh my God! You mean that bitch was doing her own brother?" Frank exclaimed with a look of disgust on his face. "How could she?"

"She was a strange one, that's all I can say," Tony added.

"Is Holly around today?" I hoped Ophelia's friend might be of some help.

"Sorry, toots, but Holly's gone to New York," Frank informed me. "She picked up a gig there for a few months."

I sighed, feeling discouraged. "Well, that about does it then." I thanked them and took a taxi back to the hotel in time for the start of my afternoon shift.

While I changed in the locker room, I took another good look at the photo and suddenly experienced a sense of familiarity with the man in the image. I was sure I had seen him somewhere before. When I tried to capture a memory that might lead me to remembering where I'd seen him, however, my mind went blank.

I shook my head in frustration and went to see Dobbs in his office to tell him about my car. The horrified look on his face needed no interpretation.

"I'm calling Smythe," he said, and picked up the phone.

I put my hand over his and made him hang up the receiver. "What for? I have no evidence, and I doubt whoever did this left any fingerprints. Besides, there is the possibility it could have been pranksters. You know what this area's like."

Dobbs looked unconvinced. "I don't think even you believe that, Ferrari. You'd better tell me what's been going on."

I knew he was not going to approve of what I had done; that is, searching Mark's apartment plus Ophelia's dressing room. I was right. Dobbs winced when he replied worriedly, "Never mind what Smythe will say when you tell him what you've been up to, but do you still really believe pranksters got at your car?"

His look of disbelief made me shake my head. "Of course not," I admitted. "I know someone's after me. I can feel it—but look on the bright side, I'm getting warm."

"Warm?" Dobbs raised his voice in alarm. "If anything, you're going to get killed! There's no 'warmth' in that, Ferrari!"

I put up my hands in a placating gesture. "Okay, okay. I agree with you. Call Smythe if you must." I wasn't happy about this, but the fact that someone wanted me dead had me spooked.

While Dobbs got on the phone, I took the photo out of my jacket pocket and looked at it again. Then I froze. I didn't know how long I sat there, staring at the half face of the man in the photo, but I jumped in fright when Dobbs spoke.

"He's on his way."

"Dobbs," I said, with my eyes still on the photo. "Look at this man's face and tell me who he reminds you of."

Dobbs took the photo and frowned. "So this is the famous photo you've been talking about."

"Never mind about that! Just look at his face," I urged.

Dobbs took his time; he even used a magnifying glass and examined the photo under a powerful desk lamp. After a few minutes, in which I could hardly keep my seat due to impatience, he put down the photo and looked at me. "Best guess, it looks like an Asian or Eurasian male."

"And what's the name of a Eurasian man you've met recently?" I prompted with excitement in my eyes.

"Get the hell outta here!" He dismissed what I said with a wave of his arm. "Have you totally lost your marbles? Smythe's going to have a coronary when you tell him you suspect Sean Webb."

"Right now, it looks like you're having a coronary," I quipped.

"Ferrari, sometimes you try a man's patience too far," he chided me. "This guy could be anybody—look at Alan, the drag queen. He's Asian. For all you know, it could be him in this photo."

"Yes, I know," I acknowledged wistfully. "In fact, it could be any Asian or Eurasian person. But there's something familiar about this guy."

"There's something familiar about which guy?" A voice asked from the doorway, and Dobbs and I looked up to see Smythe standing there. The fact he arrived so quickly meant he must've been in the area.

I was thankful he hadn't taken it into his head to bring Sean along for the ride. Dobbs greeted him and ordered coffee through room service. Then he instructed me, as a father would a child, to tell Smythe absolutely everything that had happened. I felt like a five-year-old, having to tell *Mr Smythe* why I had bashed his son.

The changing expressions on Smythe's face while I recounted my story made me squirm in my seat. He looked ready to save the killer the trouble by murdering me himself, but I did manage to detect a fleeting look of concern in his eyes when I told him about the cut brake line in my car. He looked almost as if he cared.

Smythe took a long time examining the photo, by which time Dobbs and I had finished our coffees while his remained untouched. I rolled my eyes at Dobbs and he shook his head as if berating me.

Finally, Smythe looked up from the photo and spoke, addressing me. "So what's familiar about this guy?"

I felt more uneasy than I thought when I replied, "At first, I thought he looked rather like Sean Webb, but now I'm not so sure."

I didn't know what to expect of Smythe, but it wasn't his serious, questioning look. "What makes you think this is Sean when on the back of the photo it clearly says 'Shane'?"

"It's just a hunch I have." I knew what I said sounded lame since I had no proof, but he looked thoughtful even though he didn't voice his opinion.

"I'm going to have to confiscate this," he stated, and placed the photo in his pocket.

"I knew you'd say that," I replied dryly. "About Sean, though, do you believe me?"

"I don't see how it could be him, but I never discount anybody as a suspect." He eyed me pointedly. "Not even you, Ferrari."

I was taken aback. "Me? You don't think I had anything to do with these murders, surely!"

"It was just a figure of speech, so you can drop the wounded look and calm down," His voice sounded stern. He then picked up his cold coffee and drank it down in one gulp.

"Anything new come up?" Dobbs finally spoke.

"Funny you should ask," Smythe said as he produced what looked like a small photo from his jacket pocket. He handed it to Dobbs to look at. Dobbs then passed it on to me. The image was a head and shoulders shot of an attractive, young Asian woman.

"Don't tell me Shane's a transsexual now!" I exclaimed.

"No, Ferrari." Smythe rolled his eyes. "You've been hanging around with the fairies for far too long." I threw daggers at him but didn't say anything. Smythe went on, "What you're looking at is a passport photo of Lana Hart, Shane's mother. As you can see, she's Asian, which would explain Shane's looks. Therefore, the evidence so far points to the fact that Sean Webb is not the only Eurasian man in

Sydney."

"Smartarse," I grumbled under my breath at his patronising manner.

"How did you get this photo?" Dobbs asked, but Smythe hadn't heard as he was gazing at me in the strangest way, like he was looking at a specimen under a microscope. I felt like punching him in the mouth.

"Phil," Dobbs called his attention away from me. "Where did the photo come from?"

"I managed to track down Lana's older sister and only living relative. It seems the sisters had a falling out when Lana married Robert Hart, so Mrs Chi and Lana were no longer on speaking terms. Mrs Chi didn't have any other family snapshots except this one, which she kept for posterity or some such nonsense."

"You get more and more sensitive with time, Smythe; and you move me to tears." My voice dripped with sarcasm.

"Give your mouth a sabbatical, Ferrari," he warned. "Much as you've provided invaluable information to this case, it doesn't make you a cop; and you're still out of your league as far as I'm concerned. In fact, I'm getting rather tired of your interference."

"Someone's got to save the taxpayers' money," I threw back at him, eyes flashing. "If you cops keep running around with your thumbs up your arses, this country's going to go into major debt!"

"Time out, you two," Dobbs interceded. "For God's sake, do I have to put up with your bickering every time I have you together in the same room?"

I shrugged and protested sulkily. "It was your idea to invite him."

The look I got from Dobbs was enough to shut me up. Smythe shook his head at me and stood. "I have to get going now," he spoke to Dobbs, totally ignoring me. "We've had no luck tracing anyone on Robert Hart's side of the family. Shane's still missing, no passport or driver's licence to speak of; but we did manage to get a passport photo of Tim Meadows, Mark's half-brother." He produced another photo from his pocket and showed it to Dobbs without bothering to let me see it. "As you can see, this is a Caucasian male, so he can't be Shane."

Dobbs returned the photo to Smythe and he pocketed it. "Oh," Smythe said as he turned to go, "and Tim Meadows has been living in the US these last six months, so he's got a solid alibi." With this, he left.

"What a monumental arsehole!" I remarked harshly as soon as Smythe was out of earshot. This earned me a lamenting look from Dobbs.

I finished at eleven that evening and left the hotel shortly thereafter. On my way home, I thought about the big mechanic's bill I was going to have to pay in order to have my car repaired. Great, just what I needed right now! On top of it all, there was obviously some wack job out there trying to bump me off, and I didn't even know who it was. If, indeed, the man in the photo was Shane Hart and he was the killer, he must be in disguise and following me around without my knowledge. I still thought Shane looked like Sean Webb, but this was probably because Sean showed a resemblance to Shane Hart. A resemblance to someone in a photo, however, didn't exactly make him guilty of anything.

I supposed what made me suspicious of Sean in the first place was his expensive taste in cars and his gambling. On a cop's salary, this was a lifestyle he couldn't afford, but for all I knew, he could have come from big money. Perhaps, he had wealthy parents or he inherited from a rich relative. I had obviously jumped to the wrong conclusion about him because of what had transpired between us, plus my desire to make him pay for the way he treated me.

As I walked along Macleay Street with all kinds of thoughts in my head, I started to feel warm so I peeled off my jacket. It was a rather humid evening for March, and it was a full moon. I noticed the usual crazies were out in good form: sex workers, bikers, druggies, and of course, a whole bunch of tourists snapping photos at anything and everything. The traffic was quite heavy considering it was now almost eleven thirty, and I glanced at my watch to confirm the time when suddenly I felt a hard push from behind and next thing I knew I was lying on the road in front of a taxi.

An Indian man appeared in my field of vision, on his knees, and he was feeling the back of my head while a group of people gathered around me. I felt slightly dazed, but as far as I could tell, I was okay.

"Miss, are you all right?" The Indian fellow kept touching my head and I shooed him away as I sat up.

Someone in the crowd said, "She looks okay to me."

"What happened?" I asked the Indian, who turned out to be the owner of the taxi.

The man looked confused. "One minute I was driving; the next I had to break to avoid hitting you. Good thing the traffic's heavy tonight and I was driving slowly."

"Help me up, please," I said, feeling angry at my invisible stalker; for I was sure this had been yet another attempt on my life.

The taxi driver helped me up and I thanked him. "No harm done," I reassured him now that I was on my feet and no longer feeling dazed. My body felt a bit sore from the fall, but I didn't think there was cause for worry.

"Can I drive you home?" the cabbie offered.

"No, thank you. I'm just a couple of blocks away." I then looked at the group around me and asked, "Did anyone see who pushed me?"

They all shook their heads; I thanked them anyway. I had to reassure the driver, yet again, that all was well, and when I finally convinced him he could go on his merry way, he jumped into his cab and drove off. The group of onlookers dispersed and I walked home. I didn't think my stalker would make another move tonight, but of one thing I was positive; this matter was no longer "warm". I was now getting to the "hot" stage, very fast.

When I walked into the apartment, Mandy screamed and ran to me, feeling my face, shoulders and arms. I shook her away. "What are you doing?"

"Mia, what happened to you? Did you see your face?"

Before I had a chance to respond, she ran into the bathroom and came back with a hand mirror, which she proceeded to hold up to my face. I was shocked at what I saw.

"Fuck!" I swore as I took in the purpling bruise on my right cheekbone, which was rapidly spreading to my eye.

"Go and change." Mandy took charge. "I'll get you an icepack."

I had a quick shower and jumped into my pyjamas while Mandy prepared the icepack and met me with a cup of chamomile when I came back to the lounge room. My cheekbone was throbbing from the pain and when I applied the icepack to it, it hurt like hell.

Mandy regarded me with concern. "What happened?"

"He tried again," I told her, and saw the horror in her eyes.

"You mean the one who cut the brake line in your car?"

"I don't know, but I presume so," I answered, feeling elated, even in my state of shock. "You know what this means, Mandy—

we're getting close!"

"If anything, *he's* getting close," her voice shook with fear. "Close to killing you!"

I thought for a moment while I sipped my tea and then turned to her. "You're right, of course. He's getting far too close for comfort. So it's now time for us to get up close and personal with him," I announced with conviction.

"What are you talking about?" She looked puzzled.

"I'm saying enough is enough." I felt my anger mounting. "This bastard's been playing the game his way for far too long. Now, he's going to learn there are two players!"

# CHAPTER 21

Chris sat on the sofa opposite and regarded me with concern. "That looks pretty bad, Mia. The area around your eye is deep purple and your cheekbone still looks swollen."

"Thank you," was my caustic comeback, "I would never have realised it until you pointed it out."

Mandy walked into the lounge room carrying a tray with a coffee pot, cups, sugar and milk, and set it down on the coffee table in front of me. "Don't mind her, Chris. She's been in a filthy mood ever since she came in last night."

"I take it you're not going in to work looking like that," Chris stated.

"No, I arranged for a couple of days off—at least until the swelling goes down a bit and I can hide most of the damage with make-up."

"Did you alert the police?"

Mandy jumped in before I had a chance to reply to Chris's question. "Do chickens have lips?"

Chris and I cast a strange look her way. "Never mind," she said, and proceeded to serve the coffee.

"*Do* chickens have lips?" Chris queried out of interest.

"I think not," I responded, "therefore, there is your answer. No, I didn't go to the cops; they're a bunch of useless drones."

Brows went up and Chris smirked. "I take it you had another run-in with Smythe."

Mandy cast me a quick look, and I replied, "Something like that. Now, did you bring your computer?" I felt rather than saw Mandy's sigh of relief when I mentioned nothing further about Smythe. She didn't want anybody to know about her involvement with him.

"Of course," Chris said, taking the cup of coffee Mandy offered him. "But I thought you didn't want me to do anything that would put me in danger or piss off the cops."

"Fuck danger and fuck the cops!" I declared angrily. Then I explained, "First of all, this won't put you in any danger as there is no connection to you in this case; second, the cops wouldn't know a computer even if it stared at them in the face, let alone hack into one."

Chris grinned and cast me a look of admiration. "Now, that's the Mia I know!"

"Nevertheless," Mandy stated as she took a seat next to him, "you must be careful, Chris."

He nodded and asked me, "So what am I looking for exactly?"

"Two things: first see if you can somehow find out anything about the sale of the Eye of Krishna. I don't know how you would go about doing this, but my hunch is the killer had it cut into smaller pieces in order to sell it. The whole gem would be easily recognised by those in the know; after all, it is a rare piece."

"That's going to be rather difficult," Chris informed me. "The black market doesn't exactly reveal its activities on the web, at least, not openly."

"I realise this, but try anyway. Distant as the chance may be, it might give us a clue as to who's involved in the cutting and selling process, and they could identify the killer." I took a sip of coffee and then remarked with asperity, "Of course, with that bastard Smythe confiscating the Polaroid shot of Shane Hart, we don't have a photo to show anybody now."

Mandy asked, "So I take it the police couldn't get a clear photo of him as in a passport or driver's licence?"

"No. But they did come up with a picture of Shane's mother, who was Malay. This explains Shane's Eurasian looks."

"I may be able to do more digging on this and see if I can get a picture of him," Chris put in.

"How?"

"Everyone has a history, even if they try to hide it. Shane would've gone to school at least, and schools have student magazines, yearbooks, and so on. It's possible there might be a photo of young Shane in there somewhere. These days, student records and other school documentation are kept on computers."

I exclaimed with a look of praise in my eyes, "Brilliant! You're wonderful, Chris. I would never have thought of that, and I doubt the cops would waste their time on it as it's such a long shot."

"It's certainly worth a try," Mandy remarked.

"Sure is," Chris glowed from the praise I had given him. "What's the second thing?"

"What I'm about to tell you stays in this room," I warned them. "This time, I won't even share it with Dobbs as the poor man is already terrified that the killer's going to get to me."

The other two sat forward, their faces wearing an attentive look.

"This is purely a hunch, of course, but even though I dismissed it several times from my mind, it keeps coming back to haunt me. So, Chris, I need you to find out who Sean Webb is?"

"What do you mean, who he is? He's a cop," Mandy asked, confused.

"No. I mean who he really is," I replied and saw Chris nod in understanding. "He might be a cop, Mandy, but who is he really?"

Mandy looked thoughtful. "You mean the gambling, expensive clothes, that sort of thing?"

"That's a part of it. The man has expensive tastes that are not possible on a cop's salary, but for all we know he could've come from money. This is the reason we need to find out who he is."

Chris was already working on his laptop and seemed lost in a world of his own.

I spent the next couple of days sightseeing with Mandy as I wasn't yet ready to go back to work with my eye the way it was. My car was fixed and it cost a small fortune, but there was nothing I could do about it. Chris holed up in the penthouse and advised he would call as soon as he had any results.

As soon as the swelling went down, I planned to return to work and tell everybody that I tripped and hit the pavement with my face. I knew Dobbs wouldn't believe me, but he would have to accept it whether he liked it or not. If I told him the truth, he would freak out and bring Smythe into it.

It was a beautiful Sydney morning when I drove Mandy to the Koala Park Sanctuary at Castle Hill. I covered my bruise with make-up as best I could before we left the apartment. The good thing was because it was sunny out I could wear my sunglasses most of the time, and they pretty much hid the entire area. One other thing I did before we left was to pack my Swiss army knife. I figured while it wouldn't protect me from a bullet, it would certainly come in handy if someone attacked me. I doubted the killer was going to make an attempt on me while I was with someone else; it was when I was alone that I had to be careful, but it always paid to be cautious.

I had asked the mechanic to show me how to check for a cut brake line so I could do this before I drove my car anywhere. I found that by lying flat on the ground, I was able to reach with my arm under the car and touch the brake line that fed into each wheel. If one knew where to feel for it, it wasn't so difficult.

"Will I be able to hold a koala bear, do you think?" Mandy asked like an eager child as we drove in the sunshine. "I want you to take loads of pictures of me, Mia. I'm going to post this all over Facebook and my blog. It's just so exciting!"

"It won't be so exciting if the koala pees on you or claws your face to ribbons." I hated to dampen her enthusiasm, but I had to warn her. "Cute as they are, their pee stinks to high heaven and their claws are sharp as scalpels."

"Oh." Mandy sounded disappointed.

I smiled in encouragement. "But don't worry, the animal handler will ensure you hold the koala safely." Then, I added, "Mind you, I don't even know if they let you handle koalas anymore these days. I think they let you take photos next to them while they're perched on the branch of a gum tree or something."

"Well, even if I can get close to one, it should be good enough." Mandy smiled back.

As it turned out, the park didn't allow the handling of koalas, not only for the visitors' safety, but for the welfare of the animals. The bears became distressed if held by people. Mandy managed to get close to one of them while it was asleep on its tree branch, and I snapped away with her camera while she posed this way and that. Later, she had the opportunity to feed a few kangaroos that seemed so used to tourists they almost offered to take photos for the public, that's how bored they looked.

I took multiple photos of Mandy feeding the 'roos and patting them. She also had me take pictures of her at the Tasmanian devil enclosure and the crocodile pool. Finally, when I thought we couldn't take any more photos, Mandy asked a passing tourist to take some photos of us both with some talking sulphur-crested cockatoos. They were really funny as they called out "Hello" to everyone who passed by their cage, and if a tourist stood close and talked to one, the cockatoo would respond in kind, often repeating what the person said or simply rattling off a series of words it had picked up from other people.

On our way out through the tourist shop, Mandy purchased T-shirts, caps and key rings for the folks back home. I couldn't help but smile at her exuberance as she went from item to item on the display shelves, exclaiming in delight like a young girl.

We then drove to Darling Harbour for a late lunch, we relaxed while we sat by the waterfront in a Cockle Bay restaurant sipping cool Pellegrino water.

"I'm stuffed," Mandy announced happily. "The food was great."

I agreed. "You seem a lot more cheerful these days. How are things in the romance department?"

She took her time answering as if she were examining her feelings. "I know now I'm not in love with Phil," she declared.

"Which Phil are we talking about?"

"Smythe," she clarified. "Mia, I know you hate his guts, but he's a gorgeous, sexy and considerate man. Even so, my heart's still with my Phil. I realise this now. The thing with Smythe was on the rebound, you might say. I guess my head was turned when another man other than my husband found me attractive."

"Does he know this; Smythe, I mean?"

"No," Mandy sounded sad. "I thought it best if we no longer have any contact. He's aware my heart is elsewhere; and that's all he needs to know." She sighed with melancholy. "If I were single right now, I'd snap up Phil Smythe in a jiffy," she confessed, "and even though I made a terrible mistake in having an affair and hurting those around me, I don't regret it. Phil's a wonderful lover, and he gave me so much of himself. I'll always treasure this in my heart."

I tried to maintain a normal countenance, but when Mandy talked about Smythe as a man and lover, I felt like puking. To me, Smythe was just a bastard cop. "So where to from here?"

A big smile suddenly appeared on her face. "Oh, Mia, I'm so happy! I've been talking with Phil, my hubby, and he's been ever so romantic! He told me he's been missing me big time and that he's going to take time off work to join me in Sydney for a second honeymoon."

A lump rose to my throat and tears stung the back of my eyes. I was happy for Mandy and sad for myself. My marriage had been a failure, and my love for David consisted of a brief affair in Venice—and even this, it seemed, had nowhere to go from here.

I patted Mandy's arm before I became too emotional. "I'm so glad for you, my friend. A second honeymoon is sure to work wonders; and of course, you must let me get you a super special rate at the hotel so you two can rekindle your passion in the lap of luxury."

"That'd be so great! Thank you, Mia." Mandy beamed at me.

I went back to work the following day and Dobbs put me through the third degree. "I don't believe you." He looked disappointed when I told him my story of falling on the pavement. "Why won't you tell me the truth about what happened?"

My heart broke for him. He regarded me as a daughter and here I was, lying to him. He knew it, and I could tell his feelings were hurt. What he didn't realise, however, was that I was doing this to protect him. I didn't want him worrying about me night and day.

"Dobbs," I insisted, "I know it sounds suspicious, but I'm telling you this is what truly happened." I justified the lie by telling myself it was true that I had fallen on the pavement—the only thing I left out was that someone had pushed me.

Dobbs sighed and gave in. "Fine. I'll have to take your word for it, but promise me you won't do anything crazy."

I felt guilty as I nodded. "Very well."

"And until this whole thing is over," he added, "I'll drive you home when you work evenings."

I agreed to this wholeheartedly and was grateful I had someone who cared enough to look after me. "Have you heard anything else from Smythe?" I thought Smythe might have updated Dobbs by now.

"Only that the police are not making any progress with tracking the diamond," was his response. "I don't hold out much hope it'll ever resurface."

What he said was true. The chances of finding the diamond whole, or even in pieces, were very slim as far as I was concerned. Whoever took it had by now disposed of it and was enjoying the fruits of his unsavoury labour—that of killing three innocent people. I sincerely hoped if curses really did exist, that the diamond itself would take care of the killer even if the police never caught up with him.

The rest of the evening passed quickly and promptly at eleven, Dobbs met me in the duty managers' cubicle. I was just updating the DM log when he arrived. "Ready for your ride home?"

I smiled at him. "Give me a moment to finish off here and we'll go."

Dobbs pulled up outside my place at just after quarter past eleven and I bade him goodnight.

"You working the evening shift again tomorrow?" he asked as I made to get out of the car.

"Yes. I'll see you then." I climbed out and he waited until I entered my building before he drove off.

Mandy was on the phone to her hubby when I walked in and she waved hello as I made my way to my room. She looked chirpy and energised since Phil had announced he would be arriving in Sydney in five days' time.

Five more days of having my friend with me and then I would go back to being all alone, I thought while I undressed and jumped in the shower. I had gotten used to having company around my home once again and I didn't relish the thought of having to go back to the loneliness. Not that I was alone so much, I consoled myself; I had a full on and interesting job, Chris and I enjoyed a great relationship akin to that of mother and son, although I definitely made a wicked mother; and then, there was Dobbs—my dear friend who had taken me into his family and was like a father to me. I didn't count on David, though, as he flitted in and out of my life these days.

As for excitement, I could always count on Smythe to insult me in such a way that it brought out the worst in me, but with this also came my strength and fighting spirit. Therefore, even Smythe had his place in my life—who would have thought it!

I heard my mobile ringing and came out of the shower, hastily throwing on a bathrobe. "Chris," I said when I saw his name on the caller ID, "what news?"

"Well, it's not what I expected, but I have a photo of Shane Hart for you, and it gets even better." He paused for my response.

The suspense was killing me. "Well?"

"Shane Hart and Sean Webb went to the same high school."

# CHAPTER 22

Chris arrived early the following morning and while Mandy made breakfast, we sat at the kitchen table with our first cup of freshly brewed coffee.

"I spent a long time in the Department of Education system," Chris explained, "trying to find Shane Hart." I nodded and let him continue. "Finally, I hit pay dirt, and not only do I get Shane Hart at Sydney Boys' High School, but when I looked at one of the student lists, I found the name Sean Webb."

"Oh my God!" I could barely keep my seat.

"The boys were in high school together between the ages of sixteen and seventeen. After this, I lost track of Shane; it doesn't look like he went to university. However, Sean Webb went to the University of New South Wales to study law and criminology."

"So what happened to Shane?" Mandy asked when she joined us at the table with a large serving platter full of bacon, eggs and grilled Roma tomatoes.

Chris served himself and tucked in like the hungry young man he always was. "I have no idea where Shane went from there, but at least we now know there's a common denominator for Shane and Sean. Quite unexpected, huh?"

"You mean, them having attended the same high school," I clarified.

"Yes," he replied and buttered some toast. "I was able to track down some of the class lists, too; and the boys were in most classes together. I have a feeling they were friends."

"Why do you say that?" I couldn't yet eat because I wanted to hear it all without being distracted, so I went on sipping my coffee.

Chris drew out a large envelope from his laptop bag and slid it along the table to me. "I printed these in high resolution colour. Take a look."

I tore open the envelope and drew out two A4-sized sheets of paper. What I saw rendered me speechless and after a few moments of gazing at the images, I passed them on to Mandy.

"Fuck me!" she exclaimed and blushed. "So sorry, I've been hanging around Mia for too long," she excused herself without taking her eyes off the pictures.

"Are you sure you got the right photos?" I questioned Chris before I allowed myself to become too excited.

"Straight out of their high school graduation pics," he confirmed.

"But they're almost identical! I mean, they could be twins," I declared.

"They could be, but they're not," Chris replied as Mandy lay down the photos of Shane Hart and Sean Webb face up on the table so we could all see them.

"What else do we know about Sean?" I still couldn't believe the resemblance between the two faces.

"Well, he certainly doesn't come from money," Chris informed us. "He did university on some kind of funding scheme for bright students plus he took out a loan to complete his degree. His birth certificate indicates he was born to Peter and Sharon Webb; Peter was a welder and Sharon, a homemaker."

"Of course, things could change," Mandy piped in. "There could have been a family inheritance or they might have won Lotto."

"It's possible," Chris agreed, "but I can't verify this. Besides, Peter and Sharon died when Sean was around sixteen, so I don't think he inherited anything from them seeing as they rented a home and had no other assets. I checked that out, too."

My breakfast was growing cold and I ate for a few moments while I thought what this meant. Mandy refilled everyone's coffee cup.

"Okay." I sipped on the fresh coffee. "We have two young men, who were possibly friends, but we definitely know they were classmates. They look so similar they could easily pass for brothers, and some might even consider them to be twins. Sean lost his parents when he was quite young, but we don't know who looked after him after he was orphaned. Perhaps, he shared a place with friends. What else do we have?"

"I couldn't get anything on the diamond side of things," Chris reported. "I did, however, manage to find a news article about Lana Hart's death. I printed it for you." He reached into his computer bag again and drew out a piece of paper, which he handed for me to read.

I scanned it and passed it on to Mandy. "So Lana was involved in a fatal car accident where she lost control of the vehicle and smashed into a sandstone embankment on the F3. The car burst into flames and if the impact didn't kill her, the fire sure did. This happened in ninety-eight, when Shane was fifteen years old," I pointed out, "and the article says that Lana was survived by her husband, Robert, who passed on two years later, leaving his entire estate to Concord Repatriation Hospital. No mention of his son or why he was disinherited."

"I know," Chris concurred. "I searched everywhere I could think of but couldn't get any information as to why Shane didn't get his inheritance. I mean, he was a minor at the time, but you'd think he'd contest the will."

"Maybe they had a falling out of sorts," Mandy suggested. "This happens in a lot of families and they end up writing each other out of their wills."

I agreed. "That is a possibility, but as far as we know it seems Shane didn't try to contest the will. So let's go back to Sean now. We know he doesn't come from money, unless he received an inheritance or won money somewhere. Therefore, my question is where did he get the money for his very expensive car and to keep up his kind of lifestyle?"

"You can always take out a loan for a car," Chris observed.

"Yes, I guess you can," I stated, and thought for a moment. "Tell me, Chris, can you find out whether Sean owns property?"

"That's an easy one," he smiled. "Just give me a few minutes." He took out his laptop and went to work.

Mandy cleared up in the kitchen and I brewed more coffee and took it to the lounge room, waiting for the other two to join me. In the meantime, I started to make notes in a notepad; writing down points always helped my mind to focus.

Around fifteen minutes later, Mandy and Chris joined me and we had our third coffee.

"Okay," I said, "this is the plan."

"The plan? What plan?" Mandy asked, looking confused.

"We have a large amount of information," I explained, "but we keep hitting dead ends. The only real lead is that Sean has an expensive lifestyle. So we need to find out whether he's borrowing or if he's come into money."

"I can answer that," Chris interjected and scrolled through a couple of sites on his computer. "Sean Webb is the owner of a terrace house in Paddington valued at approximately two million."

My heart quickened. "Does he have a mortgage on it?"

"It seems so, as far as I can tell. These sites are not always updated regularly, and bank records are near impossible to hack into."

"Okay, but even if he does have a mortgage, can you imagine the size of the repayments? And this is on top of what his car costs. A Porsche Boxter S goes for around a hundred and fifty thousand. How can he afford all this? Does it say when he purchased his home?"

Chris checked one of the screens on his laptop and replied, "About two years ago."

"In that case, he didn't come into money recently; otherwise, he would've paid off his home by now," Mandy pointed out. "You're saying he's the one who stole the diamond, right?"

I shook my head. "I'm not really sure what I'm saying right now, but even if the guy did steal the diamond, he'd have to be very careful not to spend his money too soon."

Chris nodded. "Exactly. How would it look if he suddenly went around spending heaps of money and acquiring all sorts of things? It'd be a dead giveaway."

"Shame you can't hack into banks." I sighed with disappointment.

"So what's the plan?" Mandy brought up her earlier question.

"The plan is you guys are going to help me break into Sean's home."

Mandy looked at me with horror on her face. "Are you crazy? Do you know what he'll do to you if he finds you there?"

"This is the only way to see whether he's involved," I argued. "I'm afraid there's no other alternative."

Mandy did not look happy, but Chris threw me a knowing smile. "So how do you want to do this, boss?"

"I say this calls for more coffee," Mandy announced, probably knowing that nothing she said was going to deter me.

As she went into the kitchen, Chris and I sat closer together and while we discussed our next move, I made notes.

I went to work at three and made sure to catch up with Chris over dinner to finalise our plans. David was back in Hawaii and we had the penthouse to ourselves. We had a pizza delivered from Giuseppe's, Chris's favourite pizza place, and while we ate, we discussed the finer points of what we needed to do.

"You know you'll be arrested for break and enter if Sean catches you," Chris warned.

"If and when I do get caught, I'll think of something," I replied with bravado, hoping all would go well.

"Are you going to tell Dobbs what we're planning?"

"No." I threw him a serious look. "Dobbs is my dear friend and I want to protect him from all this. For one thing, he's pals with Smythe; so how would it look if he sanctioned our plan? Besides, he worries too much about me; and God only knows what he'll say if I involve you!"

We finished our dinner and I got up to go. "You need to do me one other favour."

"What's that?"

"I want you to ring the Kings Cross police and ask for Sean; just say you're a colleague who has some information for him that he's been waiting on. If they put you through, hang up; but if they say he's on his day off, find out when he's due back. We need to make sure he's going to be on duty so the coast is clear for us," I instructed. "Oh, and make sure you ring from a public telephone just in case they get suspicious and try to trace your number."

I left and went to do my rounds. Then, I joined Dobbs for a late evening coffee before home time.

"Your face looks much better," he remarked.

"Yes, the bruises are beginning to fade."

"Everything okay with you?"

"Of course, Dobbs," I reassured him. "Since the time you dropped me off at home last night and this afternoon when I came in to work, there's been no incidents. I admit the brake line incident was probably someone wishing me harm, but the fall—"

"Do you expect me to believe that?" he exclaimed as he eyed me with suspicion. "You're hiding something, Ferrari."

I sighed impatiently but didn't want to have an argument with him. "Dobbs, I can't control what you think, but I'm telling you I really did fall on the pavement," I insisted while I convinced myself this classified as a "white lie".

Dobbs gazed at me for the longest time and this made me feel uncomfortable, so I glanced at my watch and stood from the table where we had been sitting in the staff restaurant. "Man, I forgot about some room checks I have to do before my shift's over. Meet you at eleven in your office?"

He nodded, still gazing at me as if trying to read my thoughts.

Chris called me just as I was about to fall asleep that night. I looked at my bedside clock and saw it was way past midnight. "Is there a reason why we can't keep to civilised hours?" I complained when I picked up the call.

"I rang the police after dinner, but Sean was on duty so I had to hang up," Chris defended himself. "Then, I waited until after eleven and called again after the shift change."

"And?"

"And I've been told he won't be back on duty until tomorrow night."

"You mean tonight," I stated.

"Oh, yes, it's past midnight now," Chris replied. "So he's back on duty today from three in the afternoon."

"Good," I said. "We have a lot of work to do, so I'm going to call in sick at work. This'll give us all day to sort things out."

"What time are we going in?"

"You mean what time am *I* going in," I corrected. "I thought around eight in the evening."

"That's a good time," he agreed. "Most people will be home from work and having dinner. The streets should be quiet."

"Exactly."

"What if there's an alarm in the house?"

"Then I'm in deep shit," I answered. "I can pick a lock, but I'm not so advanced that I can disarm an alarm."

"Well, I guess we won't know until we go in," he commented.

"You mean until *I* go in," again, I corrected. "We'll just have to play it by ear. Anyway, get some sleep; we have a long day coming up," I ordered. "And Chris," I added in a softer tone, "thank you."

We rang off and I was about to go back to sleep when there was a soft knock at my door. "Mia?" Mandy called out. "Are you awake?"

"I am now, come on in." Mandy walked into the room and I flipped on the bedside lamp. She looked troubled. "What's the matter?"

She sat at the foot of my bed, her eyes full of worry. "I couldn't sleep thinking about this whole plan. It's just so risky, and I'm afraid for you."

My heart warmed toward her. "You're sweet, Mandy, but I can take care of myself."

"Yes, but we're talking about something illegal that could land you into trouble," she insisted.

I said in amusement, "I'm always doing something illegal that usually gets me into trouble; you know me."

"I guess it's different when I used to read about your exploits via email, but to actually take part in a covert operation in the flesh..."

I laughed. "You're talking like we're MI6."

Mandy didn't join in the laughter. "You can't deny what you're trying to pull is dangerous," she argued.

I felt my blood begin to boil as I thought about the inefficiency of the cops. "Well, someone's got to do something about this whole situation. The cops are fucking useless! All they're good for is eating McDonald's."

"You don't mean that," she chided me gently.

"Okay," I sighed, "I don't mean it, but you must admit they haven't come up with much; not when you compare all the information we've unearthed plus the stuff Chris accessed."

"You're right, of course." She stood and gave me a caring look. "I know you're doing what you think is right, and I'm here to help in any way I can. But Mia, be careful. I don't want to lose my best friend." She became teary-eyed when she said this and it had a contagious effect on me because I felt tears gathering in my eyes, too. She leaned over and gave me a hug. "We are family," she stated, and left the room.

I watched as she closed the door behind her and knew that though I no longer had blood family, I was blessed with the best of friends. I sniffed back my tears, switched off the light and lay back down; but sleep wouldn't come. So I went through all the details of our plan in my mind, right down to the smallest one.

There were two things that could happen tonight at Sean's, I thought with the conviction of someone who knew she was on the right trail—I would either catch myself a killer or my life would come to a violent end.

# CHAPTER 23

Sean Webb's home in Paddington was a freestanding stucco Victorian terrace with sandy-coloured walls and Federation green trelliswork, making up the front wrought iron fence and the balcony rail on the second floor. There was a small garden just inside the fence with a narrow path and a few stone steps, which led up to a front veranda with a period-tiled floor and a front door inlaid with two stained-glass panels covering the top half.

"Give me a look," Chris grabbed the binoculars out of my hands.

"Nothing much to see," I reported. "I only hope he doesn't have a security door with bars out back because this'll make my work doubly difficult."

"You could always smash a window," he suggested, handing the binoculars back.

"And alert the neighbours?"

"He might have a dog, too, for all we know."

"Thanks for bolstering my confidence," I replied sarcastically. "Right now, I need your observations like a hole in the head!" I checked my small backpack to ensure I had everything I needed, though I had already checked it a zillion times. "Well, wish me luck."

"Be careful," he admonished.

"You remember what you have to do, right?" Again, we'd gone over our plan a thousand times, but I had to make sure.

Chris nodded and I gave him a smile. Then, I opened the car door, without making a sound, and got out. I wore black jeans, a long-sleeved black body shirt and a black cap, hiding my blonde hair in order to avoid detection.

I waved at Chris and looked up and down the street before I went across toward Sean's house. All was quiet in the leafy street and there was no one about. The house was dark, except for a soft light showing through one of the windows. I guessed this was a timer light located in either the hallway or lounge room.

I let myself in through the front gate and slipped immediately around to the side of the house. The paling fence bordering this side was topped by large and leafy frangipani and jacaranda trees, providing cover from the neighbours next door; so I was in luck. I stopped here and looked through a couple of the windows, which were protected by plantation blinds on the inside. I peeked through the partly open slats of the first window and noted that the lamplight was coming from the lounge room. I quickly took in the furnishings of the room: mainly contemporary with an Art Deco piece here and there; polished timber floorboards covered in fine Persian rugs and an assortment of Turkish-style cushions bunched up on the floor near a Victorian fireplace. I wondered whether this was where Sean brought his babes for a bit of rough sex.

The second window was darkened by shut blind slats; therefore, I made my way to the back of the house and was relieved that no guard dog had come charging at me. The backyard consisted of a small paved area with an outdoor cast iron table and four chairs. A tiny bit of lawn bordered the back fence where more trees grew alongside tall banana plants. It seemed Sean really liked his privacy.

Strangely, there were no sensor lights; and not even a security door. Perhaps, he thought that being a cop protected him from burglars. I took a small flashlight out of my backpack and moved toward the back door with my Swiss army knife in hand.

The door was an old wooden one, which looked rather rustic, and it had a standard lock that I picked within seconds. I swung it open and waited in case an alarm went off. Nothing. I then entered and noticed a small laundry leading through to a modern kitchen. I looked around with my flashlight and noted the place was neat and tidy; the kitchen equipped for the most finicky of gourmet cooks. It somehow seemed out of character for Sean; I would have been less surprised had I found a babe-den, complete with red satin sheets and mirrored walls and ceiling.

Moving on from the kitchen, there was a long timber-floored passageway with rooms opening on either side of it and with the passage ending at the front door, near a narrow staircase leading to the floor upstairs. I did a quick tour of the place and decided that aside from the lounge room, there was nothing of interest downstairs. The other doors led to a bathroom and a formal dining area.

I moved silently up the stairs and onto a small landing with a door at either end. These were the bedrooms. One of them was a small guest room containing a single bed; the other, a master bedroom, was furnished with a queen-sized bed housed in a solid Jarrah timber frame.

I decided the best place to search was the lounge room, where I had espied a couple of bookcases, a filing cabinet, a desk covered with papers and a laptop, printer and phone.

Back downstairs, I switched off the flashlight as the light cast by the lamp was adequate for my purposes. I closed the plantation shutters so I wouldn't be seen from outside and went to work. First, I checked my mobile was switched on and had a full signal. I placed it back in my jeans' pocket and kept my Swiss army knife and flashlight handy. I put my backpack on the floor, near one of the bookshelves, and left it open so I could reach in to grab any of its contents at a moment's notice.

I then attacked the desk and flipped through every paper on the surface and searched inside every drawer, including under the drawers and desk, before I powered up the laptop. I was sure the computer would be password protected; if so, there would be little I could do with it unless I took it out to Chris. But I wasn't prepared to risk this. The welcome screen came up and asked for a password, so I switched off the laptop and turned my attention to the bookshelves. Sean had a good selection of books, ranging from the classics to the more contemporary plus a large amount of literature about criminology, psychology, forensics, chemistry, and so on. He also seemed to be a history buff as I noticed a large amount of titles starting with the major wars and going back through to the middle ages.

Having found nothing of significance, except the study of a well-educated man, I finally turned to the filing cabinet. It was locked, but I knew I would be able to pick the lock with my knife. Still, I hesitated before going ahead, hoping I'd be able to relock it later. A front door was easy enough to relock because all I had to do was shut it behind me, but a filing cabinet was different, and sometimes difficult to do. At least, I had found this to be the case in the past;

this was the reason why I generally stayed away from filing cabinets. In Sean's case, however, it was imperative that I find some vital clue and so far, I hadn't been successful in finding anything, not even his filing cabinet keys. Therefore, the cabinet was my last hope and I decided to bite the bullet and pick the lock.

The cabinet contained three-drawers; the top drawer revealed neatly-labelled suspension files containing documentation relating to Sean's taxes, business expenses and insurance policies for the building, home contents, car, and so on. Everything seemed to be above board and nothing caught my attention. The second drawer held files for bank statements, educational records and a whole array of other files containing warranty documents for household appliances, cameras and electronic equipment. There were also travel brochures, road maps and a file marked miscellaneous. I checked the bottom drawer, but only found stationery supplies so I went back to the second drawer and straight into the bank statements.

Glancing at my watch, I took note that I had already been here for almost thirty minutes. I had given myself an hour tops and yet, there were so many papers I wanted to delve into. The bank statements were for the current tax year and showed nothing out of the ordinary. I began to feel disheartened. So far, Sean Webb seemed like a law-abiding citizen with a nice home and car.

The educational records told me nothing I didn't already know, so I quickly flicked through the rest of the documents until I reached the miscellaneous file. This folder held some more road maps, a couple of brochures on evening courses at Sydney University and other unimportant bits and pieces. I thought it strange that so far, I hadn't come across any family photos. The house was bare of framed photos and I couldn't see any photo albums on the bookshelves. So unless Sean kept his photos in digital format, I would have to search in his bedroom as this was the only other possible place that could reveal something of interest.

Another glance at my watch and I decided I still had a bit of time to search his room. I went to replace the manila folder into the miscellaneous suspension file and almost dropped it. Thankfully, I managed to get a tighter grip on it and replaced it, shutting the drawer. I even managed to successfully relock the cabinet.

It was when I turned to retrieve my backpack that I espied the corner of what seemed to be a sheet of paper sticking out from under the bookshelf nearest me. I fleetingly wondered where this had come from as I didn't recall it being there before. Then I realised the paper might have slipped out of the file I had almost dropped and the sheet had gone sliding along the timber flooring and under the shelf.

I crouched down and pulled it out. It was a rather old-looking, A4-sized, light grey sheet of paper. I stood up and read its typewritten contents. What I saw made the hair at the back of my neck stand on end.

It was a death certificate for Shane Hart, who had died at age seventeen from multiple injuries in a motorbike accident. I stood rooted to the spot as my mind was suddenly flooded with hundreds of pieces of the puzzle I had been trying to put together—and it seemed that now I had finally found the missing piece.

An image of the photos of Shane Hart and Sean Webb, which Chris had obtained, flashed before my eyes and then I knew everything.

"Breaking and entering is a prosecutable offence." Sean's voice came from behind me and I instantly turned, dropping the paper to the floor.

He took one look at it and sprung into action before I had the chance to move out of the way. His hand shot out and with one sharp pull, he brought me up against his chest. Something fell from my back pocket and Sean kicked it with his foot so he could see what it was. My mobile phone. He didn't bother to pick it up but shoved me against the bookshelf with my face into the books. "Put your hands behind your head, you bitch!" he ordered roughly and pushed into me with his body to spread my legs with one foot. "You couldn't leave well enough alone, could you? Good thing I decided to follow you tonight," he whispered in my ear and his lips lingered there, making me shiver with fear.

He then stepped back and started to frisk me slowly, running his hands over my breasts and kneading them in the process. I felt sickened by his touch and he must have sensed this because he laughed and moved his hands lower, across my midriff and down to the waist of my jeans. He slipped one hand inside the waistband and reached right down to my panties and between my legs. I tried to push him off me, but he shoved me even harder against the shelf and continued his exploration of my body.

He pressed himself against me so that I could feel his hardness against my buttocks and then, two of his fingers entered me. I held my breath, my body rigid, while he moved his fingers inside me for what seemed an eternity, until I felt his hardness turn soft and he withdrew his hand.

I gagged at the thought that he had come into his shorts in anticipation of what he was going to do to me and did everything I could to control my fear as images of Clee and Mark's dismembered bodies flashed into my mind.

"Nothing suspicious in there," Sean whispered against me once more, his tongue licking the outer shape of my ear. "So you just had to be smarter than the cops, didn't you?" He was panting as if he was sexually aroused again. "Well, I'm going to make sure you don't get to share your information with anybody. But first, I'm going to show you what happens to inquisitive wannabe detectives who can't mind their own fucking business."

He grew hard again and this time, he unzipped my jeans and pushed me so roughly against the desk that I sent his laptop and printer crashing with a loud bang to the floor. I tried to free myself from his grip, but he gave me a stinging slap across the face that split open my bottom lip. Blood spurted all over the front of my shirt and my ears rang from the sting of his assault.

I felt momentarily disoriented as he forced my body forward so that I was bent over the desk face down. He then pulled my jeans almost to my knees, and I pushed upward, hoping to hit his face with the back of my head. But he was too strong for me. He pushed me back down again and held me with one hand at the back of my neck, while the other went back to my panties and pulled them down. He then shoved his fingers into me again, this time making sure it was quite rough and that it hurt me.

"Yes, definitely nothing in there," he said harshly, enjoying the power he had over me. "But I'll remedy this in a moment."

He withdrew his fingers suddenly, and I remained still and silent. He may rape and kill me, but he wasn't going to get the satisfaction of hearing me scream.

Sean climbed on top of me then, and I fully expected him to enter me from behind. But surprisingly, he didn't. At least, not yet. It seemed he wanted to toy with me further.

"Let me reintroduce myself so you know who's going to fuck you this last time," he taunted me. "Shane Hart at your service."

I tried yet again to push him off me and this earned me a knock to the back of my head that sent stars exploding before my eyes.

"You're a very fiery wench." He laughed maliciously. "I'm really going to enjoy doing to you what I did to that slut of my half-sister. I fucked her every orifice, and she enjoyed it."

I still remained silent, feeling bile rise to the back of my throat and I prayed I wouldn't vomit.

"She wouldn't share her precious diamond, even after Mark and I pleasured her in every way possible. And how does she repay me? By taking incriminating photos and blackmailing me to stay away from her or she'd reveal all." He spoke with derision. "I bided my time for a while and got on with my life, or rather with Sean Webb's life."

"Sean was your high school friend," I finally spoke, and my voice came out muffled as he was still pressing me hard against the desk.

The weight on top of me eased off suddenly and I thought he was going to dispense with the rape and simply kill me straight out. But much to my surprise, he pulled me up and adjusted my panties and jeans, though he left the latter unzipped. There was an imperceptible look of admiration in his eyes as he gazed into mine mixed with what I could only describe as derangement.

He said, "I don't think I'll kill you just yet. I rather enjoy talking to a worthy adversary of sorts. These days, it's a rarity to find one."

I couldn't believe it—in his own narcissistic madness, the man was paying me a compliment!

"Why did you change identities with Sean?" I asked carefully, ensuring I didn't antagonise him in any way. I had the feeling he wanted to tell me the whole story because he thought I would appreciate him the better for it. It was like he wanted praise for his cleverness before he killed me off.

"Sean was my best friend and when he died, he gave me the perfect gift—a new life."

"But he was poor, and you came from a rich background," I remarked.

He frowned for a moment as if he were remembering something unpleasant and I held my breath, praying he wouldn't revert back to the violent psychopath he had been only moments earlier. It was my plan to keep him talking for as long as possible.

"You probably know I was disinherited by my arsehole father," he spat scathingly. "He suspected I tampered with my mother's car, thereby causing the accident that killed her."

This came as a surprise, but I said nothing and let him talk. Sean directed his gaze at some faraway point, like he was gazing into another place and time. I figured I had a good chance to knee him in the groin and run, but I didn't want to risk it.

"Why did you tamper with her car?" I spoke softly.

"My father willed everything to her in the event of his death, and then to me, when she died. But she was young and healthy, not like the old man; so I decided to give her a bit of a helping hand. I wanted to be next in line to inherit." He stopped talking for a moment, and it seemed he was in some other space and time. He continued, "Somehow, the old man discovered I was responsible for her death and he disinherited me. That prick!" The pure hatred in his voice sent chills up my spine.

"And you knew Ophelia's mother had left her the diamond; so you went after it." I helped him along, and he nodded.

"At first, I thought I'd romance her into giving me half of it. She was very sexual and loved what I did to her. She liked it hot, rough, and in any way possible. That's why she had so many men in her life. Then, her boyfriend, Meadows, got wind that I was fucking her for the diamond and he got in on the act. He told me he'd help me get my share of it if I gave him ten percent. I agreed, and we became a threesome. Clee loved threesomes—this is why she was known as the double adaptor," he sneered.

I felt disgusted listening to his sex talk. He was boasting he could give it to her in any way she liked but at the same time, he seemed repulsed by her way of life. What a hypocrite he was. "So what happened then?"

"They got too smart for their own good, and between them they took Polaroids to blackmail me. For a long time, I left them alone and bided my time so they would fall into a false sense of security. After a while, I decided I'd had enough. It was time to cash in and skip the country."

"So you killed her and took the diamond," I replied. "But why not just steal the stone and be done with it?"

His look of fanaticism frightened me to the core. "Because she had to be punished for being such a sick slut! She revolted me with her voracious appetite for hard-core sex and wanting to be fucked by more than one man at a time. She was an incestuous whore!"

He was getting so agitated that I knew I had to keep him talking in order to buy time for myself. "Why did you kill Casey?"

"Oh, you are the smart investigator figuring that one out." His eyes gleamed with a kind of mad praise for me. "He had one of the incriminating photos Clee took of me, so he had to die. I hanged the faggot and made it look like suicide, a remorseful one. It was meant to look like he'd done away with her for the diamond, but then felt so sorry for what he did that he killed himself."

"So why didn't it stop there?" I kept my voice free of emotion because I wanted nothing to set him off at me.

"Meadows had another photo. Besides, he knew about the Sean identity, so I had to kill the bastard before he blurted it out to somebody. I knew it was a matter of time before the police decided Casey didn't commit suicide. I must say, his murder was most unimaginative," he remarked as if he were admitting to having purchased the wrong-coloured shoes but couldn't be bothered to exchange them. "So in the end, I decided to make it more interesting for the cops by killing Meadows in a similar way to how I did Clee. This would make the police start to suspect a serial killer with slight variations in his MO. I set this stage in case I had to kill others that interfered with my business." This time, he looked at me pointedly.

I cleared my throat. "I can... I can understand why you'd do that. To start that type of pattern, I mean. So you killed Mark somewhere outside, not only to make it a cleaner job but to avoid having to spend too much time in his place, in case someone noticed. All you did was bring back the body to his place and put it in the bathtub."

"You are good, my Mia." He licked his lips and I trembled inwardly. "I quickly searched for the photo, hoping to destroy it, and I left him in the bathtub, just as you said, so the cops would start thinking about the serial killer theory. I didn't want to mess about with all that blood, either. That type of killing was my one special gift to Clee."

All this time, we had been standing close to each other, like two friends having a chat, but suddenly he was on me again, this time pushing me onto the desk on my back. "And now, it's your turn, my dear," he said and climbed on top of me.

I knew it was a waste of time trying to push him off as he was stronger than I. But when he raised his hips to unbuckle his pants and pull down mine, I brought up my knee and made contact with his balls. The element of surprise worked my way and he fell off the desk, crashing to the floor.

"You bitch! You're going to wish you'd never been born," he raged, and was up in an instant and onto me before I could run out of the room.

He pulled me down to the floor and we struggled while he tried to get me on my back again. I managed to ram the palm of my hand in an upward movement from the base of his nose, and this sent him screaming in pain; but not before he managed to bring me down when I tried to get up.

My head hit the corner of a coffee table and blood started to pour down my face. I didn't feel the pain, as I was in shock, but I knew I had cut my head open.

I went down on the hard timber floor, and this time he straddled me and started to squeeze my neck with his hands.

"You interfering whore! I managed to get rid of the Shane identity in case someone became suspicious about what I did to my mother and the others. It was a sure bet no one would connect Shane Hart with Sean Webb. But then, you had to come along and spoil it all!" he screamed with such deep rage that it curdled my blood.

I had to get out of here, but I went into a panic when I found I couldn't break his grip. I tried to grab one of his fingers so I could break it, and hopefully this would weaken his hold on my neck, but I couldn't do this, either. In his fanatical rage, Sean Webb was far too strong for me.

Bright lights started to explode before my eyes and I suddenly saw my father's face against a backdrop of white light.

"I'm coming to you, Daddy," I called out to him from somewhere inside my mind. The white light brightened and I felt enveloped in a cocoon of peace and happiness. "Daddy," I said, "I love you."

"I love you, too, my darling daughter. Remember, he's keeping you safe," my father's voice replied softly. Then he was holding me and as I lay in his arms, I felt safe and happy. Somehow, it didn't matter I was dying. Dad had said "he's keeping me safe".

He carried me in his arms and I could smell the aroma of frangipani all around me. My body was gently set down on a soft surface while the wonderful pair of arms still held me close, hands caressing my hair and face.

"She's coming to," a male voice intruded in on my newfound peace—and then my father's face dissolved and I felt pain in my head and at my throat. My bottom lip stung, and I couldn't talk. I took a deep breath of air and realised the frangipani aroma was still all around me, as were the arms that had offered such peace and safety. Where was my father, and what had he meant by *he's keeping me safe?*

I finally opened my eyes and the first thing I saw was a pair of blue-green eyes gazing down at me with deep concern. Detective Sergeant Smythe smiled with relief and held me tighter to him while I lay on the ambulance stretcher in Sean's small front garden, under one of the frangipani trees.

## Entry from Mia's Case Book

### Case No 2 – The Eye of Krishna

It was Smythe who shot Sean Webb clean through the forehead as he almost succeeded in strangling me. Then, while waiting for the ambulance to arrive, he didn't leave my side until I was safely transported to hospital.

I came away with a cut lip, ten stitches to my right temple, where I had gashed my head open, and a bruised ego for not being able to overpower my attacker.

Smythe behaved like a mother hen toward me all the way through the ordeal, and we somehow reached a silent agreement that in future we would be more respectful toward each other, and even share our information more openly.

The police had smashed the front door of Sean's house when they received a call from Chris, who had been listening to the whole interchange between Sean and me through his Smartphone. This was the idea Chris had come up with when we planned the whole operation.

He proposed I carry two Smartphones, one programmed to call the second one, which had been sitting just inside my open backpack. The phone that fell out of my pocket was a decoy in case it was taken away from me. Even so, the decoy had been programmed to dial the phone in my backpack—which it did.

The call was silently received by the phone in my backpack, which in turn immediately dialled both Chris's phone in the car and Mandy's phone at home, where she recorded the whole interchange between Sean and me so we would have the proof we needed for the police.

Chris's role was to monitor the conversation and call the police if things got sticky. He had strict orders from me not to come into the house, no matter what he heard. I wasn't sure at what point Chris dialled the cops, but it had been timely because Smythe and his uniforms arrived just in time to rescue me from being strangled to death.

When his father disinherited him, Shane Hart had gone to live with friends while he attended the high school where he met Sean Webb. The two were instantly drawn to each other, not only because they were always mistaken for brothers, but because both had lost their parents early in life and were now living with friends. Sean was not to know, however, that his best friend was already a murderer responsible for the death of his mother.

The real Sean's passion was for motorbikes, and shortly after his parents' passing from illness within months of each other, he lost his own life in a motorcycle accident. Smythe found this out once the police managed to track down classmates of both Sean Webb and Shane Hart.

Because the accident that took Sean's life occurred right after high school ended and the boys were not likely to see their classmates again, Shane Hart was the only one who was in a position to identify the body. This was when he took the opportunity to become Sean Webb—he simply identified his friend's body as that of Shane Hart.

The real Sean had not been carrying any identification with him at the time of death as the bike was unregistered. So when Shane Hart was asked to identify his friend, he decided fate had given him a chance to start life anew; and this he did by switching identities.

The new Sean Webb went on to university and then entered the police force. It was during this time that he decided to track down Ophelia and the diamond. He had learned about the diamond from an old letter he found prior to his father's death, where Robert had written to a friend in the UK that Oscar (or Ophelia) had been a great disappointment to him, and this was why he had disinherited her. He went on to state he still felt redeemed from his actions because Ophelia would always have Rachel Hart's diamond, The Eye of Krishna, which had been in his first wife's family for generations. This letter was found hidden inside the cover of a book on the bookshelf by the police after they carried out an extensive search of Sean's property.

So Sean finally had a chance to regain what he thought was his birthright, even though the diamond was never meant for him. Despite this, he tracked down Ophelia once he entered the police force. He also found it easy to further cover his change of identification by erasing Shane Hart's death records from the system in case anyone ran a search on Shane. This way, the name would not show up as a deceased person, but a live one. Therefore, any suspicions raised in future, such as Ophelia's death, would be thrown in Shane Hart's direction as the police would presume he was involved once they discovered he was her half-brother.

Sean was a very clever, narcissistic psychopath who had planned all his moves with excellent precision. The only mistake he made had been with Jim Casey, trying to cover the killing as a suicide. But as Sean had said to me, this was one of his unimaginative killings. Even clever psychos made mistakes in judgement every now and then; and Sean was no different.

Although Sean never fully explained what drove him to murder Ophelia, by making such a bloody mess as opposed to the way he killed Mark Meadows, I decided that judging by his deranged personality, the Ophelia homicide had been a rage killing (Sean had certainly expressed his strong hatred towards her). So when he murdered his half-sister, it was an act driven by rage and a will to punish her for her so-called deviant sexual behaviour.

The Mark Meadows murder had more purpose in the killer's mind; to start establishing the pattern of a serial killer in case Sean had to murder others that knew too much. When Sean did away with Mark, he didn't experience the rage he had felt with Ophelia, so he simply drugged his victim, took him somewhere out bush, cut him up without creating a bloody mess, as he had with Ophelia, and then took the pieces in a plastic bag and dumped them in Mark's bathtub.

The Eye of Krishna was never found. However, an amount close to twenty million dollars was traced to a Swiss bank account with the co-operation of Interpol. It was believed the money had been laundered and later deposited into the account by parties as yet unknown. Interpol was now engaged in the process of tracking down the money trail.

Sean's expensive tastes had come from borrowing heavily after all, but the money came from the black market, not from a bank; and he obviously had every intention of paying off his debts and leaving the country inconspicuously once the case was closed and he could use the diamond money.

One thing about the diamond that stood out in my mind was that although it had disappeared, obviously sold by Sean through the black market, it had caused the death of both Ophelia and her half-brother at a relatively young age. Therefore, it seemed there might be something to the so-called curse; and those who had possessed or tried to steal the diamond ended up losing their lives.

I spent a couple of days in hospital, under observation, due to concussion as a result of the knock to my head against the coffee table. During this time, both Dobbs and Smythe guarded me as though I was made of fragile china. I had fully expected this treatment from Dobbs, but to see this in Smythe was something new to me. More shocking, was the fact that he congratulated Chris on a job well done in finding out so much information through his hacking activities and for his part in the execution of our plan to catch the killer with proof for the police. I had the feeling Smythe would keep turning a blind eye in future to both mine and Chris's activities as long as we shared our findings with him.

Mandy was ever so relieved she didn't lose her best friend. Once I returned home, she moved into the hotel for a few days to have a second honeymoon with her own Phil. The two had a grand time and when I went to see them off at the airport, I knew they were in love all over again and that upon their return to the UK, they would go on to live and love each other forever more. This made me happy for my very dear friend.

Ophelia and Casey were finally laid to rest; and we held a graveside service for them organised by the Stonewall family. The queens performed an outrageous number as the coffins were lowered into the ground, which had the funeral attendants' eyes popping out of their heads at the skimpily clad Tit Elating Follies, singing *That's what friends are for.*

Dobbs, Smythe, Chris and I were invited to attend the service and we all shed tears and hugs with those around us for the tragedy that could have been avoided had Sean simply taken off with the cursed diamond without having to kill for it.

Mark Meadows was given an indifferent burial, the cost of which had been borne by his half-brother, Tim, whom the police in the US had managed to track down.

I came away from this experience with a lighter heart. I saw my father in what I thought were my dying moments and he seemed to indicate that *he* would keep me safe. I was fairly sure Dad had been referring to *him* who had been holding me in his arms—my archenemy, Detective Sergeant Phil Smythe. It was a humbling experience to realise that under all his bravado and apparent dislike of me, Smythe really cared for the interfering wannabe cop, Mia Ferrari.

In the end, what was even more humbling was my discovery that one doesn't need the love of a lover or a spouse in order to have a happy life. As long as a person has friends who care, then the person is blessed.

I had a family in Dobbs and in my friends Chris, Mandy, and even Smythe. I no longer felt the need to wonder whether David Rourke and I would ever reignite our love. As far as I was concerned, I had all the love I needed—after all, *that's what friends are for.*

## The End

# About the Author

Sylvia Massara is a multi-genre author based in Sydney, Australia. She loves to dabble in wacky love affairs, drama, murder, sci-fi (or anything else that takes her fancy) over good coffee.

Born in Argentina from Italian and Spanish descent (with a bit of Swiss thrown in) and transplanted to Australia at age 10, Sylvia describes herself as a bit of a "moggie" cat by way of mixed pedigree. She is also a citizen of the world as she has travelled widely throughout most of her life and she's the proud owner of three passports.

From a creative perspective, Sylvia has been writing since her early teens and her work consists of novels, screenplays and freelance writing. She has also dabbled in acting on and off, songwriting and even had her own band during her teens/early 20s where she performed at various venues.

As with most authors, Sylvia draws on her varied experience from the often puzzling tapestry of life. A few years ago Sylvia resigned from the human race because she discovered the animal kingdom was a much nicer place to be.

Currently, Sylvia lives with her cat, Mia; and always vicariously through the many characters in her head. Occasionally, Sylvia ventures into the world of humans, and she cherishes genuine friendships as they are a rare find.

Sylvia has recently released her 7th novel, The Stranger, a sci-fi apocalyptic romance with moralistic issues that involve the fight of love vs evil in the cosmos.

**Please visit the author's website to keep up with her latest novels or to contact her at: www.sylviamassara.com**

# About Massara's Novels

## The Mia Ferrari Mystery Series

### Playing With The Bad Boys

A woman plunges ten floors down an atrium and lands on a baby grand piano in the luxurious Rourke Hotel Sydney. The police rule this as a straight case of suicide; but 48-year-old hotel duty manager and wannabe investigator, Mia Ferrari, thinks otherwise.

As Mia sets out to unravel the mysterious death and prove the cops wrong, especially her archenemy, Detective Sergeant Phil Smythe; she comes up against an unsavoury cast of characters who will do anything to shut her up. But with a little help from her friends, Mia will not stop until she unearths the truth.

Mia Ferrari is a "wiseass", older chick with determination and an attitude, and she never takes "no" for an answer.

### The Gay Mardi Gras Murders

Mia Ferrari, smartarse, older chick, super sleuth, is back in her 2nd murder mystery, and this time, she is up to her neck in drag queens, a rare diamond with a curse and murder most foul against the backdrop of Sydney's world famous Gay Mardi Gras.

A female impersonator is found dismembered in her hotel suite bathtub, and a rare diamond worth twenty million dollars is gone. The Gay Mardi Gras is fast approaching and Mia Ferrari, senior duty manager of the exclusive Rourke International Hotel Sydney, has to juggle a bunch of drag queens, a number of fabulously handsome gay men, a transsexual with a dark mystery, a young cop with sex on his mind, a close friend from the UK who is having marital problems and a mounting body count.

As Mia pits her investigative skills against her archenemy, Detective Sergeant Phil Smythe, to solve the case, she not only becomes embroiled in the life of the people around her, but it looks like she is the next target for a serial killer with a grudge against gay men.

## The South Pacific Murders

It's a well-known fact that wherever Mia Ferrari goes trouble always follows, and going on a holiday cruise to Hawaii is no different.

A killer is on the loose onboard ship. A number of doctors from a medical convention are being murdered one by one. The captain of the cruise liner asks Mia and her travelling companions to take over the investigation while the ship is in the middle of the Pacific Ocean toward its final destination. A secret sex club and horse racing bets are the only clues that can uncover the identity of the killer, but will Mia be able to solve the mystery before the killer strikes again?

Join Mia and her friends, plus her sexy detective archenemy, on a cruise to murder, mayhem, and sizzling hot sex.

## Science fiction romance

### The Stranger

The Stranger is a sci-fi apocalyptic romance with moralistic issues involving the fight between love and evil and its repercussions.

Rhys is on a mission on Earth in order to determine Earth's destiny, but his judgement is in danger of becoming clouded when he meets and falls in love with Carla, a human. The balance of life on Earth depends upon Rhys's recommendation to the League of Galaxies. But how will Rhys choose between his mission and his love for an Earthling? Rhys is forced to weigh up the collective evil on Earth and its causal effect on the greater good of other life in the universe against the love he has for one woman.

This is not simply a tale of love between two beings but a story of the unconditional and sublime love, which is the force that drives the cosmos.

The Stranger was dedicated to the Loving Memory of David Bowie.

# Romance

## Like Casablanca

What does internet dating and Casablanca have in common? Nothing, unless you go to Rick's Cafe and find out what antiques dealer and dating blogger, Cat Ryan, is up to.

Cat's doing research for her internet dating blog gig, and the place she chooses to meet her many dates is at Rick's Cafe in Sydney. But what of its disturbingly handsome owner, Rick Blake?

Cat wonders what he thinks, seeing her with a different male all the time. What's more, why does this bother Cat so much? It's not like she wants any involvement after her recent break up with Josh, her cheating ex. Besides, it looks like Rick is trying to get back together with his ex-wife, Denise. So Cat decides to play it safe, but her heart has different ideas.

## The Other Boyfriend

Sarah Jamison is on a mission to find a boyfriend for Moira, who is her lover's partner. And Sarah's best friend, Monica, comes to the rescue with the perfect solution. Enter the enigmatic Mike Connor. Monica is sure that Mike will sweep Moira off her feet, leaving the way open for Sarah to be with her true love, Jeffrey.

Sarah hates Mike on sight despite the fact that her body tells her otherwise. He is a romance novel "hero-type" who is smug and full of himself. But the only way to accomplish her mission is for her to work with Mike so she can be together with the man she loves.

Jeffrey has promised her that the minute he can end his platonic relationship with Moira, he will be with Sarah for good; but he is having trouble letting go of the wretched woman, and Sarah feels her time is running out. She is terrified of the pending big "M" (menopause), and seeing as she's just turned forty, and her hormones are driving her to do insane and desperate things, she is sure that it is not too far off into the future!

So here she is, building a multi-level marketing business in Taiwan, and struggling with it all: a stranger in a foreign country, away from her mother and friends back in London; a reluctant lover; a drop-dead gorgeous man who might have ulterior motives for helping her, and finally, a business that seems to be dwindling.

Sarah is doing it all in the name of love and the last chance to have a family, and if this means scheming and working with the devil himself, then she will do it! What she doesn't take into account is the fact that instead of getting closer to her goal, Sarah's feelings take a turn, and she finds herself increasingly thinking about the very man she despises the most – "the other boyfriend".

## Contemporary fiction – drama

<u>The Soul Bearers</u>

Partly inspired by real life events, this is a story of courage, the gift of friendship and unconditional love. The story involves three people whose lives cross for a short period of time and the profound effect which results from their interaction. Alex Dorian, freelance travel writer and victim of child abuse, arrives in Sydney in an attempt to exorcise the ghosts of her past. She shares a house with Steve and the disturbing Matthew, a homosexual couple. Alex finds herself inexplicably attracted to Matthew, and she must battle with her repressed sexuality and her fear of intimacy.

Matthew, extremely good looking and an inspiring actor/model, lives with Steve, who is dying of AIDS. Matthew has his own battle, that of dealing with the rejection of his socialite parents, and facing a future without his partner. Steve is the rock to which the troubled Matthew and Alex cling as they examine their lives and beliefs. Steve finally dies, but his legacy lives on in the strength which both Matthew and Alex find to face their own pain. Alex learns to love again, thanks to the gift of friendship from Matthew; and in turn, with Alex's love and support, Matthew learns to forgive the past and move on to follow his dream.

This beautifully told story explores the true meaning of unconditional love--for both one's self and for others. Readers of "The Soul Bearers" will come away with a deeper understanding of human relationships and of what it means to truly love without condition.

www.lngramcontent.com/pod-product-compliance
Lightning Source LLC
Chambersburg PA
CBHW060052260626
47160CB00005B/1658